sex *as a* second language

ALSO BY ALISA KWITNEY

On the Couch

Does She or Doesn't She?

The Dominant Blonde

sex *as a* second language

•

a novel

ALISA KWITNEY

ATRIA BOOKS
New York London Toronto Sydney

ATRIA BOOKS
1230 Avenue of the Americas
New York, NY 10020

Library of Congress Cataloging-in-Publication Data

Kwitney, Alisa, date.
   Sex as a second language : a novel / Alisa Kwitney.
      p. cm.
    1. Divorced women—Fiction. 2. Middle-aged
    women—Fiction. I Title.
PS3611.W58S495 2006

813'.6—dc22   2005055895

ISBN-13: 978-0-7432-6890-5
ISBN-10:   0-7432-6890-3

First Atria Books hardcover edition April 2006

10 9 8 7 6 5 4 3 2 1

ATRIA BOOKS is a trademark of Simon & Schuster, Inc.

Designed by Jaime Putorti

Manufactured in the United States of America

This book is for Holly Harrison,
my non-resident adviser since sophomore year
at Wesleyan

●

PART ONE

openings
and closings

•

Opening a conversation and bringing a conversation to an end are essential parts of our everyday language. You already know how to say hello and good-bye, but in this lesson you will study in more detail how Americans perform these functions. You might notice some similarities, as well as some differences, if you compare American conversation openings and closings with those in your native culture.

—SPEAKING NATURALLY:
COMMUNICATION SKILLS IN AMERICAN ENGLISH

chapter *one*

•

You're too young to retire from sex."

"But I'm too old to put up with all the bullshit that's in-volved," said Kat, leaning back in her chair and crossing her legs. "Besides, the only men I find attractive are the ones I'd be insane to get involved with."

This comment received a mixed review from her friends— a wry smile from Zandra, a look of concern from Marcy. *Shit.* Kat had learned the hard way that if she didn't present her de-pression in a sufficiently amusing manner, she'd wind up hav-ing to sit through a steady barrage of unsolicited advice. *See a therapist. Take an evening course. Try the new generation of mood-altering drugs.*

Yet as much as Kat longed to avoid being on the receiving end of any more prepackaged wisdom, she wasn't sure that she could sustain the requisite level of wit to satisfy her friends. Her feet were sore from walking ten blocks in three-and-a-half-inch heels and her head was beginning to throb from the drone of fifty other peoples' dinner conversations.

"But Kat," said Marcy, "the last time you were single was ten years ago. Are you saying your taste in men hasn't changed at all?"

"Well, I no longer fantasize about Kevin Costner."

"No, seriously. Let's talk about what would attract you now." There was a look of missionary eagerness on her pretty, fine-boned features.

"Marcy, I beseech you, no in-depth analysis." Underneath the table, Kat surreptitiously slipped out of her stilettos. "How about a nice, safe topic, like the pros and cons of government-sponsored torture?"

"Very funny." Zandra reached for her martini, jangling the silver bracelets on her arm. "Am I allowed to mention that there's a guy over at that table who's checking you out?"

Kat tucked her bare feet under her chair. "You always think men are checking us out. He's probably looking for a waiter."

In contrast to Marcy, who seemed to have lost all her fashion sense, Zandra was improving with age. Ten years earlier, when they'd first become friends while watching their toddlers in the playground, Zandra had concealed her hair in bandannas and her body in baggy overalls. Then, sometime last fall, Zandra had stopped trying to restrain her abundant curls and started wearing fitted clothes that flattered her generous, hourglass figure. Not surprisingly, her transformation had coincided with the advent of a new man in her life. Well, not actually *in* her life, Kat thought, since the man only made sporadic guest appearances. But it was this very unpredictability that kept Zandra on constant French-bra-and-matching-panties alert.

Marcy, on the other hand, had gone from gamine short hair

and funky vintage dresses to a lank bob and shapeless designer shifts. Looking at her now, Kat could hardly recognize the bohemian waif she'd met fifteen years earlier in a summer Shakespeare production. It was a classic case of mommification, but in Marcy's case, she hadn't managed to have the child yet.

Thinking about it made Kat realize that she probably needed a style overhaul herself. She'd been wearing the same tailored, mannish chic for over a decade.

"No, he's definitely looking at you, Kat," said Zandra, gesturing with a toothpicked olive. "See, the blue shirt, over there?"

Kat wondered if she should try something different with her hair. Layer it? Lighten it? Cut it all off? "I see him."

"You're not even looking, Kat."

"I'm using my peripheral vision. Not my type."

Zandra looked skeptical. "And what exactly is your type?"

"Borderline." Now that her divorce was almost final, Kat was aware that her friends felt she ought to be past the stage of obsessive thinking and intense bitterness. Without ever saying so directly, Zandra and Marcy had let Kat know that there was a rough timetable for adjusting to breakups. After six months, Kat had reached the point where she was expected to provide a few sardonic anecdotes about her soon-to-be ex, as well as some fresh tidbits of carnal misadventure with new, prospective mates.

But she couldn't find the motivation necessary to give a convincing performance. Kat no longer believed she would discover some magical fit with a man. Sure, if she looked hard enough, she could probably find a partner for some mutual genital friction, but she'd given up all hope of someone taking her through the hot, sweaty crucible of transformative sex.

Kat turned to Zandra. "Why don't we talk about *your* love

life? Are you still seeing the semi-famous guy?" As the man in question was also semi-married, Zandra had kept his identity a secret.

"We're taking a break right now. He says he needs some time to be on his own and figure out what he wants."

Translation: He was blowing her off. Kat tried to think of a tactful way of putting this. "I hate to say it, but I think you'd better brace yourself. When men say that, they almost never decide that what they really want is more intimacy."

Zandra lifted her chin a fraction. "Well, I'm not as certain as you are that it's all over. But you don't see me just sitting around, refusing to meet anyone new." This was true enough. Zandra believed that romance came to those who pursued it, and her quest for an enlightened partner seemed to entail a never-ending array of workshops with titles such as Tantric Vegan Cookery and Spirit Guide Hiking.

Marcy, on the other hand, had been dating the same passive-aggressive underachiever for seven years. As far as Kat could tell, his main attraction was that he gave Marcy something to complain about.

"And how are you and Steve doing, Marcy?"

"We're talking about going to Iceland this winter."

"Iceland? In winter?"

"It's actually supposed to be very pretty, and not as cold as people think." Also, Kat assumed, it was cheap. Steve was a forty-two-year-old struggling jazz musician, and his refusal to stop temping and get a steady job meant that he lacked the funds to travel anywhere nice with Marcy, let alone get married and have a child with her.

"So, what do you do on a winter vacation in Iceland?"

Marcy stirred her martini. "Well, there's supposed to be a fabulous nightlife."

Which meant that Marcy was going to wind up alone in her hotel room while Steve drank himself into a stupor. Looking at Zandra (trying too hard in an African beaded choker and low-cut red blouse) and Marcy (not trying hard enough in a gray velvet chemise), Kat wondered why the hell she'd been voted the sick puppy of their trio. She also wondered how long she had to stay before pleading a headache and heading back home.

Adding to Kat's general feeling of malaise was the fact that the restaurant, Carnivore, was dark and hot and packed tight with college students and young professionals, all bombarding one another with flirtatious pheromones.

Kat couldn't even get her drink refilled, as the waitstaff were making only brief appearances at each table before vanishing into the back, presumably to play a hand or two of poker before returning.

Zandra had said that a night out was just what Kat needed. If grouchy was an improvement on miserable, then her plan was working.

"Where is our waitress, anyway?" Kat scanned the room. "We should never have told her we needed another minute to make up our minds."

"Speaking of making up one's mind," said Zandra, "have you decided what you want to do about your birthday next week?"

"Yes," said Kat. "Ignore it." It wasn't the fact of leaving her thirties that disturbed Kat. The way she saw it, she was still youthful enough to wear her hair long and her jeans low, yet old enough to know not to flash her thong when she sat down. After spending much of her twenties in open auditions, Kat no longer fretted about her looks, her talent, or her ability to withstand rejection.

But with her personal and professional lives on hold, Kat wasn't quite in the mood to celebrate the fact that her life was now approximately half over.

"But Kat, you can't just ignore the big four-oh," said Zandra. "Marcy and I were talking about throwing you a surprise party, but we decided you'd probably kill us."

"Oh, dear God. Promise me you aren't going to do anything like that. You aren't, are you? This isn't some elaborate deception where you pretend to be really frank and open while secretly plotting to confront me with a cross section of my past?"

Marcy put her hand on Kat's arm. "Are you having feelings about reaching middle age?"

Kat laughed. "Yes, I feel this incredible urge to go buy elastic pants and start shopping in bulk. No, Marcy, I'm not depressed about getting older. In fact, I kind of like the fact that for the first time in over twenty years, there isn't a man in my life and I don't care."

"Of course you don't *need* a man in your life," said Zandra. "But I get the impression that you've closed yourself off. I hate the idea that your experience with Logan has made you hate all men."

"Oh, Zandra, please." Kat pushed away from the table, her chair scraping along the floor. "Listen, it's not that I hate men. I don't. In fact, there are many ways in which I prefer them to women. Men tend to be more direct than women, more decisive and goal-oriented. I like the fact that men seem to worry less than women about other peoples' opinions. And, since I am heterosexual, I do find myself physically attracted to them from time to time."

Zandra raised her eyebrows. "Okay, if you admire them so much, then explain why you've decided to keep them all at arm's length."

"Because," Kat said firmly, "I don't trust men. I figure it's best to keep a lion tamer's attitude—you never know when the other half of your act is going to forget its training, revert to instinct, and bite the hand that feeds it."

"So you assume that all men are going to wind up disappointing you," said Marcy.

"It's a safe assumption. If you're married long enough, you should expect periodic unreliability, chronic disappointment, even an occasional lapse in faithfulness. In fact, just to be on the safe side, I always figured it was best to have a few flirtations going on the side. I didn't actually sleep with any of them, but it reassured me to know that if Logan ever did cheat on me, I'd know where to go."

"Wait a second. You never said anything about this before." Marcy leaned forward. "Who were they?"

"My trainer, an old college friend, and the carpenter who built our living room bookcases."

"But you didn't actually have physical contact with them?"

"Well, there was a lot of meaningful stretching with the trainer, and my old friend gave me a foot massage. But no sex. And now that I'm single, I don't find any of them appealing anymore."

"Did you ever wonder if you might have protected yourself *too* much?" There was an expression in Zandra's eyes that Kat couldn't quite read. "Do you think maybe part of the problem was that you made yourself emotionally unavailable to Logan?"

Kat shook her head. "I'm sorry, no, I'm not buying that. Maybe I didn't trust Logan completely. The way I see it, intimacy is a pretty hazardous occupation, and you'd have to be delusional not to know that you can wind up getting hurt. I just never anticipated the extent of Logan's betrayal."

"But you were always complaining that your marriage wasn't working," said Zandra, her tone almost accusatory.

"And he kept saying that I was being too negative! Still, I can accept that he'd want to leave me without any attempt at working things out. But it would never have occurred to me in a million years that Logan could just walk away from his only son. Do you realize that it's been over four months now without so much as a phone call or an e-mail? Four months!" Kat paused to take a slug of her drink and wound up draining the glass. "You know what? On second thought, maybe I do hate men."

There was a moment of uncomfortable silence, saved by the appearance of their waitress.

"How are you doing, ladies? Need any more drinks, or are you ready to order?" She paused, peering at Kat. "Hang on a moment. Didn't you used to be on that show . . . what was it called again, it's on the tip of my tongue . . ."

"She was Helen Jessup on *South of Heaven*," said Marcy. Kat kicked her in the shin with one stockinged foot.

"Oh, my God!" The waitress stared at her, wide-eyed. "The bitchy rich girl, right? I used to watch that. You hired North Sullivan to investigate kidnapping threats, but it was just a ploy to keep him away from your sister." The waitress gave her a thorough visual assessment. "Your face looks great."

Was this a compliment or a suggestion that she'd been nipped and tucked? Kat decided she didn't want to know. "Thanks."

"I've tried out for a few of the soaps, but so far, nothing. Not even a day part." The waitress was young, a dyed blond, with a large jaw and a blotchy complexion. Kat wondered if she was supposed to say something encouraging.

"It's a tough business," she murmured, remembering how much she had hated people telling her that when she was younger.

"But what can I do to improve my odds?"

Kat decided to be truthful. "Well, you're not conventional-looking. That can be a problem—you're not quite ingenue material, but you're a little too young and sexy for most character roles. If you gained some weight, you might be able to land a quirky first role that would allow you to . . ."

"Right. Well, I'll come back when you're ready to order."

"But we are ready . . ." Kat began, but the waitress was already storming off, indignation in every bounce of her lithe, young body.

"Great going, Kat," said Zandra. "Ever consider laying off the truth serum?"

"She wanted advice. What was I supposed to do, lie?"

"Kat, there are times when it's kinder not to be honest."

"Oh, please. That's such a cop-out."

"So what good did it do to tell the waitress what you really thought? Now she's hurt and insulted and we're not going to get decent service."

Reaching under the table, Kat slipped her feet back into her high heels. "You know what? I think I'm going to call it a night." Wincing a little, she fished a twenty out of her purse and laid it beside her drink.

"Oh, come on, Kat, don't be so dramatic." Zandra tried to hand Kat her money back. "Sit down, we'll get another drink. The waitress is bound to come back eventually."

"I'm not being dramatic, I have a blister on my foot." Kat pulled on her navy blue French Officer's coat. "Look, I'm just a little tired tonight. Enjoy yourselves. I'll call you tomorrow."

"Are you going to be all right?" Marcy looked so concerned that, for a moment, Kat worried that she was doing something socially inappropriate.

"Of course I'm going to be all right."

"Come on, Miss Diva," said Zandra, patting her seat. "Sit your butt back down. If that shithead Logan's still bugging you this badly, then damn it, we'll talk about him."

"It's not that. Look, we'll talk tomorrow. Marcy, I suppose I'll see you at work?"

"Actually, I'm teaching the afternoon and evening classes this session. But we can still meet for lunches."

"Sounds great." As Kat made her way through the obstacle course of chairs and tables and busboys, she was aware of her friends' eyes on her. Well, she thought, now they're free to analyze my inert sex life. It occurred to her that she had just cemented her position as the odd one out.

Which was strange. Without considering it before, Kat had always thought of herself as the axis of their trio. She was the one the other women called. She was the one who'd brought them all together.

When had it changed? Thinking it over, Kat realized that there was no precise date, but at some point during the past six months her friends had drawn away from her and closer to each other.

Outside the restaurant, Kat paused to ask one of the smokers standing on the threshold for a cigarette. Was her reaction to the divorce really that inappropriate? Not as far as Kat could see. She exhaled a plume of smoke into the soft October night, thinking that, from now on, she would have to make more of an effort to conceal her feelings from her friends.

After the second block, her shoes hurt so much that she tried to hail a cab. No luck—they were all off duty. Walking slowly and painfully past the crowded sidewalk cafes along Columbus Avenue, Kat noticed that despite the deceptive, springlike warmth of the evening, some of the trees planted along the sidewalk were changing color. I shouldn't have worn my long coat, Kat thought. This is probably one of the last nights I won't need it. Everywhere she looked, Kat saw people taking advantage of the good weather—older couples strolling hand in hand, buxom mothers and proud new fathers pushing baby carriages, young couples embracing each other with blissful obliviousness in the middle of the sidewalk.

It had been a lovely day in April when Logan had announced that he was leaving. Kat took one last drag of her cigarette before stamping it out, wishing the rain and cold would come and chase all the happy people away.

chapter *two*

•

Kat used her key to open the inner lobby doors and greeted the night doorman, who was carefully trimming his luxuriant mustache with an assortment of specialized tools. He put down the tiny scissors and mirror and smiled with a shade too much enthusiasm. "Hello, Miss Miner."

"Hello, Pedro."

"Hot date tonight? All dressed up, looking good."

Kat murmured something noncommittal and kept moving toward the elevator, her heels clicking on the marble floor. Lately, she'd begun to feel a disconcertingly lascivious vibe from Pedro, and suspected that he might have been viewing the newly released DVD of *Zombie Prom Queen*, which contained her one brief topless scene. She missed Pedro's predecessor, Kurt, who had watched her grow up in the building.

Kat stood, quietly watching the numbers change on the elevator display.

Pedro continued to observe her. "You making more movies, Miss Miner?"

"Not at the moment."

"But you're not too old."

"Thanks." Kat said, as the elevator finally opened its doors. Pedro had a talent for backhanded compliments.

"You have sweet dreams, Miss Miner!"

"You, too, Pedro." *But please don't think of me while you're having them.* Kat had made her topless horror film when she was twenty-two, and although her breasts looked much the same, thanks to a certain Dr. Berman on Park Avenue, her attitude about casually revealing herself to strangers had changed completely.

Which was one reason she didn't expect to be having sex again in the foreseeable future.

Another reason was that she was living next door to her mother, which made for convenient babysitting but awkward explanations.

"Kat? Is that you? You're back early." Lia Miner lowered her reading glasses so that they dangled on a gold chain between her formidable, silk-covered breasts. Like Sophia Loren, Lia had gradually exchanged the sultry beauty of her youth for a solid, affluent handsomeness.

"Is something wrong, honey? Don't you feel well?"

"I was just a little tired, Mom," said Kat, bracing one hand against the wall as she removed her shoes.

Lia walked over, gesturing at the location of her daughter's hand. "You're going to leave marks on the paint if you keep doing that. Not that it matters, considering the state of that wall, but you do need something to sit on there."

Kat shoved her heels in the bottom of the closet, on top of a pair of old sneakers. "It can wait." Just before Logan had left her, Kat had embarked on a major renovation scheme. The electricians had already started drilling holes in walls when she discovered that Logan had invested their savings in Internet start-ups. Since their ensuing argument and breakup, the apartment had remained like Pompeii, a perfectly preserved record of the moment disaster had struck.

Lia bent down and arranged Kat's shoes more neatly. "They're not going to last if you treat them like that, Kat."

Kat grunted. She didn't plan on wearing them again in a hurry.

Straightening up, Lia muttered something about shoe trees and organizers. Then, more clearly, she said, "Listen, Kat, you can't just keep living like this. It looks terrible. If money's the issue, I could give you something—that little chair of grandma's?"

"No, thank you, Mom."

"But it's a lovely chair," Lia persisted. "I had it right there for years. Why not take it for now? Or I'll advance you the money so you can repaint the apartment."

"I don't think that would be a very good idea."

"Why isn't it a good idea? I know you'll pay me back when the divorce is final."

For a moment, Kat was tempted to say yes. In the final analysis, it didn't really matter that she'd given up gourmet takeout, seasonal accessories, and taxi cabs. Well, okay, she hadn't completely given up taxis. But the main point was that she needed to bring in more money.

Lia took Kat's coat off the back of a chair and hung it in

the closet. "And next time, Kat, I hope you'll listen to me when I tell you I have a bad feeling about the guy you're dating."

Ah, there it was—the hidden cost of taking out an interest-free loan. If Kat accepted her mother's offer, she knew she'd wind up fighting to retain even a vestige of control over her own life. Kat had a nightmarish vision of herself arguing with her mother over how to pack Dashiell's suitcase as he headed off to college. *Socks down the side, Kat, you never take full advantage of the space.* And then Dashiell would be gone and it would be just Kat and her mother, squabbling over how long to cook the meatloaf.

Kat shuddered. "Thanks for offering, Mom, but I just don't think it's healthy for us to be any more enmeshed than we already are."

"What's enmeshed? We're close. And why are you so worried about my helping you? I know it's only temporary. By next year, you're going to find something better than that *fershlugginer* teaching job, but until then, why should you live in a dump?"

"Because I refuse to mooch off of you." Kat walked into the kitchen and poured herself a glass of seltzer. "Want some?"

"I'll just have a sip of yours. And don't insult us both with this mooching nonsense. I know you're a very hard worker, it's just that at the moment, you're not in a job that pays very well. Of course, every time I suggest that you stop wasting your time there, you ignore me."

Kat sighed and poured her mother her own glass of seltzer. Ever since the day last spring when Marcy had suggested the idea of working at the language institute, Lia had been throwing up objections. It was a waste of Kat's time and energy; it didn't pay enough; she was never going to meet anyone new to date there. In the back of her mind, Kat wondered if her mother's real objection was that it was not something she herself would have done. Saying so out loud, however, would simply cause a major argument. "I don't ignore you, Mom, you ignore me. What other job could I find that would allow me the kind of flexibility to be there for Dash and go on auditions?"

"Copyediting, for one."

"For you, you mean. Come on, Mom, I can't work for you as well as live next door."

"It wouldn't be for me, precisely. Well, maybe in the beginning, before you had experience . . ."

Kat folded her arms under her breasts. "Mom." It was complicated enough, living in the apartment she'd grown up in and paying off her mortgage to her mother. The fact that her mother had moved to an apartment across the hall added an extra dimension of weirdness.

But in the savage world of Manhattan real estate, leaving home was a complicated equation. There was a serious dearth of affordable apartments, and once you found a place you liked, you soon discovered that co-op boards were like country clubs, able to refuse you without explanation.

Of course, if you were an actor, that was explanation enough. Most Manhattan co-op boards had a prejudice against actors, since the struggling ones had trouble paying the maintenance and the successful ones attracted gawkers and paparazzi.

Which was why Kat and Logan had been happy to purchase the big, six-room, prewar apartment Kat had grown up in. Or, at least, Kat had been happy—Logan had later claimed that he'd had misgivings from the start. He also claimed not to have realized that his mother-in-law was moving just one apartment away until after the closing, when it was too late.

As if reading her mind, Kat's mother said, "You've gone awfully quiet. Are you thinking about Logan again? Because you can't let him convince you to sell this place. He may make it sound like it's a way of declaring your independence, but believe me, all he cares about is reaping a profit. And where could you and Dashiell afford to move?"

Kat took a leftover pastrami sandwich out of the fridge and unwrapped it. "Don't worry, Mom, I have no intention of selling, no matter how much Logan's lawyer tries to drag things out." If Logan wanted to tie up their divorce in an endless discussion of major assets, then that was his choice. It wasn't as if Kat were dying to resolve the issue so she could run out and get married again.

"I'm glad to hear it, honey. If you ask me, you're already letting him take advantage of you by not asking for alimony."

They'd been through this before. "I don't need him to support me, just to help support his son."

"Very noble, except that he's rich and you can't afford to repaint. By the way, this came for you earlier, certified mail. I signed for it." Lia held out an envelope.

"Who's it from?" Kat took another bite of her sandwich. "I have mustard on my hands."

"Don't squint like that, it causes wrinkles. It's from your father." Lia, who tended to overreact to minor events and underreact to major ones, suddenly looked at her daughter suspiciously. "You're starting to need reading glasses, aren't you? You're at that age now."

"Can we please stay on topic here?" Kat turned off the tap and dried her hands on a kitchen towel. "What do you mean, it's from my father? What is it?" Considering the fact that she hadn't heard from the man in thirty years, it seemed unlikely that he'd remember that his daughter had a birthday coming up.

"I have no idea. Do you think he actually sent you a card? Maybe he's dying. Did I ever tell you that in eleven years of marriage, he never once remembered our anniversary or bought me a birthday present?"

"I believe you might have mentioned it, yes."

Lia raised her eyebrows. "Oh, so it's boring to hear me complain about my lousy ex? Remind me of that the next time you get going about Logan."

"Yes, but this is just six months later. I believe I'll get over it by the time Dashiell needs bifocals." Taking the envelope from her mother, Kat stuck it in a drawer, on top of a growing pile of bills.

Lia stared at her. "You're not going to open it?"

"I need to digest a little first." The truth was, Kat hadn't thought much about her father in the past decade, and she wasn't sure she wanted to think about him now.

"But it might be important."

"He waited thirty years. I think I'm allowed to wait a couple of hours." Jesus, what if it *was* important? What the hell was she supposed to do with something important from her father? She'd accustomed herself to having one absentee parent, with whom there was absolutely no contact. She was used to being fatherless at every single parents' visiting day at school, on all her birthdays, at her wedding. She'd had to endure reading those awful kids' books on divorce, which all insisted that both your parents still loved you, even though, in her case, this was clearly not the case. On the cusp of turning forty, she didn't want to try to form a relationship with the man.

Lia polished her reading glasses on the hem of her shirt. "I still think you ought to open your father's letter right away. Maybe it gives us some clue as to how we can get the money he still owes us."

"God, you're obsessed."

"I am not obsessed!"

"Mom, it's been thirty years, and you're still complaining that my dad didn't buy you a birthday gift."

"Honey, at least I didn't renounce the entire male gender."

Oh, great, now her mother was getting on her case about that, too. "Sure, you dated, but you never found anyone you wanted to stay with."

"That's true." Lia gave her daughter a frank look. "But I did have fun."

Kat recalled that her mother had seen a few different men after her divorce. But as far as Kat could tell, Lia had reserved most of her passion for hating Kat's father. She'd talked about making phone calls to the State Department, tracking him down, attaching his earnings. "Not that it would do any good," she'd say. "He's got too many favors he can call in."

In the end, Lia's antipathy toward her ex-husband had outlasted any of her subsequent loves. Looking at the few old photographs of her father, Kat was always surprised to see how benign he appeared: a slender, small-boned, almost delicate man, with fine, fair hair, almost colorless eyes, and a way of standing that told you he wished you weren't taking his picture. He looked like a man who wasn't there, even when he was. Kat was surprised that her vibrantly attractive mother had married him in the first place, but Lia had explained that he'd had a startlingly sharp, muscular, wholly unsentimental intelligence, completely at odds with his mild looks. "I was taken by the fact that he was so brilliant and unsparing," Lia had told her. "I felt like his choosing me was a validation of my own intelligence. Of course, I was very young when I met him," she'd added. "When you're twenty, you don't realize how much simple kindness matters."

Kat looked at her mother now. "Tell me something, Mom. How old were you when you gave up on men?"

"Oh, I don't know. It happened gradually. The men just get more and more damaged and arrogant as time goes by. After a while, you meet some guy you considered a nebbish back in high school, and now he's stringing three different women along and acts like he's doing you a favor to ask you out."

"But with me, you think it's going to be different?"

Lia smiled. "Absolutely. Listen, at your age, I was still having adventures. I'm not saying you'll find someone to marry again, but I hope you'll meet someone who makes you feel wonderful for a while."

"You do realize that there's something a little ironic about getting this advice from a woman who edits romances?"

Lia gave a low laugh. "Honey, if we were all getting it in real life, then we wouldn't have to read about it." She stroked Kat's hair back from her face. "But I think you've still got some nice surprises in store for you."

"I don't need that kind of surprise. All I want is a chance to do what I'm good at again. And if I could make enough money at it to send Dash to private school, that would be nice, too."

Lia picked up her pocketbook from a chair and kissed her daughter on the forehead. "Get some rest. But you will let me know what you find in that letter from your father, won't you? I mean, I was married to the man for eleven years, I have a right to be curious."

Kat locked the door behind her mother and walked quietly into Dashiell's room. He was sleeping as he always did, with his chewed-up stuffed elephant clutched in his arms and one skinny, pajama-clad foot dangling over the side of the bed. Kat gently lifted his leg and moved it back onto the mattress, then pulled the covers over him. Dashiell instantly rolled over on top of the blanket. Kat attempted to pull the blanket out from under him, but Dash threw up one arm in unconscious complaint, and she stopped, hearing the ghost of Logan's voice: *Leave him alone, you're going to wake him up.* Kat sighed and rubbed the back of her neck.

She wondered if having a father leave was harder on a son than it was on a daughter. She suspected that it might be, particularly for a boy who was academically gifted but socially immature, like Dash. Little boys had a different culture from little girls, and there were some lessons that were easier to learn from a parent of the same sex.

Well, they would just have to make do. Leaning down to kiss her son on his forehead, Kat whispered, "It's going to work out."

Going back to the living room to turn off the lights, Kat saw that her mother had left some work on the couch. Recognizing the author's name, Kat sat down and flipped through the beginning of *The Passionate Imposter*, searching for the heroine's first encounter with the hero: "Her first thought was that he had the coldest eyes she'd ever seen."

Move this intro up a bit, her mother had written in red pen along the margin. *Nobody wants to wait two chapters to meet the hero.*

Kat swung her feet up on the couch and settled down to enjoy the sexual attention of a dangerous man in perfect safety and comfort.

chapter *three*

•

Magnus Grimmson had made sure to arrive fifteen minutes early for his first class in advanced English at the Persky Business and Traveler's Language Institute. At six feet four, he'd felt he would be more unobtrusive if he were already seated when the rest of the students arrived. He'd also wanted to claim the strategic advantage of a corner seat.

The first student to arrive after him was a beautiful Japanese woman with long black hair that nearly reached her waist. She was wearing a bright green Izod shirt and white Capri pants, and she was still young enough that her face didn't reveal anything much about her. When she spotted Magnus, she gave a startled gasp, then sat herself down as far away as possible, smiling and apologizing but making no eye contact. Magnus couldn't tell if hers was the kind of shyness that came from insecurity or cautiousness or from a quiet, deep-seated conviction of superiority.

Of course, she could also be having a reaction to being alone with a strange man. So hard to tell what was personal and what was cultural. Which was the point of this class, actually. According to the Persky catalog, "The Advanced American English Communication Skills course provides instruction in the idiomatic phrases, subtle social cues, and unwritten rules that underpin most social and business interactions."

Magnus figured there would probably be about an hour's worth of useful information stretched out over a month of lessons, but was willing to be wrong. God knows he'd certainly missed a few subtle social cues on his last job.

The door opened, and a well-upholstered lady of around sixty walked in, her light brown wig a perfect match for the mink collar on her wool suit. She sat down across from Magnus, fixing him with her sharp, dark gaze. "You are joining the class?" Her accent was Russian.

"Yes."

Magnus didn't think she seemed thrilled by the news, but had no idea why that should be the case. Since the advanced English class was geared for proficient speakers, the institute had a rolling admissions policy, meaning that students could join at any time. The woman Magnus had spoken to on the phone had added that this class was supposed to be more informal and social that the other levels, with the clear implication that this was the kind of class where friendships flourished and romances bloomed.

"So," said the Russian woman, "you are here on a student visa?"

"No, I am here to work," said Magnus, leaning back in his chair and allowing his legs to fall open. The Russian woman pursed her mouth in disapproval, but Magnus ignored her, taking out his *Persky Speaks English* textbook and examining it. Having spent time in the military, he wouldn't ordinarily allow himself to sit like this, but right now he was too damn uncomfortable to care. The Office of Technical Services had bought him a new wardrobe for this assignment, and while he didn't mind wearing the pale blue oxford shirts and pricey urban hiking boots, he had yet to figure out how to get comfortable in snugly fitted jeans. He'd always thought that the OTS provided agents with latex masks and cleverly disguised guns, not fashion makeovers, but then, he was new to this.

The next two students came in together. The hawk-nosed man with the long white beard and the heavy eyebrows reminded him of Gandalf the wizard; the short, extremely pregnant Mexican woman was unremarkable until Magnus looked more closely and saw the fierce intelligence in her eyes.

A sudden burst of Mozart in the small room made the Mexican woman jump.

"I am so sorry," said the Japanese girl, pulling her cell phone out of her trendy leather backpack. "I am turning it off right away."

"It's okay, I'm just tired." The Mexican woman rubbed her forehead, and Magnus could see that her knuckles were cracked and bleeding. "I began work at nine yesterday morning and didn't stop until nine in the evening." Over her head there was a poster of the Statue of Liberty silhouetted against a brilliant blue sky with the words "Persky Language Schools Give You the World!"

"I began working," said the Russian woman, her deep voice only marginally less harsh than it had been with Magnus.

"I began working at nine," the Mexican woman repeated.

"Forgive my interruption, but I believe that both are correct," said the wizard. His accent was Middle Eastern, his pronunciation British.

Wherever the man was from, the Russian woman didn't seem to like him any better than she liked Magnus. "We will have to ask the teacher."

Where was their teacher, anyway? Magnus checked his watch: 0900. Clearly, their instructor was the kind of person who would arrive just on time or late to teach a class. Not that it mattered: The class was three hours long, and a few minutes here or there hardly mattered. But Fred had said that this was the kind of thing to look out for. Human intelligence was all about understanding how people's minds worked. What mattered to them. What motivated them. What kept them up at night.

Magnus glanced up and noticed that a dry board had been wiped almost clean, although the words "lie, lay, lain, laid," were still legible, written in green ink.

Well, Magnus thought, that was one thing he wouldn't have to pretend not to know. There was only one usage of laid that he was sure of, and that was the one he hadn't used in quite some time.

"Good morning, class."

Magnus turned to the door, instantly recognizing Katherine Miner, despite the fact that she was at least ten years older than she'd been in the publicity photographs he'd seen.

"How was everybody's weekend?" Katherine moved to a seat near the middle of the table, forcing everyone else to move in closer together. "Did you visit your brother in Connecticut, Galina?"

As the Russian woman launched into a long-winded response, Magnus thought that if anything, Katherine Miner was better-looking now than she had been in her late twenties. The contrast between her dark hair and pale gray eyes was just as striking, but she seemed in some subtle way softer now, more approachable.

"And I see we have two new students. Let's see," she said, turning her full attention on Magnus. "You're either Luc Marchant or Magnet Grimmson?"

"Magnus."

"Sorry." Katherine made a correction in her book. "And you're from . . .?"

"Reykjavik. Iceland."

"Really." She regarded him with interest. "Someone I know was just telling me she's going there in November. She said that Iceland was actually very green and Greenland was completely icy."

"Well. In summer Iceland is green. In winter . . ." He shrugged. "It is cold and dark. But it is beautiful and there is a very active nightlife." Christ, he sounded like a travel brochure.

"With four months of night," Katherine said in a dry voice, "I can imagine you'd have to find *some* way to occupy yourselves."

The Japanese girl tittered. Had Katherine made a double entendre, or was Iceland just an inherently amusing country? And why the hell had Fred thought he might be appropriate for this assignment? He had fewer people skills than anyone he knew.

Katherine seemed to be expecting him to say something. Before Magnus had a chance to think of a response, the classroom door swung open, banging loudly against the wall.

"Merde." The newcomer was a lean, angular, shaggy-haired type in a black trench coat and motorcycle boots. He exuded ebullient confidence and an almost overpowering smell of stale cigarette smoke. "I mean, shit," the young man corrected himself, with more than a hint of mischief. "Only English, the Persky method, right?"

"I take it you are Luc Marchant?"

"Absolutely, I am in this class, if you are my teacher, Mrs. Miner."

"You may call me Katherine. You'll find Americans almost always use first names, even in formal business settings. On the other hand, Americans are not informal about punctuality—anything more than fifteen minutes borders on the insulting."

The Frenchman, of course, was fifteen minutes late. Magnus watched as he took this rebuke in with an easy smile and a nod, and no visible trace of discomfiture.

"Go ahead and sit down now, Luc, so we can get started." Luc glanced around the room, his army surplus bag slung over his narrow shoulder. There were two empty seats; one to the left of Magnus, the other right near the door, next to the Russian woman. The Frenchman shrugged off his leather jacket, revealing a black T-shirt underneath. "I can sit with you?"

"Of course." Magnus moved over to make room.

"Thanks, *mon ami.*" The Frenchman swung his jacket onto the back of the chair, smacking Magnus in the arm with the zipper.

"Okay, class, if we're done finding our seats, let's get down to work. Today, we're going to continue our work with standard American office slang. So take out your blue books and turn to page five."

Luc's hand shot up. "I do not have a blue book yet."

"So just read along with Magnus for now."

"Sure." Luc leaned in, his shoulder coming into contact

with Magnus's arm. Magnus pulled back; Luc did not seem to notice.

"Nabil, first example. 'You are putting me on.' Look down at the other expressions and choose an appropriate substitute."

The wizard's bushy eyebrows drew together as he stared at the page. "I am afraid I do not understand."

"Pick either a, b, or c. Which expression do you think can be used in place of 'putting me on'?"

Nabil stroked his white beard. "You are dressing me?"

"No . . ."

"Helping me out?"

"Only one choice left, and that's the right one, which is . . ."

"Not being serious with me."

It was utterly ridiculous, thought Magnus as he took his notes, his elbow too close to the Frenchman's. Why should the two tallest men in the class sit squeezed together in the corner?

"Very good, Nabil. Okay, Maria. 'He has to buckle down and do some work.' "

The Mexican woman did not need to consult her book. "He has to make an effort?"

"Excellent. Magnus, 'I want to get married a.s.a.p.' "

Magnus stared at Katherine for a moment. "Excuse me?" She had said it so conversationally that, for a moment, Magnus had thought she was confiding in him.

"It's your turn, Magnus. The third question in your book." Katherine smiled her patient teacher's smile while Magnus tried to recall his options. Instead, he found himself remembering his own marriage at its moment of implosion. *Listen, I know we've had this tacit agreement that we would see other people and be discreet about it, but this time it's different. I want to marry Dan."*

And Magnus, just standing there, the back of his head almost vibrating with the intensity of his thoughts. We had an agreement?

"Magnus?" Katherine's voice was very gentle. "The sentence is, 'I hope to get married a.s.a.p.' So the choices are, a, sooner or later; b, right away; or c . . ."

"Never." He said it with real conviction, and for a moment, everyone in the class just stared at him.

Katherine gave a quick, unladylike snort of laughter, surprising Magnus. Most people didn't recognize when he was making a joke. "On a personal level, I agree with you, but the correct answer is 'b.' The letters a.s.a.p. stand for 'as soon as possible'."

He'd made an impression just then, thought Magnus, but what kind? Fred had said that Magnus's greatest asset was that he looked like someone you could trust. Big, solid, blue-eyed, deliberate. Sounding cynical about relationships was probably not a brilliant move.

"Okay, Luc, your turn. 'Jack asked me to go out with him.' Does this mean, a, to leave the building; b, to go on a date; or c, to kiss.' "

Luc furrowed his brow. "Is it the last one?"

"No, the answer is 'b, to go on a date'."

"Ah," Luc said, just this side of innocence. "But to date is to kiss, no?"

"Well," Katherine said, "sometimes. There's another expression for that." Turning to the blackboard, she wrote: Make out = kiss. Go out = date. Over her shoulder, she added, "If you just stay in to tongue wrestle, I guess 'date' becomes a euphemism."

"Excuse me," said the young Japanese woman, raising her hand.

"Yes, Chieko?"

"What does it mean, to tongue wrestle?"

"Come over here," said Luc, "and I'll show you." Chieko's cheeks flushed red, but she giggled behind her hand as the rest of the class burst into laughter.

For the next fifteen minutes, the lesson degenerated into a discussion of how dating practices differed from country to country. A year ago, Magnus would have tuned the conversation out; he'd never had much patience for aimless banter. Except he'd come to understand that there was often a hidden agenda behind such communications. Magnus thought about all the times Guthrun had talked about vacations, where she wanted to go, what she wanted to do there. And what had he said? Just plan it and I'll show up at the airport. The look she'd given him had struck him as almost adolescent, exasperated, a little contemptuous.

He hadn't paid attention then. But now he knew better. There were patterns and indicators and signatures to identify in human interactions, just as there were in signal transmissions.

For a long moment, Magnus missed the base in Keflavik, the long dark winters, the endless sun of summer, hours upon hours to go over reports and analyze findings. Eric and Jon and Peter, fish-fry Friday, Biggie the rat.

And then he thought of Guthrun, her face flushed as she held the dish towel over her breasts. As if he were the intruder, the one with no rights to her nudity.

"All right, class, settle down."

With an effort, Magnus returned his attention to Katherine, who had moved over to the blackboard. "I'm going to write down a few idioms and I'd like you to use them in a sentence."

"Ah, Magnus? Pardon me, but I forget to bring a pencil."

Magnus handed Luc one of his three sharpened pencils.

"And paper?"

What the hell did the man keep in his book bag? Magnus ripped a sheet out of his notebook. "Anything else?"

"I'll let you know." Magnus couldn't decide if that last comment was meant to be facetious or not. Probably not; the man was simply arrogant beyond belief.

After the lesson, the two men stood for a moment outside Trinity Church, the ancient churchyard with its tilted gravestones a strangely European sight in the midst of the highrise office buildings. It was only noon, and Magnus was thinking that there was a whole lot of day left to get through when Luc offered to buy him a hot dog from a stand.

"Very American, eh, Magnus? You never see this in France, this eating on the street."

Magnus, who had consumed his frankfurter in two bites, nodded.

"You want another? Ah, excuse me, sir, would you give this man another? No, no, I pay, my gift."

Magnus forced himself to eat the second hot dog more slowly. He didn't have much to say, but Luc talked enough for both of them, lighting up a strong-smelling French cigarette and flitting from topic to topic. Did he say what he was doing in New York? Despite his resolution to attend better to idle conversation, Magnus couldn't recall a single word of it five minutes after they'd parted.

Still, he was pretty sure he hadn't missed anything of substance, because he was pretty sure Luc didn't *have* any substance, just a misplaced assurance in his ability to charm.

The second hot dog disagreed with Magnus for the rest of the afternoon.

chapter *four*

•

Kat woke up to find that something quick and brown was skittering across her belly. Despite the fact that she'd been a New Yorker for the past thirty years, she screamed, because roaches were one thing, rats quite another.

Kat scrambled up on the bed, her feet sinking into the mattress, and tore off her cotton nightgown. Her flesh was still crawling with distaste from the touch of those sharp little toes. *Where was it?* For a fraction of second, Kat actually missed her husband, because she really did not want to be naked and alone in her bedroom with a rat.

Then she reconsidered, because really, one rat in the bedroom was better than two, and at least the four-legged variety wasn't about to tell her that she shouldn't have bothered fixing her tits, because it wasn't her postpregnancy body that he found unattractive, it was her overly controlling personality.

A long, whiskered nose peeked out from under the bottom of the dresser, followed by a pair of beady eyes. Expelling her breath, Kat realized that this was no rat; her intruder was Ms. Nibbles, Dashiell's gerbil, who must have escaped yet again from her red-and-yellow Habitrail.

Ms. Nibbles stood on her hind legs and twitched at Kat, as if to say, Ha ha, you fool, I am the rodent you willingly brought into your home.

Still, Kat was relieved, because no matter how much she disliked her son's pet, at least she wasn't worried that Ms. Nibbles was going to give her rabies. Moving slowly, Kat came down off the bed just as the gerbil scrabbled under the radiator. *Great.*

"Dash? Dash, where are you? Did you take Ms. Nibbles out of the cage again?" Kat suddenly recalled how Logan used to accuse her of shrieking like an Italian fishwife: Is this really the example we want to set for our son?

Well, no. But every time Ms. Nibbles became agitated, she ate another of her babies.

Right after Logan had left, Dash had started asking for a dog, and Kat had finally broken down and bought her son a pair of supposedly female gerbils. It had taken them two weeks to find out that they had a breeding pair, four weeks to realize that Ms. Nibbles had a tendency toward infanticide and cannibalism, and three months to come to terms with the fact that Ms. Nibbles had become pregnant yet again, this time by one of her surviving offspring. They had given all the gerbils back to the store, except for the pregnant Ms. Nibbles, whom Dash had insisted on keeping.

Maybe it was time to reconsider the dog idea.

Kat pulled on a short, white, terrycloth bathrobe and went to find her son. Dashiell was in his room, hunched over his

Game Boy, and Kat thought he bore a faint, disturbing resemblance to the creature Gollum from *The Lord of the Rings*, fixating on his precious ring. *What was it about these electronic games that turned boys into obsessive compulsives?*

"Your gerbil is out, Dash. Honey, how long have you been up? Dash? Dash?" Kat raised her voice to be heard over the electronic pings and blips of the game. "Dashiell? Can you hear me?"

The phone rang in the other room. Kat looked at her son for a moment, torn between exasperation and concern. It seemed to her that Dash had regressed recently, tuning her out more, paying less attention to people and more to games, crossword puzzles, and math riddles. It hadn't escaped her notice that he was the exact same age that she had been when her mother had decided to leave her marriage, and that wasn't the only similarity; just like Logan, Kat's father had pulled a Houdini.

Other divorced dads lavished their children with toys, trips, candy-coated guilt offerings. Kat's father had simply vanished into some shadowy place called Europe, doing top secret work for the U.S. government. At least that was the cover story Lia had maintained for the first year or so, explaining why Ken never tried to contact his daughter.

Somehow, it didn't sound quite so convincing to say, Honey, your dad's off making a movie, that's why he doesn't call.

As if on cue, the phone rang again. Kat ruffled her son's soft, dark blond hair, so like his father's in color and texture. "Get ready now, okay? I'll go fix your breakfast. Dash? Nod if you hear me."

Dash gave a jerky nod. Kat went down the hall to the kitchen and picked up the phone on the fifth ring. "Good morning, Ma, what is it now?" Kat's mother usually called at least twice a day, once in the morning, when Kat was struggling to get Dashiell ready for school, and once in the evening, when Kat was struggling to get Dashiell through his homework.

"Good morning, dear, it's a work call." It was her agent.

"Oh, God, sorry, Daphne, I wasn't expecting you."

"Well, I'm sorry to be calling this early, but I have some news. *South of Heaven* is looking to bring back your character."

"They are?" Kat poured herself a cup of coffee. "But Logan's gone."

"Exactly. Hang on a sec, I'm on the train and we're going through a tunnel. Okay, that's better. So, with Logan gone the producers need to focus on other people. And the idea they've been batting around is to have Helen Jessup return, wanting to avenge Logan's death and claim her share of her father's business empire."

Kat took a carton of orange juice out of the refrigerator. "Oh, Daphne, that's great, but I'm not sure . . ."

"Are you kidding? Kat, this is just what you need to get your name out there again."

"I don't know, Daphne, it feels a little like going backward."

"Well, I can always tell them you're not interested, but I think you should at least consider it as a stepping-stone. You've basically been out of circulation for about nine years. You need to reestablish yourself."

Kat stopped fixing her son's breakfast. She had to force herself to focus on what Daphne was saying, and on what she was not saying, which was, *This is your shot, Kat, take it or leave it.* Staring at the souvenir Bronx Zoo mug in her hands,

Kat realized that there had to be a reason Daphne was calling her this early. She was excited for Kat; Kat ought to be excited for herself.

"You're right," she said, trying to inject a note of enthusiasm into her voice. "Of course you're right. And it would actually be great to play Helen again." And who knew, thought Kat as she inserted a Pop-Tart in the toaster, maybe it *would* be great. It had been a while since she had felt anything but flat or angry. Well, with the exception of when she was with her son. With him, she still felt other things.

"And remember," Daphne continued on the other line, "this doesn't mean you can't do other work, Kat. In fact, this opens the door to other work. Only one thing, though: They want you to do a test."

The coffeemaker had finally finished brewing; God, did she need a cup. "A test? But I originated the character. When I left to have Dashiell, they begged me to come back."

"There's a new male lead, they need to see how you two work together on film. It's a formality, Kat."

"Like being asked to fill out a work history form before joining the family firm."

"Exactly. You know you have a home there, so why worry?"

Kat glanced at the clock over the stove. Even if they hurried, Dashiell was going to be marked late for school, which meant she'd be late to the Persky Language Institute. "I trust you, Daphne. If you tell me not to worry, I'm not going to worry."

"You are the most absurdly gorgeous thirty-nine-year-old I know, and so talented I could shake you for not taking on more work all this time. You absolutely do not need to worry."

"All right already, I'm not worried. When do they want me there?" But Kat already half knew the answer. They knew she was hungry for the job, and they were going to drive the point home. "Let me guess: They want to see me immediately."

"Ten o'clock today, if you can make it," said Daphne, and Kat thought that her normally imperturbable agent sounded the slightest bit embarrassed. "They've just had a big meeting and decided to move up their timetable on this story line, and they want to get going right away."

Kat considered making an excuse; it was only the second class of the session, she couldn't find anyone to sub for her on such short notice. Instead, she forced herself to say, "I'll need to find someone to teach my class today."

"Well, call me if you have a problem. Otherwise, just go be your wonderful self."

Kat hung up the phone, took a deep breath, then phoned Marcy, who said she'd be happy to take her morning class. Then Kat raced back into her bedroom, where she exchanged her sports bra for something that gave her a better shape. Searching frantically through her closet, she settled on a pair of low-cut jeans that flattered her legs and backside. Yanking on a clingy dark red top, Kat stuck her head into her son's room. "Dash, are you dressed?" He was exactly as she'd left him. Grabbing the Game Boy out of his hands, she ordered, "Bathroom, clothes, late, now!"

He finally looked up at her with his father's startlingly green eyes. "Aw, Mom." Movie star eyes. Hero eyes. "You didn't give me a chance to save it!" Maybe he'd become an actor like his parents. Horrible thought.

"I have an audition in just over an hour, please Dash, make it easy on me today."

A slow, pleased grin spread over her son's handsome face. "You've got a job? Cool!" He grabbed her in a bear hug, too hard, but instead of correcting him, Kat just held his thin, gangly body close, inhaling the musty, slightly sour childhood smell of him for one good, long moment.

"Watch me get ready, Mommy, I'm going to be super-sonic."

"You're my good boy."

"I like that shirt. The color is nice on you."

Kat laughed. "Hurry up, you!"

"You have to let me go first."

But suddenly, paradoxically, Kat did not want to relinquish this embrace, did not want her son to have to head off to fourth grade where his teacher might ask him questions he knew but couldn't answer easily, where his classmates might not be kind to him at recess. "I love you, you know that? I *love* you." Enough for two parents, she did not say.

Reaching up to tickle her neck, Dash said, "I love you more."

"No way. Mothers always love you more than you love them."

"And fathers," Dash said easily.

Kat hesitated, thinking of all the years she had said "your father and I," because that's what you did when you were married. Her mother had done it, too. Your father and I love you. Your father and I are proud of you. Your father and I bought you this lovely doll-house for your birthday. Before he left on his business trip, of course. He wanted to be here, honey, and if there weren't such a big time difference, he'd call.

And if there was a gap between what was said and what you perceived to be true, you learned to live with it, the same way you learned to live with all the traditional lies adults told you about how the world works.

Kneeling down, bringing her face on a level with his, Kat tried to think of something to say that was neither painfully honest nor reassuringly false. There wasn't a lot to work with. "You'll be the kind of father who loves his children more, Dash. You'll be a wonderful dad."

And then Ms. Nibbles skittered across the wood floor, and Dash shouted, "Cannibal mom on the loose! Shut the doors! Dangerous animal at large!"

This was the problem with real life, Kat thought: Scenes never ended where you wanted them to, promising plotlines fizzled out, and nobody ever revealed the big secret that makes everything else fall into place.

chapter *five*

•

Magnus had learned one new fact about Katherine Miner this morning. She had perfectly proportioned breasts: full, with a slight, natural slope, and small, dark pink nipples at the precise angle to most tempt a man's mouth. She had the kind of breasts that made a man want to spend the best part of a day just learning their shape and taste.

Or, at least, she'd had them back in the late eighties, when she had filmed *Zombie Prom Queen*. For sheer sexiness, though, he preferred the early nineties love scene in *The Lying Time*, where she played the role of a pregnant widow who takes in a boarder. Pressing rewind, Magnus let the scene play out again, admiring the way Katherine turned and looked over her shoulder, acknowledging that she'd known she was being watched all along; the delicious, wary tension in her eyes when the drifter reached out and touched her cheek; the sudden ferocity of her response when he kissed her.

You couldn't see her bare breasts in this scene; they were pressed up against her co-star's chest.

Magnus pressed pause on the DVD player and stretched out on the cheap floral sofa bed, which had come with the rental apartment, along with two chipped duck lamps, a paint-by-numbers landscape, and a small, unsteady table surrounded by folding chairs.

It felt a bit decadent, lying around in his briefs, watching a twenty-nine-year-old Katherine running around topless. But he'd woken up at five AM, his body clock still adjusting, and this was homework. Intelligence analysis, after all, was a bit like handicapping horses; you accumulated as much information as you needed to make a prediction about how a given individual was going to behave in the future. If he could just watch these images of her long enough, Magnus thought, he might begin to catch a sense of the underlying pattern, see what common element she brought to each role.

Of course, he'd also gotten a bit distracted by her breasts.

But upon repeated viewing of the love scenes, Magnus had found that what was below her neck wasn't as riveting as what was above it. On-screen, Katherine Miner's face reflected a frank, earthy, open sensuality. In person, however, she came across as one sharp, witty, extremely well defended woman.

Running the ancient shower until the rust-colored water ran clear, Magnus wondered if this dichotomy had always existed, or whether it was a recent development. Either way, he thought, it wasn't going to be easy to gain this woman's confidence.

He figured he might as well begin by examining his own

preconceptions. In Magnus's experience, when you didn't look at your own bias, you just wound up convincing yourself that the evidence proved what you'd known all along.

That was how you wound up with reports that said "Of course the Shah of Iran isn't in any real danger" or "The only reason the inspectors can't find Iraq's weapons of mass destruction is because they're not really looking." That was how you bought the story that your wife was always driving along the coast to Hveragerdi and coming back exhausted because she was a dedicated horseback rider, instead of recognizing that she was sore from athletic bouts of sex with other men.

The shower sputtered and then abruptly the water flow slowed to a trickle. Upstairs, somebody must have decided to run a bath. Magnus stepped out of the stall and filled the sink with lukewarm water. Okay, he thought, splashing water on his face and under his arms, what do I *think* I know about Katherine Miner?

Grew up attending English-speaking schools in Spain and Italy. No contact with her father from the age of ten, when her mother brought her back to New York, leaving Miner in Italy. Probably not much of a relationship with her father beforehand, either, since he was usually off on assignment. Extremely close with mother, both literally and figuratively. Had a fairly successful acting career consisting of some off-Broadway and small, supporting TV and film roles, culminating in a three-year stint on a soap opera. No long-term romantic relationships before Logan Dain. Devoted herself almost exclusively to raising the kid, who had an early speech and language delay. Delegated all financial dealings to the husband, who lost their savings in bad investments and then left her to pursue a career in movies. Five months ago, her friend Marcy helped her get a job at the Persky Institute, but finances were still a problem.

At the present time, no hobbies or sports or extracurricular activities.

Christ, Magnus thought, how the hell am I supposed to establish rapport with this woman? She makes *me* look like the life of the party.

The phone rang and Magnus answered it on the third ring. "Hello?" The caller ID said "out of area."

"Good, I got you before you left for class."

"What's up, Fred?" Magnus supported the phone between his chin and shoulder as he pulled on his jeans.

"News flash: Your potential source is ditching class and heading out for an audition at her old soap on Sixty-fourth and Columbus."

Magnus paused. "So you want me to approach her?"

"It's a good opportunity to get her on her own, but you're going to have to figure out a reason why you weren't in class."

Magnus rubbed his hand over his chin, wondering if he needed a shave. "Any suggestions?" Grabbing a razor, he decided not to bother with shaving cream.

"You could say that you just found out that your ex-wife's getting remarried."

"I'm so upset by that I skip class? Makes me sound a little high strung." Magnus scraped the blade over his jaw.

"You also found out that she's pregnant."

"Ouch." Magnus patted his chin where he'd nicked himself. "This wouldn't happen to be true, would it?" After twenty years of working in signals intelligence, Magnus was used to interpreting photographs, not people. Still, he wouldn't put it past his handler to use news like this to his advantage. Fred was a strategist.

"Actually, it is. Dan just filed a request for married housing, said they were expecting a baby in early February."

Magnus tried not to imagine Guthrun's slender belly swelling with pregnancy. "Gee, thanks for breaking it to me gently."

"You know a gentle way to tell a man his wife's knocked up with another man's kid?"

He had a point there. Fred waited, and when Magnus didn't say anything, he added, "Contact me as soon as you've got something to report."

The line went dead, and Magnus stared at it for a moment, wondering if he had made a mistake in accepting this assignment. He knew a hell of a lot more about nuclear stockpiles than he did about cultivating human sources of intelligence. And no matter how many times Fred had reassured him, Magnus still felt certain that Katherine was going to notice that his English was just a little too good to be a second language. Which, of course, it wasn't.

"It's not a problem," Fred had insisted. "First of all, you're not exactly a big conversationalist. Second of all, you've managed to pick up a bit of your ex's accent."

I hope he's right, Magnus thought as he buttoned a pale gray Armani shirt that a team of highly trained disguise experts had distressed until it appeared as if he'd owned it for a decade. Even without the question of whether or not he belonged in Katherine's class, he had a feeling that she was going to be suspicious of any man who started getting too friendly.

Ken Miner, on the other hand, wasn't in the least suspicious. No, he was one hundred percent convinced that everyone was out to get him.

As Fred had explained it to him, Ken Miner had gone from

being one of the Agency's top field agents to becoming a paranoid recluse who lived in a small apartment in southern Israel, where he chain smoked and worked on a memoir that he never seemed to finish.

Of course, Magnus thought as he tied the laces on his leather sneakers, that was the problem with the spy business—a certain amount of paranoia went with the territory, but when you got to the point where you assumed everyone you knew was out to get you, you weren't much use to anyone. Contrary to popular belief, the CIA didn't snuff out old agents. Either you were important, and they kept you on the payroll, or you weren't, and they let you get on with civilian life.

So no one had cared about Ken Miner until about two months ago, when the tiny, central Asian country of Kyrgyzstan underwent a sudden, violent change of government. Scrambling to figure out what was going on, the Agency learned that a fellow by the name of Muhammed Oybek had emerged, seemingly from nowhere, to become a major political player. It turned out that Oybek hadn't been on anybody's radar screen, in part because none of the agents actually spoke the country's native language. Then Fred had remembered that Miner had actually recruited the man back in 1980. At the time, Oybek had been a low-level Soviet party member. Very low. So low, in fact, that no one had been very impressed with him, and the man was let go, his file permanently closed.

Now Oybek was a power to be reckoned with, but no Westerner was able to get within spitting distance. Was he loyal to Moscow? Did he want to strengthen ties with the Arab countries, and how did he feel about nearby Afghanistan?

All of a sudden, Ken Miner was the go-to man. Not only did he know Oybek, but he spoke some Kyrgyz, a language no one else could even pronounce.

So Fred had gone to Miner's Eilat apartment, only to find that his man had vanished. Fred had speculated that Miner had spotted him coming, jumped to the conclusion that the Agency was out to get him, and bolted out the back door. For a crazy old guy, Miner was certainly resourceful—Fred hadn't been able to locate him.

But going through his computer files, Fred had found a clue as to where Miner might be now. There was an email to the ex-wife, expressing an interest in seeing her and their daughter. Lia's response had been to threaten Ken with non-payment of back child support. Which meant the daughter was their only real lead.

Magnus yawned, stretched his hands over his head, and walked four steps over to the apartment's tiny kitchenette area. This consisted of a narrow, filthy stove, a tiny refrigerator, and an electric kettle whose heating element was caked with white scale from the calcium in the water.

Opening the refrigerator, Magnus pulled out a carton of orange juice. He felt a lot more confident about his ability to convince Ken Miner that he was on the level than he did about his chances of impressing a former movie actress. Magnus was used to dealing with brilliant but mentally unbalanced folks—his staff in Iceland had been filled with them. His track record with women, however, wasn't so great.

He hadn't even noticed that his wife was cheating on him until he'd come home to find her lying spread-eagled on the kitchen table as Lieutenant Colonel Dan Saunders slammed into her. It was a setup, of course. Even Magnus understood that, dim as he was about such things. She'd wanted to forcibly demonstrate her unhappiness, because he'd been too blind to notice that she'd been cheating on him for two years. And yet he'd stood there, not saying anything for a moment, just watching as his superior officer screwed his wife. The twist in his belly, strangely enough, hadn't just been pain, or even disgust. It had been mixed with desire, at the rawness of it, his delicate wife making harsh little grunting sounds as Saunders thrust in and out of her.

That was the part he still couldn't understand. He didn't even like porn, for God's sake. He'd loved his wife. He'd been betrayed. The memory was still painful. So why?

He knew what Guthrun thought, because she'd said it. *So that's what it takes to wake you up.*

That memory had pretty much put his libido into cold storage. Until he'd met Katherine. Magnus took a sip of orange juice from the carton. Maybe all he'd needed was to get away from Guthrun and that whole sick situation. Besides, it wasn't as if he needed to do anything other than charm Katherine a little. He knew how to do that. He just didn't know how to handle all the stuff that came after.

Shit, he'd spilled some juice on his shirt, and because the damn thing had been tailored to his body, the stain showed clearly across the front. Irritated with his clumsiness, Magnus began undoing buttons. Why the hell couldn't he have gotten a disguise that hid things rather than revealed them?

chapter *six*

•

Kat, oh, my God, I didn't know you were coming in today! I was just going to call you to see if you were free for lunch this week." Suzette Morris, an ebullient, gym-toned redhead who played *South of Heaven*'s most-married woman, gave Kat a hug and then pulled back, still holding Kat's hands. "Get a load of you. You look amazing, as usual." Kat had considered Suzette a friend, until she'd left the show and Suzette had stopped calling her back.

"So do you," said Kat, taking in Suzette's careful makeup, off-the-shoulder blouse, and plaid mini-skirt. Suzette was putting a bit too much effort into looking casual, a sure sign of age. Kat, who had barely had time to apply undereye concealer and lipstick in the cab, was glad that she'd at least managed to find her good brown leather jacket, which was as thin and soft as fabric and cut like an English riding coat. The jacket made her feel as if she'd had all the time she needed to get ready and decided to dress with deliberate casualness.

"Oh, and you wore that leather jacket of yours! I always loved that piece," said Suzette. "I wish I could just wear my old favorites the way you do, without worrying about what's in fashion."

Ouch. "Oh, I always figure it's better to follow your own sense of style. By the way, I like your new haircut. Very flattering." Of course, Kat was very much aware that Suzette's new shaggy red bob just happened to hide all the places a surgeon's knife might leave a scar. Kat suddenly felt much better about her own messy ponytail, which revealed that she hadn't had any work done on her face.

"Yeah," said Suzette, ruffling her bangs, "I thought it was time for a change. Hey, have you seen everyone yet?" Suzette took Kat's hand and threaded it through her arm. "Come on and let's see who we can surprise."

Kat allowed herself be led along, hoping that the fact that her jacket wasn't this year's cut didn't really matter. She figured that the main reason she was here was to reassure some newbie executive that a nearly forty-year-old could still play a major vixen. She didn't want to appear out of date.

"So," Suzette said, "what *have* you been up to these days?"

"Working on a screenplay," Kat lied. "An independent filmmaker approached me about adapting something for him." Actually, a Columbia filmmaking student had suggested this to her, and she'd told him she had no time.

"Oh, really?" Suzette looked intrigued. "Anyone I know?"

"Probably not yet, but you will." Kat turned the subject back on Suzette, pleased to hear that she'd given her cover story the right note of authority. *You know how to do this, Kat.*

As Suzette led Kat down the hallway, she reminded herself that this just another role, playing herself in the theater of the real. All right, so she'd discovered her first gray pubic hair this morning and her right foot was developing a bunion. Kat knew that projecting self-assurance and an air of relaxed sensuality was the best beauty trick of all.

Of course, it helped if you'd had sex within the last calendar year.

"Here we are," said Suzette, stopping in front of the actor's lounge. "Probably the same stale doughnuts as when you left."

Dean Marcovici, who had been a minor player ten years earlier but was now an established star, gave a whoop when he saw Kat, lifting her off her feet and whirling her around. "Oh, thank God, Kat, I've had no one to scheme with since you left. Boring, boring story lines. Oops, did a writer just walk by the door? Oh, fuck it," he said, raising his voice. "Boring!" As he put her down, Dean gave her a squeeze with his left hand, which was directly under her breast. "I cannot tell you how much I've missed copping a feel of your delicious zeppolis."

Kat swatted at Dean's hand. "I thought you were more a connoisseur of cannolis."

"Oh, Lord, you think I'm gay, don't you? Why does everyone always assume that? Is that why you never even gave me a chance?"

For a moment, Kat just stared at him, nonplussed. Then Dean punched her in the arm. "Just kidding, I am gay. But I know, when straight guys start waxing their eyebrows, how's a person supposed to tell?"

"Katherine!" Isabel Lash, the show's executive producer, walked into the lounge with her arms outstretched. "Welcome back!" She had let her hair go gray, a light, silvery color that matched her linen suit.

"Oh, Isabel, it's great to be back," said Kat. "And I love your hair." The instant the words left her mouth, Kat became conscious of having said the same thing to Suzette, still standing behind her. Never mind, she told herself, keep going, same rules for life as for improv. "So you forgive me for leaving after I had Dash?"

"I was just sorry to see all that talent going to waste," said Isabel. Behind her back, Dean pulled a simpering face; he knew as well as Kat did that Isabel, miffed at Kat's departure, had informed the show's head writer that Kat didn't have to do much acting to play a bitch.

"Well, initially I thought I'd do some theater when Dash got older, but as it turned out, he was kind of a full-time occupation for a while."

"I know motherhood hits some women that way—they just feel they can't leave their kids for a moment." Isabel smiled. "Others find a balance."

Was it hostility or was it Botox, Kat wondered, that made Isabel's expression appear slightly frozen? A bit of both, she decided. "Well, Dash had constant ear infections and then got diagnosed with a speech and language delay, so balance was a little hard to find there for a while." She smiled back at her former boss. *Yes, I still bite back, Isabel.*

"Yes, I'm sure. But all that's over now, isn't it? Now, why don't you go on ahead into makeup and we'll introduce you to Matteo, our new bad boy."

Dean leaned in and stage-whispered, "But this time you have to promise not to let your hunky co-star knock you up, sweet-ums."

Kat gave a little snort. "As if." She waved good-bye to her

friends and walked the familiar route to makeup, glancing at the show's various awards on the wall, pausing at an old still of herself as Helen Jessup in her big wedding scene with Logan.

It felt better than she'd imagined, being back on set. Ten years ago, she'd felt that her role didn't allow her to stretch as an actor; now, she'd be content to make a living while practicing her craft. And it would be nice to have a whole social network at work again. Teaching English to foreign students might be rewarding, but the other instructors kept to themselves. She needed to get back into the swing of things again, go to the theater, attend parties. Dashiell was old enough now for her to concentrate a bit on her own life.

Kat walked into the makeup room, sat down in front of the lighted mirror, and began removing the concealer she'd applied in the back of the taxi. She heard rather than saw someone enter the room, and turned to see if it were Allie or Josie who was working today.

It was neither.

The young woman who'd just seated herself in the room's second chair was a long-legged, fresh-faced brunette in a strapless yellow sundress. She appeared to be in her mid- to late twenties, with a graceful lithe bearing that suggested a background in dance.

Kat returned the girl's smile, taking in the younger woman's sharply arched eyebrows, the slightly almond cast of her dark eyes. Feature for feature, this twenty-something did not resemble Kat, but Kat knew instantly what she was looking at: a younger version of herself.

"I don't suppose you're here to do makeup, are you?" Kat kept her voice dry and knowing, Bette Davis in *All About Eve*.

"No, I'm here for a test. Oh, my God," said the woman,

"aren't you Katherine Miner? But I thought . . ." there was an awkward silence. "I kind of got the impression that you'd passed on this role."

"Well," said Kat, "they gave me a bit of a different impression, too. What's your name?"

"Bo. Bo Johnson." She held out her soft young hand, and Kat leaned forward to shake it. "I loved you in that film you did in the early nineties, *The Lying Time?* We studied it in my acting class and I always thought that you were so underrated."

"Thanks." Kat was irritated by the girl's hesitant tone, but really, what else could this Bo do? If Kat was going to play the cynical fading star, then Bo had to be the breathless ingenue or the scheming chorus girl.

But as Kat looked at their reflections side by side in the mirror, she perceived a certain blandness in this girl's expression, a lack of spark. So what if this Bo were ten years younger? Kat knew her own abilities. Had the breakup with Logan really made her so unsure of herself that she'd walk away from a challenge?

Bo looked at her watch. "It's taking a long time, isn't it? What do you think they're doing out there?"

"Yelling at each other," said Kat, "for putting us in makeup at the same time."

Bo gave a startled bark of laughter. "Oh, my God," she said. "You are so right. Too funny, really. Well, Katherine, if we're being honest here, I have to say that I nearly pissed myself when I saw you in here. I really am a fan of your work, you know. I used to watch you as Helen all through senior year of high school! So, I don't know how to put this, because I can't see how you wouldn't get this job if you want it, but good luck."

Kat smiled without bothering to involve her eyes. "Same to you, Bo."

Just then Josie came into the makeup room, babbling apologies and telling Kat how perfect her skin looked. "It's so great seeing you again! It's kind of like old home week, isn't it? What with you and Logan both coming by."

Kat's initial response was one of confusion. "Logan's coming here today?"

Josie's brown eyes went wide. "Oh! Oh, you didn't know." Josie's skin was too dark to reveal a blush, but nervousness made the hint of Alabama in her voice stronger. "Me and my big mouth."

"Josie, I don't understand."

"Just forget I said anything." Josie smoothed some foundation under Kat's eyes with a sponge.

"Are you joking? There's no way I can forget this now." Conscious of the other actress in the room, Kat kept her voice neutral. "So Logan is here in New York. Is he coming by today? Has he been here already?"

Josie hesitated. "Well," she said, "he came by earlier today, and he's going to shoot some scenes sometime next week. I think. I don't know when, exactly, and you know how schedules change around all the time."

Kat tried to remember what her agent had told her. "But didn't Logan's character just die?"

"Ah, well, you know soaps. Maybe he's dead, maybe he's got an evil twin, maybe someone's had plastic surgery to look like him."

"I see. And just how long has he been back from the dead?" Kat felt a surge of anger so intense that she understood how people wound up shooting their spouses, chopping up the remains and tossing them into the marshes behind the New Jersey Turnpike.

"As far as I know, he just got in from Europe. I would've thought he'd contact you, because of your son."

"Yes, I would have thought so, too."

"He's probably going to call you. In fact, I think he said something to that effect."

Kat fought a rising sense of humiliation. "Come on, Josie, if this were any other man, you'd be calling him a shiftless bastard."

"I'll call Logan a shiftless bastard. Shiftless bastard. That better?"

"Much." She closed her eyes as Josie applied a touch of eyeshadow, fighting to keep herself calm. It wasn't easy. Disturbing questions kept bubbling up: *How could I have spent so much time with a sociopath? Is there something wrong with me? Do I have any judgment at all? It's all right*, Kat told herself. *You can use it for the scene.* Kat tried to focus on channeling her hurt and embarrassment into something simpler. Helen Jessup was a goal-oriented narcissist, prone to fits of outrage. When life disappointed her, she didn't sit around analyzing her defects and second-guessing her choices.

She got pissed off.

"All right," said Isabel, striding into the room and filling it with the scent of Ma Griffe and tension. "How are we doing? Ready to meet Matteo Ortiz? He's playing Ramon, the head of a crime syndicate that's come to town. He and Helen have a major story line coming up."

Kat glanced questioningly at Josie, who was still assembling her pots of makeup. "Oh, girl, you're so beautiful you hardly need touching up." Yeah, sure, thought Kat, and this is the way you treat all your stars. "Here, just let me do this." Josie brushed a quick dusting of blush on her cheeks. "There you go."

"Thanks, Josie." Kat slid out of her chair. "Okay, Isabel. Lead the way."

Isabel peered at her. "Did she even do anything? Never mind. Here's the script."

Kat gave the competition a friendly wave as she left the room. "Bye, Bo."

Isabel glanced at Kat sideways as she made her way down the hall. "Just so you know, it wasn't my idea to audition anyone else. I just wanted you, but you know how the sponsors are."

"Of course." What Kat really meant was, Of course the sponsors had nothing to do with it, you mendacious bitch. But the fact that Isabel was covering her ass gave Kat a glimmer of hope. *Maybe I will get this job.* And on the tail of that thought came the realization of how much she wanted it.

"Okay," said Isabel, stepping aside so that Kat could enter the room first. "Here we are—Matteo, meet Katherine Miner."

Matteo, who had been deep in discussion with Hank the cameraman, turned and smiled, his eyes bright with instant friendliness.

"Katherine, so nice to meet you!" He clasped her hand, and Kat couldn't help but notice that his manicure was better than hers.

"Not all that nice—I think I have to slap you at the end of this scene." Kat channeled Helen's bold confidence as she smiled up at the handsome young man, but she couldn't quite disguise the fact that she had just figured out what everyone else in the room already knew: She wasn't getting the part.

Matteo Ortiz was all of thirty-two years old. They weren't

going to hire a forty-year-old woman to act opposite him. Wait, Kat thought, maybe I'm jumping to conclusions here. Wasn't it possible that the producers were open to casting an older woman with a younger man? Or maybe she could still pass for thirty.

"So, Kat," said Isabel, "have you had a chance to look over your lines? Ready to start?"

Looking into her producer's eyes, Kat saw that she'd been right the first time—she didn't have a chance. It didn't matter to Isabel how she looked or acted, or whether she and Matteo generated any heat.

Isabel and her team didn't want an actress who *appeared* young. They wanted one who *was* young. And why shouldn't they? Youth was cheaper, harder-working, and easier to photograph, and had the added bonus of behaving badly on the weekends and reaping the resultant publicity.

All age was good for was giving sage advice that no one wanted to hear, such as, *Enjoy it while it lasts,* and *Figure out what you're going to do when this career ends.*

"Kat? Are you ready to start?"

For a moment, Kat considered leaving. She wasn't even sure why they were bothering to audition her—maybe one of the sponsors wanted to see her back on the show, and Isabel needed to say she'd done a test.

Should I play along with this farce? Maybe there was more dignity in saying, You know, I wasn't even sure I wanted this part, and walking out. It was what the character she was playing would have done.

But Kat wasn't a spoiled heiress. She was a professional, and part of being a professional was performing, even when you'd already fallen flat on your ass, even when you knew without a shadow of a doubt that you'd lost the audience in the previous act, and that everyone was just waiting for you to wrap things up so they could go home.

Kat took a deep breath.

"Okay," she said, "I'm ready." Setting the script aside on a low table, she turned to Matteo and offered him her opening line: "I hope you realize that I have no intention of letting you walk all over me."

Kat had no sense of whether she was doing well or not, but in the end, it didn't really matter. The real test of her acting ability would be whether she could smile convincingly at everyone before she walked out the door.

chapter *seven*

•

Kat made her way down Columbus Avenue under a bright October sky, not at all sure where she was headed. As she crossed the street to get away from the noise of a jackhammer, the construction worker stopped drilling to admire a very young girl. Despite the bite of autumn in the air, the girl was wearing a tube-top blouse that revealed the tanned, plumpish curve of her stomach. *Why did her parents allow her to go out like that?*

"Yeah, baby," said the construction worker as the girl clumped by on platform sneakers, clumsy with self-consciousness. "You shake that thing."

What thing? The girl barely had breasts yet. Kat turned to scowl at him, and the man gave a mocking tip of his hardhat. "Cheer up, lady, you'd be pretty if you smiled."

"And you'd be smart if you shut up." On the other side of

the avenue, Kat paused outside a liquor store. Rummaging in her handbag for her cell phone, she noticed the elaborate Halloween window display of frolicking skeletons and cobwebbed bottles of red Transylvanian wine. As a child, Kat had loved this time of year, when school was just beginning and relationships hadn't been sorted out yet. Funny how that vague feeling of excitement persisted, long after there was any reason for it.

What I need, Kat thought as she speed-dialed Zandra's cell phone number, is some emotional support. "Hey, Zan," she said, "any chance of your meeting me for some lunch?"

"I wish I could, Kat, but I've got other plans today." Zandra's voice was nearly vibrating with excitement.

"Ah, the return of semi-famous man?" Passing the drugstore window, Kat caught a glimpse of her reflection in the mirror. The makeup Josie had applied appeared garish in daylight. "When are you two getting together?"

"I'm still waiting for him to call and confirm."

"So what's the problem? Come out with me and bring your cell phone." Kat pulled a tissue out of her purse and wiped off some of the blusher.

"I'd better not. His schedule's pretty tight, so he's not sure when he has a window to see me."

"Hang on a moment. You mean, you're just supposed to sit there and wait for his summons?"

"You're making it sound as if he's doing it on purpose, Kat. This is a business trip, and he has commitments."

"Zandra, are you trying to tell me he can't make a definite appointment for food and sex? There isn't a man alive who can't make time for food and sex. Either he's running a power trip or he's hedging his bets."

"No, Kat, he's trying to juggle work and his personal life.

And I'm not just sitting around waiting for the phone to ring, I'm working." Zandra was a freelance documentary film-maker, a career made possible by a sizable trust fund. "You know, just because you feel let down by men doesn't mean that all men are going to let you down."

Kat took a breath. "You're right. Sorry, Zan, I just wish you'd meet a man who treats you the way you deserve."

"And I keep telling you, I have! Now what's going on?"

Kat crumpled the tissue and chucked it into a garbage can. "You mean, other than the fact that I've just discovered that I've passed my sell-by date? What I want to know is, why can thirty still be young and flirtatious and rife with possibility while forty's a quick slide off a steep cliff?"

"You didn't make an audition?"

"I lost out on my role, the role of Helen Jessup."

"I thought soaps were supposed to be good for actresses in their forties."

"Only if they stick around to defend their territory." On Kat's left, a handsome young man walked past wearing a baby in a sling across his chest. "Oh, and it turns out that Logan is in town, shooting a few scenes. A fact he didn't care to mention to me or his only son."

Zandra inhaled sharply. "Oh, Kat, that's awful. What can you do to make yourself feel better?"

"Hire a hit man?" From the opposite direction, Kat saw another, older man with thinning red hair talking animatedly to his young daughter. Typical. When you were upset about getting older, every woman you passed looked like Lolita. When you were dealing with father issues, every third man you saw seemed to be doting on an infant. "Or maybe I'll just go home and barricade myself inside my apartment for a month."

"How about some retail therapy? You could buy some fall clothes."

"First of all, I can't afford it. Second of all, there's nothing that even tempts me." Kat stopped in front of a boutique and stared at a sweater dress that looked exactly like something she'd worn twenty years earlier. "How can I cling to an illusion of personal progress when they're showing fuchsia ankle boots again? Doesn't anyone remember that we decided these were ugly back in eighty-eight?"

Zandra laughed. "We've changed our minds. Now they're playful."

"I'm too old for playful. I need flattering."

"Well, why not go buy yourself a lipstick?" Zandra's concept of economizing was splurging on smaller, less expensive items.

"I guess I could, except what's the point? Every other actress my age has had her eyebrows lifted up to her hairline. I don't even think it's attractive and I'm beginning to wonder if that's why I'm not getting any work."

In the background, Kat heard the sound of Zandra's doorbell. "Shit, Kat, that's him. Listen, how about I call you back later? We can talk this evening, okay?"

Before she could reply, Zandra had hung up. Kat checked her watch—almost twelve. She thought about calling her mother, but suddenly she felt drained of all energy. *Maybe I should just find someplace to sit and eat.* Kat inspected the menu in front of a small French cafe and considered a *salade niçoise. But with my luck, Logan will walk by with some new girlfriend just as I've stuffed my mouth full of tuna.*

It was just so fucking unfair. Nearly ten years after having Logan's child, her career had fizzled out, while Logan's star was on the rise, his commercial viability enhanced rather than reduced by the attractive crinkling of crow's feet around his blue eyes and the touch of gray in his hair.

And it didn't stop there. The self-serving bastard was able to just ditch his old family, secure in the knowledge he could meet a new woman, start a new family, and, if the woman or kid proved unsatisfying, well then, hey, he could just start over again.

She'd known all this before, but it hadn't bothered her quite so much, because she'd assumed that she would at least have the opportunity to channel her raw emotions into acting, which would lead to more and better job offers, which might conceivably lead to her meeting a new man who was smarter, kinder, and more reciprocal about oral sex.

It hadn't seemed likely, but it had seemed possible. Now Kat realized just how much she had depreciated in value over the course of her marriage. She had thought she was just taking some time out from her career to focus on Dashiell, but she'd really been aging in dog years.

Blinded by emotion, Kat walked straight into somebody's chest.

She made a sound halfway between "oh" and "oof" and the man she'd bumped into steadied her with two hands. "I'm so sorry, I wasn't paying attention."

"No, no, it's my fault." It was only after the man spoke that Kat realized who he was. Out of the context of her classroom, she hadn't recognized her new Icelandic student. *Christ, he was big.* "Magnus? Aren't you supposed to be in school?" In the daylight, she could see that his thick, shaggy blond hair was shot through with liberal amounts of silver.

Magnus looked uncomfortable. "I had . . . a work call." He hesitated. "And there was some news about my wife getting married."

Well, that was more information that she'd expected. "You mean, your ex-wife? If you two are divorced, she's your ex-wife."

Magnus looked even more uncomfortable. "Of course. My ex-wife."

Kat wondered if the Scandinavians were like the Germans and the Japanese, who hated getting caught in errors. "Listen, it's okay to make mistakes. That's how you learn."

"Yes," said Magnus, with a rueful smile. "You learn not to get married."

Kat smiled back. When you got past the deliberate way of speaking and the faint, lilting accent, the man had a sense of humor. "If it makes you feel better, I'm in the same boat."

Magnus frowned at her. "Excuse me?"

"I mean, I'm in a similar situation." Magnus continued to look puzzled, so Kat added, "I also got some news about my ex-husband. My almost ex." And that was more information than Kat had intended to be giving.

"Do you want—" Magnus broke off as Kat started saying "Well, I guess I'd better—" at the same time. He gestured that she should finish her sentence.

"No, really, what were you going to say?" As Kat waited for Magnus to speak, an elderly couple walked around them, peering with unabashed curiosity into their faces. Kat wondered what they thought they were seeing: a disagreement? a flirtation?

Magnus nodded, thanking her for letting him go first. "I was going to ask if you'd like to have lunch with me."

"Oh, that's very kind of you, but I don't think I can."

A deep line appeared between his fair eyebrows. "You don't think you can? Or you don't think you should?"

Kat hoped he paid this much attention to her in class. "A little of both, I guess."

"Is it against the rules?"

Kat shook her head. "No, not really, but it's not customary for the teachers and students to meet outside of classes."

"But it's not against the rules, correct?"

Kat tried to think of a way to reject him more firmly without hurting his feelings. She was reminded of her son, who also had trouble picking up social cues. And then she thought, Why am I making such a big deal about this? She'd had lunch with students before, usually right after they took the final exam.

"Well, all right," she said, at the same moment that he said, "I understand." They both laughed. Kat remembered something she was always aware of inside the classroom: Some cultures have longer conversational breaks than others. New Yorkers tended to overlap sentences, which meant that someone like Magnus probably had to struggle to get a word in edgewise.

"All right," she said to Magnus, "let's get something to eat. But just to make things perfectly clear, in America, a lunch between a man and a woman is not considered a romantic date."

Magnus nodded as they began to walk toward the French cafe. "I see. It is the same in Iceland. Unless, of course, the woman slaps the man with a herring."

Kat stopped in front of the restaurant and stared up at him. "You're joking."

Magnus gave her a sideways glance as he held the door open. "Actually, yes."

Kat wasn't certain whether Magnus was telling her indirectly that she was being too pedantic, or whether in some subdued, sardonic, extremely Scandinavian manner, he might be flirting with her.

Oh, crap, what if he's taking the wrong message from my agreeing to eat with him? Kat decided to order a hamburger with onions, just in case.

chapter *eight*

•

How the hell did she manage to eat so neatly? The tiny cafe
served an enormous portion of meat that kept slipping out of
its bun, and Magnus's fingers were covered in ketchup.
Katherine, on the other hand, was managing to take such delicate bites that it was a pleasure to watch her.

"So," she said, picking up a French fry, "what do you do?"

"What do I do?" For a moment, Magnus thought she was
asking him how he was coping with his divorce.

"What kind of work? By the way, in America, that's not
considered a personal question. In fact, it's one of the first
questions you'll probably get asked by people you meet."

Which was why he'd rehearsed his cover story until it
sounded natural. "I'm a chemical oceanographer. I've been
working on a climate record for the seas around Iceland."

"Ah." Katherine took a sip of her Coke. "But you don't do it anymore?"

Magnus swallowed a bite of hamburger, along with a residual sense of unease at lying. He had always believed that one should be as honest as possible with people, and it had come as a surprise to him to discover that not everyone felt that way. "I'm on leave," he said, surprised to hear how plausible it sounded. "As soon as my English is good enough, I start teaching at Columbia." At some point, of course, he was going to have to tell Katherine the truth, or some version of it. He would have felt a hell of a lot more comfortable just coming right out and telling her that the Agency was interested in making contact with her father, but Fred had been adamant. Make the human connection first, then hit her with the sales pitch.

"That should be an interesting change. Assuming you want to teach." Magnus wondered what Fred would make of the fact that she was the one driving the conversation. *Take control. Get her talking about herself again.* "What about you? Did you always teach?"

"I just started in the spring. I used to be an actress."

"But not anymore?"

"There aren't a lot of roles for women my age." Katherine picked her burger up, looked at it, then put it down again. "I think I'm full."

"Why not?"

"Excuse me?"

"Why are there no roles for women your age?" It seemed to Magnus that forty was the age at which everything got complicated, and complicated was interesting.

"I don't know. *Desperate Housewives* is a huge hit, and all the magazines say forty is hot right now. But that's just one show, and unless you're on it, there isn't much to choose from."

"But don't the studios like to copy successful formulas?"

"Sure they do. And then, when the copycat gets lousy ratings, they decide that forty isn't so hot anymore." Katherine pushed her plate away. "I could probably get a commercial playing a frowning mother or a happy Viagra wife, but that's about it."

"But there are a lot of roles for men your age?"

"Yes. There are." Katherine gave him a look that said, Don't be fatuous.

So much for that topic. *Shit.* Could he ask her something about her son? No, she hadn't mentioned him yet. What about fathers? Was there any way to work the conversation around to fathers?

The silence was stretching on too long. "Well," Katherine said, "this was nice." She turned and caught the eye of their waiter, holding up two fingers to signal that they needed two checks. "I think maybe the whole class should go out and eat together sometime. It's good to practice conversational skills like this."

"This is my problem with women," Magnus blurted out. "I never know what to talk about."

Katherine glanced over her shoulder, clearly hoping to see their waiter return. "What do you mean? You're doing just fine."

As uncomfortable as lying had been, this level of honesty was worse. "I do fine for five minutes. After that, I don't know what to say. When I met my wife—my ex-wife—she did all the talking. She was very . . ." Magnus hesitated, not wanting to sound too articulate.

"Outgoing? Friendly? Extroverted?"

"Yes," Magnus agreed. "In the beginning, that's how she was."

"And afterward?"

Magnus tried to think of how a non-native English speaker would describe his volatile, needy, narcissistic wife. "Her moods went up and down a lot."

"That's the problem with dating. You're on your best behavior and so is the other person, and by the time you see their worst behavior, you're already committed. If I ever get involved again, I'd want to know what the other person's faults are from the beginning."

"Well, as for me, I'm boring."

Katherine laughed as if he'd made a joke. "So is it just women you don't know how to talk to? What would you talk to a man about?"

The question took Magnus by surprise. "I don't know," he said slowly. "I suppose . . . you know, now that I think about it, men don't sit and talk. They do things."

"Okay, so what do men do?"

"Sports. Rock climbing. You talk about which climb you're going to do, and what equipment you need."

"My son likes to rock climb. Indoors. There's an atrium with a climbing wall just a few blocks from here."

"Do you climb?"

"Not since I was ten. And back then, it was trees." The elderly waiter arrived with their check.

Was it a coincidence that she'd been ten when she'd last seen her father? Magnus leaned forward, getting ketchup on his sleeve. "Why didn't you climb with your son?"

"I don't know. I just never thought about it." Katherine looked at the bill, scowling slightly. He liked watching her changing expressions. A lot of women in New York seemed to have curiously immobile faces. "I asked him to bring separate checks."

"Let me pay." Magnus reached for the check and she snatched it away.

"No, absolutely not."

"Please, I want to."

"Thank you, Magnus, but no." Katherine took a pen out of her handbag. "Let me just figure out what we each owe."

"But—"

"Do you have any singles? I think fourteen should cover your share."

Magnus handed her a twenty. "You know, it's not that hard, climbing an indoor wall." This was exactly the kind of bonding activity that agents were supposed to do with potential sources.

"I'll get you change." Katherine stood up and took her jacket off the back of her chair.

"If it's close by, and you have a little time, why don't we go take a climb? I could belay you."

This finally got Katherine's attention. "You could what?"

"Belay you. With the ropes." He mimed letting a rope out. This was perfect, he thought. *She doesn't have any hobbies of her own; I'll loan her one of mine.*

"No, really, thank you for the invitation, but I'm not in any shape to climb a wall today."

Magnus instinctively glanced down at her body. *No, don't do that, she'll think you're ogling her breasts.* "You look like you're in great shape." *Ach, that had come out sounding kind of sleazy.*

"Thanks," Katherine said in a dry tone, "but what I meant was, I'm not really prepared to do something that makes my adrenaline flow today." As Katherine slid her arms into her leather jacket, Magnus realized he should have offered her a hand. "But that's just the kind of thing you should do with women. There are lots of sporty things you can do in this city so you don't have to worry about sitting around and talking."

Okay, now she was giving him advice on how to pick up other women, never a good sign. "That's a good idea. What sorts of sports do you like?"

"Oh, don't go by me. I don't do anything anymore. But try the rock climbing wall. That was a great idea." Katherine reached down and handed him a napkin. "By the way, you have a little lettuce on your front tooth."

"Oh. Thanks." Magnus swiped at his tooth with his tongue, feeling as if he'd been catapulted back into adolescence.

"I hate it when people don't tell me," Katherine said apologetically as she stepped away from the table. "All right, see you in class tomorrow. No more playing hooky. That's an idiomatic expression for being absent without an excuse."

Magnus picked up the menu and pretended to study it until he heard the little bell over the door jingle, signaling that Katherine had left.

The instant he knew he was alone, Magnus buried his head in his hands. Jesus Christ, he was screwing it up. And there weren't going to be any second chances. After this, he was going to wind up in some dead-end job, a gray man at a gray desk, shedding flakes of dandruff and smelling of failure. From time to time, younger, brighter analysts would drop off their gruntwork, pretending to respect his years of ineffectual service. And finally, when the monotony became too much to bear, he would get an indoor cat and spend all his spare time calling the vet and worrying about its urinary tract health.

The bell on the diner's door jingled and Magnus felt a

blast of cool air. He looked up to see Katherine walking toward him. "I forgot my pen," she said, picking a Cross ballpoint up from the table. "Hey, your eyes look red."

Magnus tried to collect himself. "Do they?"

"Are you all right?" A few strands of dark hair had fallen out of her ponytail, and she absently brushed them aside.

"Well . . ." He had absolutely no idea what to say to her.

"Oh, God, your ex-wife is getting remarried. Of course you're upset."

"And she's pregnant, too." That was a legitimately upsetting thought, although Magnus wasn't sure why. He and Guthrun had tried to have a baby early on in their marriage, but when Guthrun hadn't conceived, they'd simply accepted it. Or at least he had. It suddenly struck Magnus that there had, of course, been other choices.

On the heels of that thought came another realization: *I must be the one with the problem.*

Katherine reached out her hand. "Come on."

"Where are we going?" Magnus was feeling a little stunned. Why hadn't he considered going to a fertility doctor? Why hadn't he talked things over with Guthrun?

"I don't have long, but if you want to climb that indoor wall, I'll try it with you."

Magnus stood up, trying not to let his immense relief show. He still had a shot at making this work. He could make a connection with this woman. All he had to do was have a little confidence in himself.

Which would've been a lot easier if he hadn't just woken up to the fact that his ex-wife had been right all along. He was sleepwalking through his life.

chapter *nine*

•

I'm going to fall."

"No, you won't."

"Oh, God, I'm going to fall. I can't believe I let my son do this." Katherine had climbed ten feet above the floor before the fear had set in. Now she was stuck in an awkward position on the indoor wall, her left foot supported by a small amoeba-shaped protrusion, her right foot somewhere beneath it, while she clung with both hands to a red plastic flipper. Despite the harness around her waist, she didn't feel in the least secure.

And if all this weren't bad enough, she had the sneaking suspicion that her low-waisted jeans were riding down, giving Magnus a good look at her panties. How could she face him in class after he'd seen her panties?

"Hey," she called over her shoulder. "I think that's far enough, don't you?"

"Kids do this without even thinking about it. You're doing fine, just straighten out your left leg."

Katherine glanced down at Magnus, who was standing on a foam mat, controlling the rope attached to her harness with casual assurance. His self-consciousness from the diner had vanished, and Katherine could see that the man carried himself with an athlete's energetic stillness—obviously, there was no rational basis for her fear. She was hooked up to a safety rope, Magnus clearly knew what he was doing, there was no way she could plummet to the ground like an injured bird.

Tell that to her frantically pounding heart, which was pumping adrenaline into her trembling limbs. Katherine squeezed her eyes shut. *I refuse to give in to panic.* When she opened them again, she saw that two or three people had come into the atrium, and were enjoying the spectacle of her fear as they ate their brown bag lunches.

"I want to come down now." This had been a terrible idea. She couldn't believe she'd agreed to this just because Magnus had seemed a little socially awkward. Didn't she have problems enough of her own without risking her dignity and her bones?

"You're fine," said Magnus, sounding infuriatingly nonchalant. "The climbing shoes allow you to grip with your feet, and the key is to get them sorted first. That's it, straighten your left knee."

To her right, Katherine saw that another woman was beginning to scale the wall, picking her way up a more difficult route. Within moments, the woman's gray head was level with Katherine's. "Come on," she said as she passed Katherine, "you can do it. I started climbing at age fifty!"

I will never forgive myself, Katherine thought, if I back down now. Slowly straightening her left knee, she searched for a better place to rest her right foot.

"Good, Katherine, good," said Magnus, some twelve feet below her. "There's a good hold just there, to your left. Yes." Kat reached up with her left hand, gained a couple of inches, then started the whole process again. Her fingers and thighs were shaking, and she could feel herself sweating with the effort.

"You're doing really well."

"Yeah, great, but now I'm stuck again." She remembered watching Dashiell do this last year, her usually unathletic son clambering almost effortlessly from handhold to handhold, laughing when he lost his grip and the rope connected to his harness swayed him out twenty feet above the floor, then back to the wall again. It was the one sport that hadn't made Dash feel uncoordinated or frustrated; she hadn't realized how fucking difficult it was.

"Move to your left," said Magnus. "Up there, the blue hold."

"Where? I can't see it."

"That's how I feel in conversations," Magnus called up, sounding cheerful. "I never know how to get from point A to point B."

"Yes, but you can't break your leg falling off a conversation."

"You can't fall off this wall," said Magnus, and she made the mistake of looking down at him. He made an adjustment to the black pulley device attaching her rope to his harness, picking up some slack. "See? If you let go, I'll lower you down."

"Why am I not reassured?" Seen from this height, Magnus wasn't so tall. In fact, he looked rather puny and insubstantial. Kat felt her stomach do a small, unsettled flop, and she could taste the burger she'd half-eaten in the back of her throat. Before Dash was born, she had hiked, ridden horses, gone white-water rafting. But now she felt incredibly vulnerable. "I want to get down now." She hadn't realized how much having a child had changed her. It wasn't just that she hadn't had the time to pursue her old interests; she'd also lost her nerve. "I mean, I really, really, really want to come down."

Forget pride, forget determination. Kat would gladly have paid Broadway ticket prices just to be standing on the ground again.

"So come down. Just hold on to the rope with both hands, lean back, and push off with your legs against the wall."

The part of Kat's brain that knew this was a good idea had ceded the stage to the part of her brain that wanted to curl into a fetal ball. "I don't think I can."

"Katherine, what is it you're most scared of?"

"Afraid of," she corrected him. "And what do you *think* I'm afraid of? Falling."

"So fall."

"What if the rope breaks?"

"I checked it. The rope is fine. It could hold a grand piano."

"If I kill myself, you're going to fail my class."

"Let go, Katherine. I've got you."

It occurred to Kat that there was something liberating about having the worst imaginable thing happen. At least you had nothing left to dread. Leaning back, she let go, and just like that, she stopped being frightened. She hummed the tune to the old Batman TV series to herself as she bounced gently down the wall. When she got to the ground, she wobbled a little on the foam mat.

"There you go," Magnus said, steadying her for the second time that day. Without thinking, Kat threw her arms around his neck. "Oh, God, thank you." He felt wonderfully solid under her hands, so tall and broad that she felt almost childlike by comparison.

Then Magnus gave her an awkward pat on the back, making her aware of how inappropriate this close physical contact was. "It wasn't so bad, was it?"

"It certainly took my mind off my other problems." Kat moved back, fumbling with the catches on her harness. "How do I get out of this thing?"

"What other problems?" Magnus gestured at the clasp near her crotch. "You, um, you undo this thing . . . do you need me to, uh, help?"

"That's okay, I think I have it." Kat stepped out of her harness. "I am going to have something fun to tell my son when he gets back from school. Hey, what time is it?"

"Almost two."

"I have to get home. Well, thanks for the experience, Magnus." *Talk about your awkward moment. I can't believe I just hugged him. What is wrong with me?*

"You have to go right now?"

"Afraid so." She felt sorry for him as he stood there, looking at her as if he desperately wanted to say something more. Don't worry, she felt like saying to him, You'll find a girlfriend here in no time. She thought about who was in her class at the moment, and was sorry that the nice Israeli woman had gone back to her country. He would have liked Seigal.

As Kat walked away, she saw a slight young man in a climbing harness walk up to Magnus, and as she watched, they made some adjustments to their equipment. The young man, who looked to be less than half Magnus's weight, let some rope out as Magnus took a different, more difficult route up the wall than the one she had taken. He maneuvered himself until he had his fingers at the edge of an overhang, and then began to pull himself up by sheer upper-body strength.

Well, Kat thought as she headed toward the subway, this was an unexpected ending to the day. In a strange way, though, the encounter with Magnus had made her feel better. Even though she wasn't in the least tempted by him, the fact that an attractive, sweet-natured man seemed to find her attractive was a balm to her ego.

At Seventy-second Street, Kat saw her bank and realized that she was nearly out of cash. As she opened the door, she wondered whether she would have considered Magnus as a romantic option if he hadn't been her student. Probably not. She'd always been suspicious of relationships based on mutual misunderstanding, and there were enough potential pitfalls between two people who actually spoke the same language and shared the same basic cultural assumptions.

Besides, Kat thought as she slipped her bank card into the ATM, Magnus wasn't her type. She'd always gone for extremely verbal men. With her, banter had been up there with kissing as preferred foreplay. Although, she had to admit, there was something exhilarating about doing something physical with a guy who looked strong enough to catch her before she hit the ground.

But even if he weren't in my class, Kat thought, I'd need to have some kind of mental connection, even if all I wanted was hot sex. And Magnus, while sweet, lacked a certain edge, a hint of spice, a dark side. *Although, God knows Logan had a dark side, and look where that got me.*

Punching in her PIN, Kat requested a hundred dollars. As an afterthought, she decided to check on her balance.

What she saw made her break out in a cold sweat for the

second time in an hour. Only this time there was no one around to lower her gently to safety. She had no money left. Heart racing, Kat picked up the phone beside the ATM. "Hello," said a young man with an Indian accent. "May I please have the number on your card or account?"

"My money is gone. I want you to explain where all my money went."

"First I will need your information, please."

Kat told him, feeling as if she were in shock.

"Yes, you have a negative balance of one hundred dollars, ma'am."

For a moment, distracted by the lilting cadence of the man's speech, Kat didn't process what he was saying. "A negative balance? You mean I owe the bank for the money I just withdrew?"

"Not until the end of the month."

When there would be interest due as well. "I don't understand how this could be possible. Can you check for some kind of an accounting error?"

"Just one moment, ma'am, while I check this out." Kat looked wildly around her. An old woman with a collapsible wagon and a small dog on a leash was tucking her purse into a fanny pack. A young man in slouchy jeans and a tailored shirt was withdrawing money without incident. Everything normal, except for her.

"Well? What have you found out?"

"One more minute, ma'am, and I can tell you exactly . . ." Across a telephone line and a continent, the young man paused. "Are you the only signer on this account?"

And suddenly, as her stomach knotted up like a fist, Kat realized what must have happened. "Logan Dain, my ex . . . my husband. Did he make a withdrawal?" This had always been her checking account, but now that she thought about it, she had signed Logan on back when Dash was a baby. So that he could make deposits and withdrawals for her on occasion. So that he could help her out.

"There was a withdrawal earlier this afternoon for the full amount." The young man sounded cautious. "Are you claiming this was an unauthorized transaction?"

"Yes! If it was the other person signed on to this account, he can't just close down the account without consulting me, can he?"

"Actually, I believe . . . I'm just verifying the password and . . . yes, he can."

"Oh God." Kat hung up the phone, ignoring the looks she was getting from the bank's other customers. She wasn't just low on funds anymore. She was broke. And unless she could find a way to boost her income before the maintenance was due on the first of the month, she was either going to have to give in to Logan and lose her apartment, or give in to her mother and lose her mind.

getting information

Every day we are confronted with situations that require us to obtain information from strangers. In most cases, if you need information, you can ask someone directly. However, there are some topics considered personal and private that Americans are hesitant to discuss. You can "soften" direct questions by asking indirect questions to show an interest and to gain information.

—SPEAKING NATURALLY:
COMMUNICATION SKILLS IN AMERICAN ENGLISH

chapter *ten*

•

"What do you mean, you didn't remember that he was still signed on to the account? How could you forget a thing like that?" In her purple caftan and matching turban, Lia Miner resembled an infuriated psychic, but instead of reading tea leaves, she was examining the bank statements Kat had left on the kitchen counter. "Honestly, Kat, that's the first thing you and that lawyer of yours should have taken care of."

"Please stop yelling at me, Mom. My stomach is in knots as it is."

Lia sat down on a stool next to her daughter and poured Kat a Campari. "Here, drink this, it'll settle your stomach."

"Shouldn't I take an Alka-Seltzer?"

"Trust me, right now you need alcohol."

Kat sipped her glass of bitters. "No, what I need is an acting job. I'll call my agent and tell her I won't say no to commercials anymore. No product too cheesy. Adult diapers, canned ravioli, estrogen creams—I'm desperate, I'll take anything."

Lia patted her daughter's hand. "Don't worry, I'm here to take care of you. Including a loan, if you need it. And if money remains tight for a while, you know we could always move in together. This apartment is big enough for the three of us."

Kat clutched at her stomach. "Thanks, Mom, but I'm sure I'll think of something."

"Of course you will. By the way, what's Dashiell doing right now?"

"He's playing Game Cube in the living room."

"Did he have dinner yet?"

Kat gave her mother a look. "Mom, it's eight o'clock on a school night. What do you think?"

"Don't be defensive, I'm just asking. What about you? Because I have some leftover meatballs."

"I think Logan's given me an ulcer." Kat undid the top button of her jeans and massaged her belly, which wasn't quite as taut as it had been a few years ago. *I should find the time to do Pilates again.*

"My friend Hilda has an ulcer. Take it from me, this is just heartburn compounded by heartache." The two women sat companionably for a moment without speaking. Through the open window, sounds filtered up from the street below—a car horn, a barking dog, a mysterious shriek.

Lia held up the Campari bottle. "Want some more?"

"Not right now, thanks. You know what I don't understand, Mom? How did I spend so much time with a complete shit?"

"I used to ask myself the same thing." Lia opened the refrigerator door and took out a tray of cheese. "What does your lawyer say?"

"About my taste in men?"

"About the money." Lia cut herself a slice of cheddar, silently offering some to Kat. "Not even a bite? No? Well, can't you do something to stop him? He has so much money of his own right now, with that film he's shooting."

"My lawyer says he thinks Logan is trying to force my hand." Kat's teaching salary brought in around $300 a week, one fifth of the apartment's monthly maintenance. Which was due in two weeks. Oh, God, it was hopeless. How could she possibly raise that much money right away? Give acting lessons? Wouldn't pay nearly enough. Sell her jewelry? She'd never gone in for expensive rings and necklaces. The only really valuable thing she possessed was the apartment.

Kat sat straight up. "Mom, where's today's newspaper?"

"On top of the microwave. Why?"

"I just had an idea. I could rent out the maid's room." Kat riffled through the *Times*, looking for the real estate section. "Listen to this. One-bedroom rentals, Upper West Side— nearly two thousand dollars. Studio rentals—twelve hundred seems to be standard. Rooms for rent—look at this, only one listing, and they're asking for nine hundred and fifty!"

Lia stared at her. "What are you, crazy?"

"Why is that crazy? It's what you did when I was a kid."

"I did it because I had to. Do you remember that Lana, the hippie Barnard girl who kept burning curry in my best pan? Not to mention the time I came home to find the apartment reeking of marijuana."

"That was incense, Mom."

"Please. No one burns incense unless they're trying to hide some other smell."

"Well, I liked her a lot better that that bearded guy who was always butting in when we had arguments."

"There you go." Lia replaced the cheese in the refrigerator. "Having a boarder means losing your privacy."

"On the other hand, a boarder means I could probably pull in another two hundred a week."

"But I can help you with money!"

Kat shook her head. "Thanks, but I'm going to try this first. If I put up a flyer at the institute tomorrow, I won't even have to pay to place an ad in the paper."

"God, you're stubborn."

"I know," said Kat, beginning to feel a little better. "Look, Mom. A boarder might not be a perfect solution, but at least it puts some control back in my hands."

Lia sighed. "Fine. Do what you want. Only tell me one thing before I go, what did your father write?"

"I don't know."

"You didn't open the letter yet?"

"I didn't have time."

Lia crossed her arms under her breasts and gave Kat a profoundly skeptical look.

"Okay, I admit it, I'm procrastinating. But it's not so simple for me. It's kind of emotionally loaded, his writing me after all this time, and I don't have the energy to deal with any more complications in my life."

"Kat, this is your father we're talking about. Believe me, he's not capable of sending an emotionally loaded letter."

"Fine. I promise I'll open it tonight. When I'm *alone*."

"All right then, I'm going home." Lia stood up, holding on to the stove for balance as she pushed her feet into black net house slippers. Her toenails were nicely shaped and painted a glossy dark shade of red, making Kat aware of her own neglected feet. "Unless you want me to bring you back some meatballs?"

"No, thanks."

"I'll leave you the Campari." Kat kissed her mother goodbye, then sat for a moment, wishing she could rush out and find her boarder right away. Now that she'd made her decision, it was hard to just sit around, doing nothing. *Well, maybe it is time to deal with that damn letter.* Not sure why she was so reluctant to read what her father had sent her, Kat opened the drawer where she kept her bills and took out the envelope. Her address was neatly typed by an actual typewriter, but her father had written only his name, neglecting to include his return address. Kat took a knife and slit the top of the envelope.

After this day of disappointments, it was tempting to imagine that her father might have sent her something valuable—an insight, an explanation, a check with a lot of zeros in it. Even knowing that life didn't work like that, Kat found her heartbeat speeding up as she removed the letter.

Growing up, Kat had only been mildly curious about her father. Other people always seemed to expect her to be terribly upset by his lack of interest in her, but for Kat, being fatherless was just a fact of her particular life, like living in the city. Then, when she had started acting in her late teens, she had discovered that it wasn't quite that straightforward. Forced to dig more deeply and consider what drives a character to make certain choices, she'd come to realize that there were ways in which her personality had been shaped by her father's absence. Her habit of choosing men who made Mr. Spock seem emotionally expressive was part of her father's legacy. At first, Logan had felt like a departure from her pattern—after all, there they were, getting married, moving in together, making a home. But having a child had changed her life completely, while his role in the marriage had remained essentially the same.

And now Logan had done to their son what her father had done to her. Was there a way to explain things to Dashiell that would minimize the damage?

Kat unfolded the letter and stared at it in disbelief. The page was blank. She turned it over, trying to understand. Was it a joke? A mistake? Was it meant to be symbolic? *Oh, for fuck's sake.* Crumpling the letter, she tossed it in the garbage.

I refuse to waste my time and energy trying to analyze this, Kat thought as she washed her face and brushed her teeth. She had enough to figure out without trying to decipher the motives behind her father's obscure behavior. The explanation was probably something simple, like the man had Alzheimer's. Which was not her problem, thank God. *Nobody expects you to take care of a parent who didn't take care of you.*

Lying in bed, Kat found that even though she was exhausted, her body was filled with tension. Flicking on the TV, she tried to find something to distract her. There was John Ritter, alive and young, lusting after his nubile roommates. There was a toothless nun reciting scripture. There was an attractive blonde Italian in her mid-fifties, saying something about aging skin. Kat turned up the volume.

"As your skin ages, it thins around the eyes and mouth. Fine lines become visible. The skin loses its suppleness and elasticity, and begins to look gray and tired. Your neck sags and your eyes seem sunken. Age spots appear, your lips become wrinkled like prunes, and you begin to pay for every moment you ever laid out in the sun on the beach. And menopause only makes things worse, ladies."

Seven hundred years ago, Kat thought, you could buy an indulgence that supposedly absolved you of your sins. Nowadays the only sin people worried about was looking old.

"And the appearance of your skin affects everything," said the blonde, pacing the stage and clenching her fists like an evangelist preacher. "It affects your love life. It affects whether you get hired or not. So staying youthful is not just vanity anymore. It's a necessity. And just washing your face and using a moisturizing cream is not sufficient. Now, let me explain about what a deep surgical peel can do for you."

You mean, other than leave you looking as though you'd been flayed alive? Quickly switching channels, Kat tried not to think too hard about her rapidly aging, dulling, sagging flesh. Surely there was still some island in Greece where women were allowed to age naturally. Maybe she could retire there and let the sun shrivel her up as she tended a little vegetable garden, embalming her insides with retsina as she cackled out a rousing chorus of "I enjoy being a crone."

Kat's hand stilled on the remote. She had just flicked past Logan's face. Turning back to the previous channel, she watched as her almost-ex-husband leaned against a doorjamb, smiling his bad-boy smile. His bare chest was leaner and more muscular than it had been the last time she'd seen it, and his light brown hair was longer. "When's the last time you had something this spicy for lunch," said a sexy male baritone that Kat happened to know belonged to a short, bald man named Sid. "Turn on *South of Heaven* and turn up the heat."

You shit-eating asshole bastard, I'll show you some heat! Turning on her computer, Kat fired off an email to Logan. *Have heard you are in NYC. Please write or call to arrange a visit with Dash before he finds out you are around from someone else. As for the account you closed, I advise you to return the money before I make a call to the tabloids explaining why you have left me with no money to buy your son groceries or pay the rent.*

Shutting down her computer, Kat went back to the kitchen and poured herself a second Campari. After a few minutes of calming herself down, it occurred to her that it was a hell of a lot easier to send off a blank email than to mail a blank letter in an envelope. Opening up the garbage can, Kat fished out the crumpled paper and stared at it.

Could it be some sort of practical joke? Was her father the sort of man who thought making people uncomfortable was funny? She had no idea. She had never really known him, even when he had been around.

He would be gone for weeks or months on end, phoning in occasionally from some undisclosed location. When he came back, exhausted, he was not to be disturbed while he napped or read a book in the living room. And then he was off again.

Kat could recall with perfect clarity the two times that her father had actually spent time with her, once when she'd been about three or four, when he had pretended to be a dragon, and once when he'd taken her to the zoo—she'd been five or six.

Oh, and one other time did stick out in her memory, a summer afternoon just before her parents' divorce when her father had taken her into the kitchen and shown her how to make invisible ink out of sugar, milk, and lemon juice. She'd singed her bangs on the candle, trying to warm the page up enough to make the secret writing appear. Not that she'd minded; Kat had been so ridiculously happy to be spending time with her father that it hadn't bothered her that he wasn't watching out to make sure she wasn't going to burn herself. Even now, she could recall the distinctive smell of crisping hair, her father's quick reaction, their conspiratorial laughter: Mustn't let your mother find out!

And suddenly it all made sense. Kat took her father's blank letter and went into the kitchen, where she found the remains of Dashiell's fat numeral nine birthday candle. Lighting it, she passed it underneath her father's note, smiling with satisfaction as the letters became visible.

Dear Katherine,

I have no idea what kind of person you have become, but as I recall, you were a fairly intelligent child. I assume that you are not particularly curious about me, as you have never attempted to make contact.

Perhaps you were simply waiting for me to express an interest in you. Well, fair enough. Being a father isn't something that has ever come naturally to me, and the very things that have made me good at my job have probably made me a singularly awful parent. I'm sure your mother did right to remove you from my influence.

If you wish to meet me, go to the Turkish restaurant on the corner of 99th and Broadway and sit in the far corner of the traditional section. There will be another message under the seat cushion. In the future, look for a piece of blue bubble gum on the right side of the phone booth by the restaurant. That will be a sign that I have left you a message. If you want to communicate with me, put a piece of pink bubblegum on the left side of the booth, and I will know to check the restaurant for your message.

Because there are those who would do me harm, I must ask you not to tell anyone that we are in contact.

Assume that everyone you meet is lying to you about who they are, why they are there, and what they want from you.

Dad

And that was it. No apology for all his years of neglect, both emotional and financial. No closing line of "love"—in fact, no mention of any sentiment whatsoever. And absolutely no acknowledgement of the fact that she had a son, his grandchild, whom he'd never seen. For some reason, it was this last omission that bothered Kat that most. Perhaps, she thought, children had some built-in protection against feeling the full force of their parents' betrayal until they became parents themselves.

She glanced at the clock: five past midnight. She was going to be exhausted in class tomorrow, but she couldn't imagine being able to fall asleep now. Well, at least there was one nice thing about being up this early—the time belonged to you and you alone. Kat used her nails to scrape the melted wax from the kitchen table, then folded her father's letter and put it in the drawer along with all the other bills and notes and receipts she hadn't found time to file in the past six months.

Then Kat ran herself a bubble bath and selected one of her mother's books from a pile beside her bed. After all, when you'd lost all hope that men could act like human beings, there was nothing like a bit of transgressive vampire sex and the delicious fantasy that the guy was only cold and unfeeling until you came along and warmed him up.

chapter *eleven*

•

a vague feeling of having dreamt something pleasant evaporated the instant Kat opened her eyes. Before she could pin down the details of her dream—there had been a man in it, and she thought he might have been carrying her in his arms—her son let out a piercing scream from the other side of the apartment.

Racing into the kitchen, Kat discovered that what she'd heard had actually been a shriek of fury. Dashiell's gerbil, it turned out, had gnawed a hole in the box of his favorite cereal. After briefly expressing her sympathy and sweeping up multicolored crumbs, Kat tried to give five different reasons why Dash couldn't just skip breakfast. In the end, she found herself yelling, "Stop making everything into a fight."

"But you're the one who's shouting," Dashiell pointed out with impeccable logic.

The morning did not improve from there. Just as Kat was apologizing for losing her temper, Dashiell recalled that he'd forgotten to complete his math homework. When Kat asked why she hadn't seen the assignment in his backpack, Dash revealed that he'd also forgotten to bring his math homework home from school. Oh, and he needed her to make him a bag lunch today, for the school trip. Did she want to come?

Looking into her son's hopeful green eyes, Kat realized that her child did not have the luxury of allowing himself to be mad at her for more than an instant. It had been the same for her, growing up. When you only had one parent to rely on, you didn't push them away too hard.

Kat was acutely aware of her son's disappointment as she explained that she'd just taken time off work and wouldn't be able to act as a trip chaperone. No, he couldn't play hooky. Yes, she did think it was important to see a bunch of old stuff. There were things you could learn better outside of a classroom.

"Yeah," said Dashiell, his jaded expression making him look years older. "You can learn that nobody wants to be your partner on line."

"I have a surprise today, class," said Kat. "We're going on a field trip."

The members of the Advanced Class glanced at each other in surprise. Maria put a hand on the firm swell of her abdomen. In her tight white "Sexy Baby" T-shirt, she appeared visibly more pregnant than she had two days earlier. "Which field? Will there be a lot of walking?" There were dark shadows under the young woman's eyes, and Kat wondered how much longer Maria would be able to keep her job cleaning apartments.

"We're not really going to be walking around a field," Kat reassured her. "A field trip is another term for an excursion. I thought we'd go to the Egyptian rooms at the Metropolitan Museum of Art." Kat let her eyes roam around the classroom. "Or has everyone been there already?"

It turned out that only Galina had visited the Met, but she had gone to see the Impressionists. It was not really possible to take in a whole museum properly in one day, Galina added, patting her short brown wig. Chieko said that she had meant to go, but had gotten confused and wound up taking a tour to the Cloisters, and Magnus said that it was on the top of his list of things to do.

Kat smiled with relief. She'd been a little worried that the moment Magnus opened his mouth he might say something about having seen her outside of class. God bless Scandinavian reticence.

"Excuse me," said Chieko, "but Miss Marcy said we would go over nonprogressive verbs today?" She sounded as industrious as she always did, but for some reason, Chieko had come to class today dressed like the little girl from the *Addams Family*, in a black Victorian dress that hit just above the knee. Her eyes were heavily made up in dark colors, and she looked as if she had just been brought over by the powers of darkness.

Kat glanced at her watch. Dashiell's class was due to arrive at the museum at ten. "I think we can do a little review on the subway," she said, deciding not to comment on her student's transformation from clean-cut preppy to sultry Gothette.

"Katherine," said Galina, "I am understanding that the museum fee is covered by our tuition, yes?"

"Actually, the verb 'to understand' is not progressive. You just say, 'I understand.' " Great, the class did need to review that section. Kat felt a moment's embarrassment that Marcy had spotted an area of weakness that she hadn't detected. But then, Marcy had more experience, and was better at teaching formal grammar. Kat knew that her own talents lay elsewhere, in the creative, expressive aspects of language. In her opinion, fluency didn't come from mastering syntax, anymore than acting came from memorizing lines. An imaginative leap was required.

"So," said Galina, a little tartly, "I *understand* that the museum fee is covered?"

"I'm sorry, it's not covered. But even though the museum posts a suggested donation, you can actually pay whatever you want—even a penny."

"Really? Even a penny?" Galina adjusted the silk scarf that had been elaborately wrapped and knotted around her neck. "Good to know."

Just when Kat thought she had pulled it off, and was going to sail through this day as both superteacher and supermom, Nabil raised his hand. The cuff of his threadbare white shirt did not quite reach the bony knob of his wrist, but there was something about Nabil that commanded respect, not pity.

"Yes, Nabil, what is it?" Meeting the gentle, intelligent gaze under the heavy grizzled eyebrows, Kat felt obscurely guilty. Nabil had been a professor of English literature back in Cairo. Now he couldn't even get a job teaching in high school, and Kat wasn't sure that her class was going to help him. Even if his spoken English became less stilted and formal, she had a feeling no one was going to hire a guy with a two-foot-long white beard to teach Shakespeare to a bunch of savvy urban preteens.

"Forgive me for asking," said Nabil, "but what exactly is the intended purpose of this trip?"

To rescue my son. "You've all been doing so well in class," Kat temporized, "but I'd like to see you all practice your language skills out in the world. Think of it as a reality quiz. Each of you will have to approach a stranger and find out something about him or her." This was actually a variation on an acting exercise she'd once been given.

"What sort of something?" Luc walked in the door, once again wearing a black trench coat, motorcycle boots, and a coolly amused expression. How cute, Kat thought, he has a look. Keanu Reeves's look, to be specific.

"I'll leave that up to you. By the way, you're late again."

Luc cocked his head like a puppy trying to make sense of some new human eccentricity. "True, but surely I am not so late I miss the whole class. Why is everyone putting on their jackets?"

Kat fished her ponytail out of her collar. "In America, when you're late, you're supposed to apologize."

"But how can anyone be on time in a city that doesn't permit indoor smoking? Anywhere I go, I must waste time finishing a cigarette, because it is certain I am not allowed to smoke when I reach my destination."

"Luc, I can't teach you how to get by in America if you're not willing to learn."

Luc threw out his hands in protest. "I am willing! Look at me, I am very excited to go wherever we are going and do whatever it is we are doing. What is it we are doing together?"

Kat bit her lip to keep from smiling. The last thing on earth Luc needed was more confirmation that he was charming. "Maria, you tell him."

"We are going in a field trip," Maria interjected as she struggled to zip her nylon jacket shut over her belly. She didn't sound happy about it. In fact, Kat realized, no one seemed particularly pleased at the prospect of an outing.

Maybe that's why I like being around foreign-language students, Kat thought: They tend to approach life with a certain base level of suspicion. After months of enduring her friends' relentless optimism, it was comforting to be around people who assumed that any plan of action would lead to some unforeseen complication.

Kat was less than comforted by the sight of Arabella Simms, the new regional supervisor, walking down the hallway.

"Well, where are you all headed at once? Coffee break?" A youthful thirty-five, Arabella was fresh from London headquarters. Like Maria, Arabella was seven months pregnant, but unlike the petite Mexican woman, Kat's boss was dressed in a crisp navy blue maternity dress and matching low-heeled pumps. She also wore a blue Alice band in her shoulder length, dark blond hair, which made her look a bit like a knocked-up schoolgirl.

"No, we have a field trip," said Nabil. "We are going to the Metropolitan Museum to practice our English outside of the classroom."

"I see," said Arabella, sounding a little too chipper. "Well! How marvelous! You are so inventive, Kat. And how ambitious of you to take everyone all the way uptown and then bring them all back before dismissal."

"Oh, well, I thought it made more sense to let everyone leave from the museum," said Kat.

"I'm sorry, Katherine, but if you review our handbook, you'll see that we always dismiss students from the institute."

Kat made a quick mental calculation. If the subway trip took them forty minutes each way, that still left her an hour to spend at the museum, with time left over to hand out the next day's assignments. "That still leaves us enough time. We should be fine."

"Excellent. And next time, let's make sure to work out these details ahead of time, to save any unnecessary confusion, all right?"

Kat mustered a smile. This was the problem with new bosses; they felt a constant need to establish themselves. Arabella's predecessor had been too preoccupied with keeping his New York girlfriend away from his London wife to fuss about his teachers' schedules. Oh, well, give Arabella some time and she'd calm down.

As they walked toward the subway station, Galina fell into step beside her. "You know, in the Soviet Union, nobody thanked you for doing your job too well. They wanted you to be a factory worker, not a star."

Kat nodded absently as she checked her watch. Shit, it was already nine-fifteen, she was losing her margin of error. "Believe me, Galina," she said, glancing back to see how Maria was doing, "being a star is the last thing I worry about."

chapter *twelve*

•

I don't understand why I must talk to strangers," said Galina as she and Magnus waited for the rest of the class to pay their donations and receive their small yellow metal buttons. "Why will talking to strangers improve my English?"

Magnus gave a noncommittal shrug. Like Galina, he was not entirely certain why they were here, but he didn't want to appear disloyal to Katherine. In addition, he had formed a slight dislike for Galina, who was wearing her mink jacket, despite the fact that it had to be seventy-five degrees inside the museum. He smiled, suddenly struck with an image of the woman going home to a little hut strewn with animal carcasses, like Baba Yaga, the witch of Russian folklore.

"What is funny about this, tell me," Galina demanded. "Because to me, it is not funny that I am paying to talk to strangers that I could talk to on my own."

"On my own, I would not come here at all," said Nabil, his tone matter of fact. "All these artifacts were stolen from my country."

Chieko joined them, pinching her metal button onto the collar of her black Victorian little-girl dress. "This is exciting, no?" She turned to Maria, who was reading a map of the exhibits.

"Look at this—a whole room of costumes. I have to come back."

"The Frick is nice, too," said Luc. "But much smaller, of course."

"All right, everyone, listen up." Magnus moved closer to Katherine, who was wearing a short-sleeved brown turtleneck sweater and faded jeans that made her look all of twenty-nine. "We're all going to fan out throughout the exhibit, and each of you has to strike up a conversation with a stranger and find out something about that person. Any questions?"

"Yes," said Maria. "What are you going to do?"

"Spy on all of you, of course. Anyone else? No? Great. We'll meet back here in front of the little gift shop in thirty minutes. Have fun!"

Magnus watched as the other students fanned out slowly, like new recruits patrolling a potentially dangerous area. After a moment, Luc began talking to a pretty redhead with a young child in a stroller, and Katherine walked rapidly down the hallway of papyrus, not really taking in the ancient inventories of oxen and crops.

She's looking for something, Magnus thought, following Katherine as she rounded a corner. Or rather, looking for some*one*. He had a childish urge to flick her ponytail, which bounced as she walked, turning her head from side to side. For a moment, he thought he'd lost her, then he saw that she had gone into a dimly lit room filled with mummies, some wrapped and shrouded, some wearing elaborately painted masks. Standing off to one side, Katherine seemed to be observing three schoolboys who were sitting in front of one of the cases. Was one of the boys her son? It was too dark to tell. Keeping himself partially blocked by a display of small animal figurines, Magnus waited to see what she intended to do next.

"Go find someplace else to draw," said the tallest of the boys, opening an artist's sketchpad.

"Yeah," said the second boy, who was wearing glasses. "We got here first."

The third boy stuck out his chin. "So what? This is the only room that has mummies out of their boxes."

"Are you deaf or something, Dashiell the asshole? We don't want you here."

"I don't care," said Katherine's son, his eyes on the mummy. "I have as much right to be here as you do."

No way was this a coincidence, thought Magnus, fighting to contain a rising sense of excitement. Katherine must have decided to take the class to the museum because she knew her kid was going to be here, too. This was it—his second chance. All he had to do was make a good impression on her son, and how hard could that be? The boy was probably longing for a father figure, and would imprint himself on any man who showed him the least bit of interest.

"You don't have to be right on top of us," said the kid with the glasses. "Why don't you go sit over there?" He indicated a spot across the room.

The tall child smiled with malice. "Maybe he's too scared to be all on his own with the scary, scary mummies."

"You're the one who's scared, you stupid butt-head!" Bad move, thought Magnus. You react, you show weakness. That was one lesson he had learned early on: show no emotion, particularly not anger or fear.

The tall boy grinned, showing teeth. "If I'm so stupid, then why did you just offer me a Pokémon card to sit next to you on the bus?"

Katherine stepped out of the shadows. "Hey, Dashiell."

Dashiell turned, his face brightening. "Mom! You said you couldn't come!"

Katherine knelt down. "I decided my class needed a field trip, too."

The kid with the glasses stared at her as if she'd just announced she was an undercover cop. "You're a teacher?"

"Yes, Riley, I teach English to adults from other countries. I brought them here to practice using their conversational skills. Sometimes my students worry that they might make a mistake and people will make fun of them." The two boys exchanged glances.

"Hey, Dash," said Katherine, "did you see this small mummy over here?" She pointed to a case across the room from the other two boys. "How old do you think this guy was when he died?"

Very clever, thought Magnus, but what is he going to do when you're not around? Sooner or later, that kid is going to have to fight his own battles. Katherine turned and caught his eye as if she'd heard his thoughts.

"Magnus," she said. If she was embarrassed that he'd found her out, she hid it well. "Dash, this is one of my students."

The boy grunted a brief greeting. Mindful of his bad knee, Magnus lowered himself carefully down next to Katherine's son. "So, your class is learning about mummies?"

"About ancient Egypt."

"That sounds interesting."

The boy turned, finally meeting his eyes. "It's not. I already read the entire *Ancient Civilizations* book. Now I have to waste a day drawing. I hate drawing. I'm not learning anything here."

Spoken like a kid who has to sit by himself. Magnus felt Katherine's gaze on him, and knew that he was probably supposed to argue for the importance of school assignments. "Different people learn in different ways," he said. "Maybe some of your classmates only learn when they're drawing."

Dashiell looked at his sketchpad with loathing. "So let them do it, and let me stay at home."

Magnus scratched his jaw, trying to regroup. Getting close to Katherine's son was not proving to be quite as easy as he'd anticipated. Maybe he should quit trying to be a good role model and just acknowledge the fact that school could be as cruel and dehumanizing as the army. But before Magnus could open his mouth, he heard a familiar voice behind him.

"*Alors*, Magnus." Luc strode into the room, looking cynically amused. *Probably practiced that look in the mirror for a year.* "So, what are you doing in here? Hiding?" Luc smiled as he spotted Katherine. "Ah, I see, hiding with the teacher."

"Actually, I am doing our assignment." *God, I sound stiff.*

Luc looked down at Dashiell. "I see." He turned to Katherine, raising an eyebrow. "He is yours?"

"Yes, he's mine." Katherine's smile was a little rueful. Magnus didn't think she'd expected to be found out by two of her students. "How did you know? Everyone says he looks like his dad."

"Then they are not looking very carefully." Luc knelt down beside Dashiell, as agile as a cat. "Show me what you draw," he said.

Dashiell held out the pad. "It sucks." He had drawn a blobby shape in the middle of the page.

Luc made a whistling sound between his teeth. "It's true, but you can fix it, no problem."

"How?"

"If you permit me . . . ?" Luc took the pad. "First, do not look at the paper, okay? You look at what you draw. Just there." Luc's hand moved rapidly over the page, making small marks. "And when you observe carefully, you begin to see how things fit together." Luc held up the page, which now looked like a mummy.

"Cool! How did you do that?"

"This is my work. I draw comic books."

"Which ones?"

"Right now, I do some Batman. Okay, now you draw."

Mouth clenched in concentration, Dashiell began to sketch the mummy's painted mask, using Luc's outline.

Magnus looked up to find Katherine standing over them. "Hey. Thank you, Luc. Dash, we have to go now."

"Okay." Dashiell, engrossed in his project, did not appear distressed at this news.

As they left the mummy room, Magnus could hear the other boys saying something to Dashiell about his drawing.

He couldn't make out the words, but there was no mistaking the tone; Dashiell's social stock had just risen by about two hundred points, thanks to his encounter with a bona fide comic book artist.

Crap. No one would ever believe that a year ago, he'd had one of the highest security clearances in the country and a job he'd been damn good at. Or, at least, he had thought he'd been good at it. Maybe the top brass had been right, and that oily, charming bastard they'd brought in over him was the better choice. No. That wasn't right. His analysis had always panned out. He just hadn't known how to play office politics. Hadn't Fred said that if he just learned to read people the way he read reports, he would be the perfect field agent? In any case, it was normal to feel a little insecure when you were trying new things, Magnus reasoned. But you didn't live up to your full potential by playing it safe.

On the other hand, there were worse things than not living up to your potential, such as discovering that you didn't actually have all that much potential to begin with.

Maybe he should've taken that desk job at Langley.

chapter *thirteen*

•

Okay, so what did we learn today?" The atmosphere in the classroom had lightened considerably after their trip, and Magnus was surprised to see the usually somber Nabil chatting animatedly with Luc, while Maria and Galina were laughing at something Chieko was telling them. "Come on, guys, I'm glad you're excited, but we only have a few minutes left and I want to hear what happened. Luc, let's start with you."

"Well," Luc said, "I talked to a woman who informs me right away that she dislikes her children and takes pills for depression—things a French person would only tell a family member or a close friend. And then, just when I start to wonder what is left to talk about next time, the woman checks her watch, says good-bye, and that is it—the end of the entire relationship!"

Katherine laughed. "So you're saying you don't like American informality?"

"It leaves no room for seduction," said Luc, clearly warming to his subject. "And also, I think it is false. Maybe you will hear all sorts of personal information, but no one here treats you like a friend. In France, you can use charm and the baker will give you the best loaf of bread, but here? 'It's all identical.' " Luc mimicked a nasal American accent. "Yes, folks, everything is regulated, pasteurized, and homogenized." Dropping the accent, he added, "It all just makes me want to dip my unsterilized finger in and stir things up a bit."

I'd like to sterilize you, Magnus thought, a little surprised by his own vehemence.

"Oh, I don't know," said Nabil. "I think Americans may not all be as direct as you might think. Every time I tried to approach someone, they backed away."

"Interesting," said Katherine. "But I have an idea why that might have happened. Can anyone tell me how close most Americans stand while talking?" Silence. "Okay, let me see— Magnus, come stand as close to me as feels comfortable."

Magnus pushed his chair back and walked toward her, feeling extremely self-conscious. "Here?" He was about six feet away.

Katherine's face gave nothing away. "Is that where you would stand to talk to me?"

"Yes, I think so." Oh, great, this was some kind of cultural test. Well, given the fact that his parents were both Icelandic and he'd spent the past ten years there, he was probably more Icelandic than he was anything else. On paper, of course, he was American, but he'd grown up on military bases in Florida and Egypt, and that was its own weird culture.

"So, everyone," she said, "does that look right to the rest of you?"

"He's standing way too far away," said Maria.

"Is he?" Chieko shrugged. "Looks okay to me."

Katherine seemed pleased—this, apparently, was the response she'd expected. "North Americans, Germans, and the British tend to converse at approximately one arm's length away. That's their body bubble, the area around them that feels like their personal space. Scandinavians and Japanese tend to have larger body bubbles, Latins slightly smaller ones, and Middle Easterners feel comfortable talking at a much closer distance. It's not a conscious thing, but as an actor, I was trained to be observant and become conscious of what unintentional messages I might be conveying. Look what happens when you move into somebody else's body bubble."

Katherine stepped forward, closing the space between them, smiling as if she were on to him. Magnus took a step back, and Katherine took another step forward. "You see," she told the class, "he's instinctively retreating. I'm also maintaining very direct eye contact, which is making him a bit uncomfortable."

I'll say. Magnus was suddenly very aware that if Katherine came any closer, the top of her head would fit under his chin. And more than that, he was suddenly aware of her as a woman.

Shit, this hadn't happened to him in a classroom since Reagan was president. *Dead fish, think about dead fish.*

Katherine carried on with her demonstration, oblivious. "Some cultures avoid direct eye contact, and some seek it out. Nabil, if you stood too close or held eye contact too long, the person you were talking to might have felt threatened or misinterpreted your intentions."

Magnus forced himself to meet Katherine's clear gray gaze, but it was difficult. No matter how many times he told himself that he was having an inappropriate reaction, or how intently he tried to visualize a two-day-old halibut, he felt a swelling sense of physical attraction. He could tell the moment Katherine sensed it, too; her face flushed, and she turned away. Katherine glanced at her watch. "Thank you, Magnus, you may sit down now. So, that was a good lesson—in order to practice our English, we may need to practice our North American body language. In any case, we're out of time today, but tomorrow we can talk more about the trip and any cultural differences we might have uncovered."

As the other students filed past, thanking Katherine for the field trip, Magnus took his time gathering his books, trying to get over feeling embarrassed. He had to be professional here. He had to focus. He had to think of something to say to Katherine that would lead to another private meeting. Unfortunately, everything that came to mind sounded like a bad pickup line. I need to work on my colloquialisms, care to go out for a drink? I love your old movies, I watch them at home on video all the time. Did you know that there's a phallological museum in Reykjavik? Although why anybody wanted to go see a bunch of shriveled whale penises, Magnus had never understood.

If only he could just walk up to her and say, I'm not really slow, Katherine, I used to routinely field emergency phone calls from the CIA. I've made snap decisions that affected thousands of lives. I've been at the bottom of the ocean, dealing with an equipment failure in my sub, while everyone around me hyperventilated.

But he couldn't, because he'd left that part of himself behind in a long-term storage facility, along with his steel-string

Martin guitar, his rock-climbing paraphernalia, and the antique chess set he'd inherited from his grandmother.

No one had told him that disguising himself as a new immigrant would make him really feel as if he'd been stripped of his career and his status and his entire frame of reference.

Magnus heard a soft laugh, and turned to see Luc saying something to Katherine that made her smile and glance down.

Walking up to them, Magnus heard Katherine say "it's not going to happen," as she made the last of a series of cuts in the bottom of a piece of paper. "And while I thank you for the compliment, I really don't think I'm in the kind of shape to be the model for Red Sonja."

Luc noticed Magnus first. "But you are perfect. Tell her she is perfect, Magnus."

Katherine didn't give him a chance. "Go pick on someone your own age."

"Who is Red Sonja?"

"A comic book warrior woman," said Luc.

Katherine put down her scissors. "Brigitte Nielsen played her in a truly terrible movie in the early eighties."

Feeling like an outsider, Magnus thought he should say something about how Katherine would make an excellent warrior woman, but couldn't find the right words. Instead, he pointed at the flyer. "What are you doing?"

Katherine squinted at the page. "Do those lines look straight? I need to find a boarder. I thought I'd put this up on the bulletin board downstairs and see if anyone needs a room."

Magnus tilted his head to read the page.

ROOM AVAILABLE
Sunny, quiet room with private bathroom
(half bath, sink, and toilet), plus kitchen privi-

leges in Upper West Side Apartment, immediate avail. No smokers, rock musicians, or opera singers. $200 a week.

Katherine's home phone number was written on the pre-cut ribbons of paper.

For a moment, Magnus couldn't speak. Things like this never happened to him. He never won prizes, or got his airplane seat upgraded, or received a free pass. He cleared his throat, reaching inside himself for calm. "You are renting a room in your apartment?"

"Mm hm."

"May I see it?"

He sounded abrupt, even to his own ears. Katherine looked slightly uncomfortable. "I really wasn't thinking of renting to a student of mine."

"Ah."

"No offense, but I think it would be simpler to rent it to a faculty member, or even to a student in someone else's class."

Magnus wasn't sure how to react. Was this an invitation to convince her otherwise, or would that be deemed impertinent?

Luc, who clearly never doubted himself, instantly launched into a litany of reasons why his was a special case. "But this is a miracle, this is just what I am praying for! My living situation is unbearable. I am sharing a cheap hotel room with an Israeli and an Australian, I have not the money to go elsewhere. The Israeli keeps spitting sunflower seeds from the top of the bunk bed and the Australian smokes clove cigarettes." Luc shook his head. "Please consider again, at least you know me a little, *n'est-ce pas?*"

"Well . . ." Katherine paused. "The room's on the small side," she said, more to Luc than to Magnus. "It's what Americans call a maid's room. The bathtub wouldn't be big enough for Magnus to soak his feet."

Magnus pretended to think about it. "But you are close to Columbia University, and I am supposed to start teaching there."

"I don't know . . ."

"But you're right, it's probably not big enough," said Magnus. If Luc was going to be the guy in hot pursuit, then Magnus was going to play it cool.

"But I don't need big enough," said Luc, using his hands for emphasis. "All I need is a little privacy."

Katherine appeared to be considering Luc's argument.

Of course, Magnus thought, there's such a thing as being too cool. "All *I* need is a place to sleep," he said. "For privacy, I have the Columbia libraries, where I spend most of my day doing research."

Katherine looked from Luc to Magnus, took a deep breath and then started to laugh, shaking her head. "Fine, then. Sure. Why don't you both come see the room?" She stood up, sliding the strap of her briefcase on her shoulder before pausing. "Hang on a moment. Luc, I just thought of something. How much do you smoke?"

Luc was silent for a moment. "Just one or two cigarettes, in the evening."

Magnus snorted in disbelief.

"Well, maybe a little more than that. But you know," said Luc, apparently sensing that he was at a disadvantage here, "I was deciding just the other day that it was time for me to quit. After all, I am not in France anymore, and here it is just an inconvenience, you are not allowed to have a cigarette anyplace."

A concerned crease had appeared between Katherine's eyebrows. "I really don't want anyone smoking in my house."

"It is a repulsive smell," Magnus agreed.

"Not to me," she said, her expression rueful. "My problem is, I love the smell."

Luc smiled. "So we will be strong together, two ex-smokers."

Magnus tried to think of some bad habit he and Katherine could bond over, but realized that the only vice he indulged in at the moment was solitary. When this job was done, he really did need to start dating again.

Luc stepped in front of Katherine and held the door open with a flourish. "After you," he said, conveniently letting go so it slammed Magnus in the face.

"Oh, pardon, I wasn't looking."

"No problem," said Magnus, rubbing his nose. "I just need to pay more attention to where you're going." Unfortunately, this bit of irony was lost on Luc, who was already three steps ahead.

chapter *fourteen*

•

If you don't mind, take your shoes off here." Katherine slipped out of her own shoes, which resembled black ballet slippers, and padded gracefully into the living room.

As he unlaced his hiking boots, Magnus noticed that Katherine wasn't exactly Martha Stewart. There wasn't a lot of furniture, but he spotted at least three large cardboard cartons shoved against a wall. In some places, the paint had been stripped down to plaster, and there were splotches of base coat here and there on the walls.

Luc had already removed his black, ankle-high boots by the time Magnus finished with his laces. Now here was something Technical Services hadn't covered. How did a man maintain his James Bond mojo while walking around in gray wool socks? Magnus kneeled down surreptitiously to check for odor, and was relieved to detect nothing offensive.

"This space is fantastic," said Luc, who appeared to have no self-consciousness whatsoever and was striding around the large and light-filled room in his black T-shirt and jeans, exclaiming over the high ceilings and the big framed picture of red and brown squares. Magnus tried to find something to comment on, but kept noticing things better left unmentioned, such as a steamer trunk passing as a coffee table and three mismatched chairs badly in need of repair.

"As you can probably tell, I'm in the process of redecorating," said Katherine.

If that were the case, thought Magnus, it was very early in the process—Katherine's apartment looked as if she had just moved in. She herself was so well groomed, and seemed so in control, that he never would have imagined that she could live surrounded by what appeared to be broken hand-me-down furniture.

"This reminds me of Paul Klee's work," said Luc, standing next to the picture of red and brown squares. It was hung crookedly, Magnus noticed, and at the wrong height.

Katherine stood next to him. "I bought it at a flea market last year, and that's exactly what I thought."

Magnus inspected the rack containing Katherine's vast CD collection—show tunes, seventies pop, ABBA, a lot of Andrew Lloyd Webber. Better not to say anything about that, he decided.

Luc walked over to a bookcase, where the books all seemed to have been placed at random. "And I see you have *Candide*. This was the only book I read in school that did not bore me. Of course, I got in trouble anyway, for making a picture of the pirates forcing Cunegonde." Luc grinned. "I don't know about Voltaire, but I know which garden I wanted to cultivate." He looked at the book again. "But this is English. You read it like this?"

"I'm afraid so."

"Ah, *quel dommage.* So many phrases don't translate. Do you know what we call the words you Americans think you know? *Faux amis*—false friends."

Katherine looked intrigued. "Such as?"

"Deception," said Luc, using the Gallic pronunciation. "It means a disappointment. *Une demande,* which means a request. *Baiser."*

Katherine raised one eyebrow. "I take it a kiss is not just a kiss?"

"Only in the noun form," said Luc.

"And when used as a verb?"

Luc was clearly enjoying himself. "It means to fuck."

There was a moment of surprised silence, as if a pebble had been thrown in a well and made an unusually large splash.

Magnus cleared his throat. "Not a lot of people know this, but some people compare the Icelandic sagas to the work of Homer and Shakespeare."

Katherine turned to him. "Really?" He might have been imagining it, but he thought she seemed a little relieved that he'd broken the tension.

"Especially the saga of Gunnlaugur the Worm Tongue." Somehow this did not sound quite as sparkling as Luc's repartee.

"You don't say."

"And Icelandic is the only Scandinavian language that is like the Old Norse the Vikings spoke."

"Hmm."

Magnus noticed that Luc was smiling and shaking his head. "And I really like this room," Magnus concluded. "A lot."

"Thank you." Katherine straightened a pair of candlesticks

with a slight air of self-consciousness. "Well, I guess I should make it clear to you both that officially, this room isn't included in the rent. Just the maid's room and the use of the kitchen."

"Of course it is not," said Luc. "In France, my mother had a lodger, and he never thought to step into the family rooms. But how very kind of you to show us the view."

Mindful of the classic Icelandic saying, Nobody is completely stupid, if he can be silent, Magnus walked over to the window and kept his mouth shut. A lot of tall buildings were visible against the wet, gray sky. There were roof gardens and penthouses on some buildings, water towers and chimneys on others. It struck Magnus as very strange and somehow artificial, like a scene from a movie.

"You know," Luc said, coming up beside Magnus, "the best thing about being here in New York is that everything is new and strange, and so I become new to myself. It's like I am a child again, having to learn what everyone else already seems to know."

"I think I know what you mean," Katherine said. "That's how I feel when I travel."

Magnus thought it sounded like bullshit. He was in a new place, and he didn't seem the least bit new to himself. In fact, he felt as if he'd never been more aware of the sad fact that he was stuck being his own big, silent self, too cynical for optimism and too morose for wit.

Katherine had joined them at the window. Up close, Magnus realized, her dark hair had reddish highlights. He caught the faintest hint of a scent from the shampoo she used and felt a return of that earlier, carnal awareness. Over her shoulder, he caught Luc grinning at him. "Of course, it is easy for me to travel, I do not have a big body bubble to carry around."

Magnus tried to ignore him. "How long have you lived

here, Katherine?" Her name felt oddly intimate on his tongue.

Katherine hesitated, but before she could say anything, the front door opened and a dark-haired woman in her mid-sixties stared at them in surprise. She was carrying two large Zabar's bags.

"Oh, hi, honey. I didn't expect you to be home yet. Did you tell me you were inviting friends over? I thought you said you were going to the gym?"

"Mom, what are you doing here?"

"It's Friday. I took a half day off and decided to do some shopping for you."

"You didn't have to do that." As Katherine walked over to her mother, Magnus observed that she was trying to conceal her irritation, while there was a faint edge to the mother's voice that said, attack me and I will retaliate.

"When were you going to do it? You'll never have time to get down to the eighties, and wait till you see what I got. A loaf of that rustic corn bread you love, and a marinated skirt steak for our dinner."

Katherine ran her hand over her ponytail, smoothing it. "Mom, I'd planned to take Dash out to dinner to the Turkish place tonight."

"I thought you were trying to cut down on expenses."

"There's a special reason I have to go."

"So go tomorrow." Katherine's mother disappeared into the kitchen with the groceries.

Katherine cast a harried glance in Magnus and Luc's direction before following her mother. "But Mom, I can't just switch things around that easily."

Magnus might not be skilled at small talk, but after twenty years in the military, he knew a power struggle when he saw one.

"So," Luc said, "that is what Kat will look like in three decades."

Magnus wasn't so sure. Physically, the two were very similar, but Ken Miner's ex-wife had an air of authority that his daughter lacked.

Which wasn't the perception of Katherine that he'd had in the beginning. His first impression of her had been that she was similar to Guthrun, a strong, practical, fiercely independent woman. Now that he'd spent more time with Katherine, he realized that she was more complicated, and conflicted, than that. She was strong, all right, but also a little frayed around the edges. And while Katherine certainly struck him as pragmatic, there was also a side of her that was warm and emotionally generous, not words he had ever associated with his ex-wife. He also got the feeling that Katherine, like him, stayed up nights worrying about whether or not she had made the right decision.

While Lia Miner, her voice carrying clearly from a room away, seemed not to have any doubts about the rightness of *her* opinion.

"You're really set on renting out the room? Oh, Kat, are you sure about this? I don't think Dashiell really needs any more change in his life right now."

Katherine's voice was softer, but still audible. "Mother, this is not the time and place for this discussion."

"Well, if you'd bothered to let me know you were planning to show the apartment, we could have talked in private! Who are these guys?" Lia's voice was louder now, and Magnus heard footsteps. He turned to the window, trying to appear as though he hadn't overheard their entire conversation. Out of the corner of his eye, he saw Luc do the same.

"The men in the other room are two of my students," said

Kat, a note of warning in her voice. As the two women entered the room, Katherine took a deep breath. "Luc, Magnus, this is my mother, Lia Miner."

Katherine's mother shook their hands and Luc told her he was very pleased to make her acquaintance, adding that she looked too elegant to be American and too young to be Katherine's mother. As Luc continued buttering up Katherine's mother, Magnus wondered if the Frenchman had the sense not to lay it on too thick. Lia Miner was nobody's fool. On the other hand, seen up close, she was surprisingly youthful-looking, despite the fact that her hairstyle had a hint of early Jackie Kennedy about it. Still, her skin was clear and her hazel eyes sparkled with intelligence and a hint of flirtation. "So, Luc, you're from France? Paris?"

"You have a good ear for accents," said Luc, much to Magnus's disgust. Everyone assumed most Frenchmen were from Paris; trust Luc to find a way to turn his answer into a compliment.

"And your family is from Morocco? Tunisia?"

"Morocco. When I was small we lived in Israel."

Lia nodded her head, as if he were merely confirming her suspicions. "Our family is Jewish, too, you know, but from Italy." Lia turned to Magnus. "Now, you I'm not so sure about. Swedish? Norwegian?"

"I come from Iceland." Magnus had a sinking sensation that he was losing this contest to Luc, as well. "I don't think my family's Jewish," he added, trying to make a joke of it.

Lia smiled wanly. "And you're from Reykjavik?"

"My mother was. My father came from a small fishing village."

"And where did you grow up?"

"These days, almost everyone lives in the capital." Magnus was trying to stick as closely as possible to his real history, omitting certain details, such as the fact that his parents had emigrated to the States in 1957, the year Magnus was born, or that he hadn't actually spent much time in Iceland as a child. He had gone back a few times to visit his maternal grandmother while he was growing up, but his family had never bothered to travel to see his father's relatives.

"And which do you prefer, then—city or countryside?"

"I like the country, but not where my father is from. It's a bit bleak." When he had first gotten posted to Iceland, Magnus had made the trip to the isolated, avalanche-prone West Fjords to see where his father had come from. His only surviving relative turned out to be a caterpillar-browed great-uncle named Jon, who held a cube of sugar in his mouth and sipped cup after cup of tea during Magnus's visit.

In between beating him at games of chess and complaining about the decline in herring, the great-uncle had talked about what a great shame it was that Magnus's father had left. Why anyone would want to stay, however, was not exactly clear. There were no young people left, Jon complained, only auks, gulls, and eider ducks. Was Magnus aware that this was the darkest village in Iceland? No direct sunlight for four months! After spending less than a day in his house, Magnus had felt as if he'd aged twenty years.

Lia was tapping her finger against her cheek, as if trying to add up a series of numbers in her head that wouldn't quite come out right. "Bleak. I see. You know, your English is so good, I'm surprised you need an English class."

Magnus tried to look as though this were a welcome compliment. "Thank you for saying so." God, she was scary. What must it have been like to be married to this woman? No wonder Ken Miner had disappeared.

"Mom, everyone in my class speaks English well. It's an advanced class."

"Ah." Lia raised her eyebrows, and Magnus didn't know whether to thank Katherine for her intercession or to feel vaguely insulted that his language skills were being disparaged.

"I'm a scientist. I need to be able to write papers in English," he added.

"Really. Now, I would have said that you were in the military. You have the look of a man who guards his privacy, and men tend to get that in the army or in prison. What kind of science?"

Jesus, this woman would have made a marvelous interrogator. "I'm a chemical oceanographer."

"Now, isn't that funny," said Lia. "I just saw a repeat of that show *Seinfeld,* the episode where George claims he's a marine biologist in order to impress this girl. But then he goes to the beach and has to rescue a whale. You would know what to do if you came across a beached whale?"

"I study the quantitative fluxes between constituent reservoirs. But if a whale beaches itself in Manhattan, I would be happy to identify its species for you."

Lia raised her eyebrows, and a second too late, Magnus realized that she thought he was being sarcastic. "Well, that's good to know. In any case, I'd better leave you boys to your competition over . . . the maid's room. Bye, Kat. Call me later. Nice meeting you, Luc." She paused, infinitesimally. "Magnus."

Shit, shit, shit, shit. No question about which of them the mother preferred.

chapter *fifteen*

•

I can't believe my mother, Kat thought as she shut the front door. First she barges in and challenges me, and then, to top it all off, she launches into the kind of third-degree questioning that says, I know you intend to do my daughter. Kat took this morning's intrusion as a sign of her mother's rapidly deteriorating sense of boundaries; at least, back when Logan had been around, Lia used to ring the doorbell before letting herself in.

"Sorry about all that," she said, turning back to the men.

"Nothing to apologize for," said Magnus.

"Your mother seems very nice," Luc added.

"Oh, she's wonderful. I don't know what I'd do without her." *Not that she would ever let me find out.*

"It's nice that she makes dinner for you," Luc offered.

Kat nodded, thinking, But not so nice when she does it

without checking with me, as if I were still fifteen. Which left Kat in the awkward position of having to explain that she had to go to Fez for dinner tonight because she was expecting a secret message from her father. Imagining the fallout, Kat reconsidered. Maybe it would be simpler to spare her mother's feelings and make up some other excuse.

Out loud, she said, "Let me show you the hall bathroom. Since the bath in the maid's room is tiny, whoever rents the bedroom can take baths or showers here." She opened the door, and both men peeked inside.

"That's a very large bathtub," said Luc admiringly. "You could fit two people in there. Maybe two and a half."

Kat felt herself flush, recalling the evenings early on in her pregnancy when she and Logan had stretched out together, soaping each other's backs and making slippery plans for the future. And then, not meaning to, Kat found herself speculating about what each of the men beside her might be like, naked in the tub. Not that she had any intention of taking things there, of course. But if she did, she had the sense that Luc would be playful, energetic, uninhibited, while Magnus would be tentative at first, then deliberate, intense, focused.

Kat realized that both men were looking at her. She cleared her throat. "Follow me and I'll show you the rest." Was it her imagination, or did that sound a little like the kind of offer Mae West used to make?

The sight of her kitchen removed any lingering sense of sexual tension. It was like stepping back in time, standing on the hideous, Brady Bunch–era linoleum, surrounded by mustard yellow walls and a dark brown stove and refrigerator. Only the wicker stools by the sideboard were new; the rest remained exactly the way Lia had arranged things back when

Kat was in second grade. "As you can see, I have a long to-do list. We were just about to redo everything when my marriage broke up." Kat thought she'd managed to sound quite matter of fact, and was taken completely by surprise when Magnus covered her hand with his.

"It's okay," he said. His palms were huge, enveloping hers, and the tips of his fingers were calloused. But Scandinavians never just reached out and touched people, she thought. Then, surprising her even more, Magnus stroked his thumb along the inside of her palm. The jolt that went through Kat made her reevaluate her earlier assumption about what this man would be like in bed. Should she return his caress? Yank her hand away?

"*Alors,*" Luc said, a bemused expression on his face, "I do not wish to alarm you, but I think I just saw a rat."

"Oh, no!" Kat broke contact with Magnus. "Where was it?"

"Over there," Luc said, pointing to a corner. "You, ah, don't normally have rats here, do you?"

Kat gave a surprised gurgle of laughter. "No! No, it's just my son's pet gerbil." As she said "gerbil," the animal in question darted across the floor again, disappearing under the stove this time. My life has just turned into a screwball comedy, thought Kat. So glad I agreed to bring my students into my home to witness this.

Magnus crouched down. "It runs around loose?"

"Not exactly. She escaped and I haven't been able to get her back into her cage."

"May I move this?"

"Please."

As Luc and Kat watched, Magnus shifted the stove away from the wall. There was a low, metallic groan, followed by a sharp internal bang, and a small brown rodent streaked across the room.

Luc clapped his hands together. "I have him!"

Kat felt a bit giddy. "Fantastic, Luc, great reflexes. Hang on to her and let's get her back in her cage. God, I don't know why people keep rodents as pets."

Magnus stood up, his right knee registering an audible protest. "In Iceland, I had a rat in my office. We called him Biggie."

Kat opened the door to Dashiell's room, trying to focus on what Magnus was saying. "You had a pet rat?"

"Not exactly. But we let him alone. And then when . . . someone else came in to replace me, he insisted that the rat be caught. So my assistants started building rat traps. Huge, complicated rat traps."

"Okay, Luc, get ready." Kat lifted the door to Ms. Nibbles's Habitrail and Luc pushed her in. "We did it! Good work."

"My pleasure."

As they made their way back to the kitchen, Kat realized that Magnus hadn't finished his story. "So what happened to your rat?"

"My assistants—my former assistants—kept on building these contraptions to catch the rat, and each time, instead of the rat, there was a note."

Luc raised one eyebrow. "A note?"

"Like from a kidnapper. Letters cut out from magazines. 'I laugh at your stupid trap,' things like that."

Kat smiled. "Sounds like you had a nice bunch of people to work with. So, what happened with Biggie? Did he get caught?"

Magnus's face didn't change expression, but Kat felt the shift in his mood, as if a shadow had passed over him. "I don't know. I came here. Probably Dan used poison in the end. Dan was . . . very efficient about getting what he wanted."

"Ah." She didn't say anything more, sensing that Magnus hadn't intended to reveal quite so much. But from the way Magnus talked about his old job, it was clear to her that he hadn't chosen to leave. *No wonder he lacks confidence.*

"So," Kat said, wanting to change the subject, "there's nothing left to show you two except for the bedroom itself." There really wasn't much to see, just a small room with a single bed and a tiny desk and chair. Logan had started sleeping there when Dash was a baby, because he hadn't seen the point in being awake when Kat was the one breast-feeding the baby. And although he'd stopped sleeping there, the marriage had never really recovered its fragile, preinfant equilibrium.

"There you are, I don't suppose either of you is all that interested now that you've seen it . . ."

"I am," said Luc. "Exceedingly interested."

"Me, too," said Magnus. "I love it. It's just what I need."

"Well," Kat said, "that does put me in a bit of an awkward position."

"No, no, I swear, not even in my imagination," said Luc, the wry expression on his face making Kat laugh.

"Well, I'm not sure how I should choose between you." The last thing Kat wanted to do was alienate a student, and both men had points in their favor. On the one hand, Luc was great fun, and she knew Dashiell liked him. On the other hand, Magnus was older, quieter, more settled. More appealing on a personal level, said a little voice. Not that she intended to do anything about it.

"Let me make it simple for you," suggested Luc. "Choose me, and I will cook delicious French and Moroccan food for you and your son."

"I don't suppose you would like Icelandic rotted shark and sheep's head jelly," Magnus said, "but if I'm living here, maybe I can help by fixing a few things around the house."

"Oh, God, I don't know what to do. Maybe the fairest way would be to flip a coin." Kind of like choosing beds in college, Kat thought. And then she remembered something about sharing living space. She'd had one roommate freshman year who had kept her awake night after night with her noisy lovemaking sessions. "Oh, um, one other thing, I don't know if either of you has a steady girlfriend at the moment . . ."

"Not me," said Luc. "I am all alone, a poor, solitary comic book artist."

Ah, the insufferable cuteness of youth. "Well, the thing is, if you do meet someone you like, that's fine, of course, but this being such a small room, and so close to the kitchen . . ." Kat left the rest of the sentence unsaid. "It's not that *I* care, but because of my son . . ."

Luc cocked his head to one side in mock innocence, clearly enjoying her discomfiture. "Exactly what are you saying?"

Kat decided to begin again. "It's not that you can't have a girlfriend over," she said, then hesitated, unsure how to put this politely. *You just can't have screamingly loud sex at all hours of the day and night?* Magnus held up one hand.

"With me, there would be no visitors. No girlfriends."

Luc's eyebrow shot up. "Boyfriends?"

"No. No girlfriends or boyfriends."

There was a speculative gleam in Luc's eyes. "Farm animals?"

Magnus glared at the younger man. "No sexual partners at all. I am celibate."

Luc shook his head, as if scandalized. "Truly? Is it a medical condition? A psychological problem?"

Kat pinched the Frenchman's arm. "Thank you, Magnus, for being so honest."

"Are you intending to take holy orders?"

"Shut up, Luc," Kat said, as if she weren't wondering the exact same thing. Turning to Magnus, she said, "The room is yours if you want it."

Looking Kat straight in the eye, Magnus said, "Oh, I want it, all right."

Luc muttered something under his breath in French that Kat couldn't translate, but which brought a flush to the Icelander's cheeks. "Well, that's great. When do you want to move in?"

"Immediately, if I may."

"Works for me," said Kat, thinking, Problem solved. I'll have the cash to pay the co-op board, I don't have to worry about my boarder and some skank making wild barnyard noises while I'm trying to get a late-night snack, and with Magnus's having sworn off sex, no chance that I'll do something stupid, like get involved with a student.

chapter *sixteen*

•

there were two choices of seating at Fez: the main restaurant area, which had regular tables and chairs, and the traditional section, which had low, cushioned benches and circular, hammered metal trays balanced on pedestals. Usually, young, physically demonstrative couples chose to dine in this area, because it was so dark. The far corner, in particular, offered a great deal of privacy, making it a perfect choice for lovers. Or spies.

And there was another similarity. As Kat ran her hand under the seat cushions, she felt a rush of guilty pleasure. It was probably a testament to just how boring her life had become, but playing secret agent was the most fun she'd had in ages. She glanced across the table to see if her son had noticed anything odd about his mother's behavior, but Dashiell continued to play his handheld electronic game, oblivious to the fact that she was poking around under the tasseled pillows.

A young waiter in a red fez, white tunic, and embroidered black vest came by, and Kat yanked her hand out, accidentally hitting the edge of the low, circular brass table, which rang like a gong. "Sorry," she said, sweating. Some Mata Hari she was turning out to be.

The waiter smiled as if he were used to customers banging into things. "Would you like a drink?"

"Sure. Thank you. A glass of house white and a Sprite."

Once the waiter had left, she put her hand in again, her heart pounding with excitement as she felt the edges of a note under her fingertips.

Suddenly Dashiell looked up from his Game Boy. "Nana was really mad at you for not eating the dinner she bought."

"Did that upset you? You know, even people who love each other have disagreements sometimes."

"Like you and Daddy used to?"

Kat put her free hand over her son's. "Yes, but Nana and I are never going to split up."

"You mean we're always going to live across the hall from her?"

Kat hesitated. "We're always going to stay close and see a lot of each other. Even if we have an argument."

Dash went back to his Game Boy, apparently content. Then, just as Kat was fishing for the note again, her son looked up. "So your student is going to live with us?"

"That's right." Kat kept her left hand, which was under her seat, very still.

"Not the French comic book guy?"

"No, the other one. The Icelander. You know, they both helped get Ms. Nibbles back."

Dashiell grunted and turned his attention back to his

game, finally leaving Kat free to fish out the note. Squinting, she tried to make out her father's message in the wavering light of the hanging copper lamp.

> Mundane excitement eventually triumphs / mediate eddies / hierophant elegance reacts egregiously / acerbic tone / synchronized impulse x-ray / post menopausal / tourettes only minion organizes reduced revenant ostrich warts.

Oh, great, Kat thought. He's written it in code. Or else my father's computer has a virus. Kat looked up to find her son staring at her.

"What's that?"

"Oh, nothing," Kat said brightly. "Now, what are we going to order?"

"Those thin beefy strips. What do you mean, nothing? Why are you hiding it?"

"I'm not hiding it. It's just a letter."

"Who from? Is it something about my father?"

Kat realized that her son wasn't going to let this go. Normally, Dashiell paid little attention to what was going on around him, but like all children, he had an almost infallible instinct for sniffing out parental secrets. "Actually," she admitted, "it's from *my* father."

Dashiell looked puzzled. "Your father? But I thought he was dead."

"Up till now, he's been as out of touch as if he were dead, but suddenly he's decided to contact me."

Dashiell took the radical step of putting his Game Boy in its case. "So, what does he say? Is he coming to visit us?"

"I don't know. He's a spy, you see, and I think he's written this in some kind of weird code." She showed Dashiell the letter. "What do you think?"

Dash examined the sheet for a while without speaking. "It's not a code," he said at last.

"It's not?"

Just then, the waiter appeared. Kat ordered a doner kebab for Dashiell, and salmon wrapped in grape leaves for herself. After this, she promised herself, no more breaking her budget with dinners out.

Once the waiter had left, Kat touched Dashiell's shoulder. "So what is it? Are you sure it isn't some kind of secret message?" It was sort of strange, deferring to her nine-year-old, but her son loved word puzzles and math games. As far as Kat knew, the only code her son hadn't been able to break was the unwritten one of social interactions.

"Of course it's a secret message," said Dash, in a tone of voice that suggested she was a little slow on the uptake. "It's just not a code."

"Try to say it without sounding so condescending, Dash."

"Sorry." The waiter put some long, flat bread on the table, along with a bowl of yogurt cheese. Dashiell tore off a piece of the bread. "This is a cipher. A code replaces every word with another word or symbol or number. A cipher replaces every letter."

"Can you decode—I mean, decipher it?"

"Of course. It's totally easy. A baby could solve this."

"But I can't, so please just tell me."

"This is a null cipher. Meaning you just take the first letter from each word, see? 'Mundane excitement eventually triumphs,' that just means 'Meet.' 'Mediate eddies' means 'me,' and so on."

Kat took the letter back. "Meet me here at six p.m. tomorrow!" She half stood up and hugged her son across the table. "Dash, you're a genius."

"So did your dad send you any cool spy stuff? X-ray glasses or bugging devices or signal pens?"

"I'm afraid he seems to be a low-tech kind of guy. If I want to talk to him, I'm supposed to put some pink chewing gum on the left side of the phone booth out there."

"You're joking."

"Afraid not."

"But that's so lame."

Kat shrugged in silent apology, but her son had already turned to watch the waiter arriving with their food. Dashiell attacked his lamb and beef dish with messy enthusiasm, bolting down his bites and then pausing abruptly. "I'm full." He started to reach for his Game Boy.

"Don't start playing, Dash. Talk to me a moment. How did the rest of your field trip go?"

"It went great. Thank you for coming, Mommy."

He hadn't called her Mommy in a while. "I'm glad it helped, honey." She concentrated on cutting a piece of her fish. "How do you feel about us having a boarder?"

"Okay, I guess. But, Mommy?"

"Yes, baby?"

"When am I going to see Daddy again?"

Kat took a breath, taken completely off guard. "Well," she said, "I don't really know. I imagine he'll come see you as soon as he gets a break from filming." Was that the right thing to say? Should she be more honest and brace him for the reality that he might not see his father for a long time? But for once, Kat couldn't bring herself to state the bald truth, that Logan was close by and didn't seem particularly interested in seeing his son. *May you rot in hell, you lousy bastard.*

"Maybe we should call him. Or write."

"Sure, we could do that." Why couldn't Logan just get hit by a truck and die? Death was such an easy thing to explain, and the perfect excuse for being out of contact. "Why don't you let me email him for you?"

"Okay."

Later, back in the apartment, with Dashiell asleep, Kat sat down at her computer. She was a little afraid to check her email, in case she discovered that Logan hadn't even bothered to respond to her message. That worry turned out to be unjustified; he had sent a reply, all right.

> *GreatDain64: I have shared your email threats with my lawyer, who advises me to avoid all personal contact until the details of our settlement have been worked out. If you really are concerned about Dashiell, I should think the last thing you would want to do is air all our dirty laundry in the tabloid press.*

Kat nearly threw the computer against the wall. That asshole! She tried to reconcile this conscienceless, disembodied voice with the Logan who used to stroke her pregnant belly. *Don't get dragged down with that, now. Concentrate.* Aware that Logan was showing everything to his lawyer, it took her an hour of revising to come up with something she could actually send, which was:

> *Kminer: It doesn't take a law degree to figure out that IT IS NOT RIGHT for a father*

earning in the high six figures to take all the money out of his wife's bank account when she and your son HAVE NO MONEY TO LIVE ON. If you don't like how that sounds in print, then I suggest you make some reasonable arrangement with me.

P.S.: Dashiell wants to know when he will see his daddy again.

When she had finished sending her message, Kat poured herself a glass of wine and longed for a cigarette. Why had no one ever invented a cigarette delivery service for mothers who used to smoke and longed to go back to the habit but couldn't leave the house to buy a pack? Pulling her hair back into a high ponytail, Kat took a sip of pinot grigio and checked her answering machine.

The first message was from her agent. "As we suspected, the soap decided to go with another actress. Presumably they want to keep their options open with Logan, and they're worried about how you two would work together now. I want you to know that I was really frank and told them that I thought there were a lot of fans who were going to be extremely disappointed. But you know what? We've got feelers out to the other soaps, and in the meantime, you've had an offer from an infomercial for a new line of skin-care products. Now, I do remember what you used to say to me about paid endorsements, but frankly so many actresses are doing them these days that I don't agree with you that it's the kiss of death to your career."

Translation: You can't kill something that's already dead.

"Now, I've heard that this particular line is actually very

good, it's an American repackaging of a French program. And you know, it's quite a compliment to be asked—clearly, they think you're looking good, and that your face will motivate viewers to buy their product. Call me and let me know what you think."

Well, Kat thought, maybe I should consider it. God knows it would be a welcome infusion of cash, and even if it was a bit whorish to get paid to compliment something for an hour, she would hardly be the first to fall from grace. The Saturday-morning cable stations were full of former sex symbols peddling cutting-edge hair gizmos, specialized martial arts sit-up machines, depilatory miracles, and makeup that could conceal the effects of age, sun damage, and the wounds inflicted by an ax-wielding maniac.

She'd be the signature face of something, like Victoria Principal and Cindy Crawford. Not the fate she'd hoped for herself, but at least it would save her apartment from the dangers of divorce court.

Suddenly Kat noticed that there was another message. She pressed play. "Hi, Kat, it's Daphne again. Just got some more details about the infomercial. A number of really good actresses are involved—the star of that BBC police show that came over here a few years back, one of the *Sex and the City* women, Sela Ward—whoops, no, sorry, Sela got an eye infection, so she had to bow out. Well, call me Monday if you're interested, you're supposed to pick up a few jars and use the products for a couple of days before they shoot the video."

Oh, Christ, Kat thought. It's come to this—I'm second choice to Sela Ward to help peddle moisturizer.

Actually, when she thought about it for a moment, that wasn't the worst thing in the world to be. It wasn't exactly "We saw your performance in that Chekhov play and we had to have you," but it was hardly the most disappointing event of recent days.

Now, Kat thought, this was actually a seldom remarked upon advantage to depression. When you were really feeling down in the dumps, every lousy thing began to carry the exact same weight, whether it was losing a pregnant gerbil somewhere in the walls of your apartment or learning just how limited your job options really were.

Kat was just thinking she might be tired enough for bed when the doorbell rang.

Kat opened the door to her mother, who was wearing her dark purple caftan and an overbearing expression of cheerfulness. "So? Which one did you choose? The Icelander?"

Kat realized that, in living this close to her mother, she had turned her life into a sitcom. All she needed now was the soundtrack and the neat, thirty-minute resolution to all her problems. "Want some wine, Mom?" Kat poured her mother a glass and handed it to her. "I did decide on Magnus, but . . ."

"Ha! I knew it! You always liked the tall ones."

Kat sighed. "First of all, Mom, I'm not getting involved with a student. Second of all, I'm definitely not getting involved with a paying boarder."

Lia sipped her wine. "Sometimes it's enough to feel an attraction. And you are attracted to him, don't bother trying to deny it."

"All right, I'm attracted."

"So why not just enjoy yourself? It's not like he's twelve and you're his sixth-grade teacher. And it's not as if he's going to be living with you forever."

"I thought you were concerned about Dash's reaction. Besides, aren't mothers supposed to advise their daughters *against* casual sex?"

"Dash is going through a hard time, but so are you, and you're *my* baby. I want you to have something good in your life. The way I see it, by the time you hit sixty, sex starts avoiding you, so you might as well take advantage of having that man in your house while you can."

Kat checked in her kitchen cabinet and offered her mother a box of thin wheat crackers. "Okay, Mom, here's the truth. Maybe I would consider doing something, but he says he's celibate."

Lia nibbled on a cracker. "Okay, this is not a good sign. When women swear off sex for a while, it's usually because they need a little time to deal with their emotions from a previous relationship. When men do it, there's usually some deep-seated psychological problem." Closing the box of crackers, Lia stood up. "Is it too late to change your mind and choose the other one?"

"Mom, I'm not shopping for a lover."

"Well, maybe it's time you were. After a certain age, the opportunities don't just happen all by themselves like they used to."

After her mother left, Kat double locked her door and changed into her nightgown. When was the last time she'd had sex, anyway? September? October? And that hardly counted, as it had been quick and unsatisfactory, and followed by the revelation that her husband no longer found her attractive. No, correction, it hadn't been a revelation, not really, it had been more of a *confirmation* that Logan had lost all desire for her, and that it wasn't conflicting schedules or tiredness or any of the other myriad of marital excuses for not having sex that was to blame.

And the sad truth was, she hadn't even missed the sex. She had missed wanting sex, and even more, had missed being wanted. She had missed walking around feeling that delicious sense of possibility that she used to get from attractive men. She missed feeling that her body was a gateway to pleasure.

Still, it was nice to think that today she had experienced a frisson of erotic contact with a man. Even if it had only been for two seconds.

Kat climbed into bed and was about to turn off the light when she realized there was no way she could meet her father and ask the questions she wanted to ask with Dashiell in tow. Kat picked up the phone and pressed the memory one button. "Mom, I'm not waking you up, am I?"

"No, I was just reading in bed."

"I never told you why I had to go to the restaurant tonight."

"It has to do with your father, doesn't it?"

Kat laughed, shaking her head in amazement. "You are just plain scary, Mom. Or psychic."

"Not really. Look, Kat, first you won't tell me anything about the letter your father sent, and then, all of a sudden, you absolutely have to eat Turkish, but you can't explain why. So, did you see him? How does he look?"

Kat rubbed the backs of her hands, which were rough and dry. "Actually, he left a note for me to pick up. I'm supposed to meet him there tomorrow evening."

"God, the complete narcissism of the man. Why is he using Fez as a dead drop? Don't tell me he's that frightened of me."

Kat smoothed some lotion into her knuckles, not wanting to admit that she wasn't sure what a dead drop was. "Why would he be scared of you, Mom?"

"Because when he got in touch with me last month, I told him how much he owed me in back child support, that's why."

It took Kat a moment to process that. "You never told me he contacted you."

Lia's voice sharpened. "I just don't see why that man deserves to have anything to do with you now when he didn't help us at all back when we needed him."

Lying in what had once been her mother's bedroom, Kat felt a momentary sense of disorientation, as if thirty years had telescoped together and she were ten again. "What if I'm curious about him, Mom? And isn't all that kind of ancient history at this point?"

"Not to me, it's not."

"Well, I want to meet him. I was going to ask you to watch Dash, but if you don't want to . . ."

"When do I ever refuse you anything? I'm just worried that he's going to wind up disappointing you. You know you can't expect anything from him, don't you?"

"Believe me," Kat said, "I'm not expecting anything."

chapter *seventeen*

•

Kat was disappointed. She'd been sitting in the restaurant for the past forty minutes, waiting for her father to arrive. In that time, she had worked her way through an appetizer of vine leaves, a shepherd's salad, and a glass of wine. Kat made a mental calculation and realized she'd just consumed about $20 worth of vegetables, and she hadn't even been that hungry. Which was strange, really, since she hadn't eaten much all day, but the prospect of meeting a parent she hadn't seen since fifth grade was a real appetite suppressant. Trying to distract herself, Kat opened her fake Kate Spade bag and took out the three containers of Rejuvenatrix she'd picked up from her agent in preparation for the infomercial.

There was a bottle of cleanser made from sea kelp, which was green and smelled like a seashell that still had something living inside of it; a jar of moisturizer, which was blue and smelled a bit like a seventies aftershave; and a small test tube of something called Intensive Care, which was a disconcerting shade of red. It smelled like a doctor's office.

Maybe the infomercial would be a greater test of her acting abilities than she'd realized, Kat thought. Even Katharine Hepburn in her prime would have had trouble selling this stuff.

The young waiter in the fez and vest appeared. "Will there be anything else, madame?"

Kat looked around the dimly lit restaurant, hoping for a glimpse of a man she only vaguely remembered. In the last pictures she had of him, her father had sported a thick, dark blond mustache clearly influenced by Robert Redford's Sundance Kid. Now that she thought about it, he must have been her age at the time of that photograph.

"I don't think so," she told the waiter, still not completely resigned to the fact that her father was not going to show. "Just the check, please." Could Dash have mistranslated the cipher? No, probably just another example of the complete and utter fecklessness of Ken Miner.

"You were here last night," said the waiter.

Curious, Kat looked up. "That's right."

"With your son, yes? The little boy."

Could this have something to do with her father? "Yes, that was my son. I'm Katherine Miner," Kat added for good measure, in case the waiter needed confirmation of her identity before he gave her his message.

"I am Malik." The waiter looked at her with his big, dark eyes. "Do you have a husband?"

Oh, no, thought Kat, I know where this is headed. "Sorry, Malik, but I'm not in the market for a one-night stand, I'm legally married, so I can't offer you any help getting a green card."

Malik shrugged. "I just thought you looked lonely," he said, walking away.

Perfect. Kat dialed Marcy on her cell phone. "Hey, I don't suppose you want to come down to Fez and meet me for dinner?" Kat knew she should just cut her losses and leave, but she felt reluctant to head home to her mother's inevitable "I told you so."

"I would love to see you, but I've already cooked lasagna. Steve was supposed to be home an hour ago."

"We're a pair, then. I've just been stood up by my father."

"I thought your father was dead."

"No such luck." Kat looked out at the tables around her. To her left, a scholarly looking young man was kissing the side of his date's neck. "What's up with Steve?"

"He had rehearsal with his jazz band, and I guess he and the guys went out for a drink." Marcy sounded tired rather than irritated, and Kat found herself wishing her friend would grow a little backbone.

"Well, why don't you come out and hang with me? The lasagna won't mind."

"If I go out, I'll never know just how late Steve made it in," said Marcy. "Why don't we get together this Sunday, for your birthday? Or are you still planning on ignoring the day completely?"

"How about I see you and Zandra Saturday night, instead? That way you can punish Steve, see me, and I can still pretend my birthday's not happening."

"Sounds like a plan. I'll call Zandra now."

Kat hung up and paid her check. As she gathered up her containers of Rejuvenatrix skin-care products, a small slip of paper fluttered to the floor. Kat leaned down, assuming she had dropped the skin-care instructions.

And then, reading the page, she realized it had nothing to do with skin care, after all. Kat crumpled the note in disgust and dropped it into her bag. *Unsafe my nearly forty-year-old ass.* She wasn't sure what game her father was playing, and she decided that she didn't really care. If he didn't have the guts to show up and face her, then to hell with him. She had too much going on in her life to waste her time trying to decipher his motives.

chapter *eighteen*

•

magnus wasn't sure which was harder, spying on Katherine or figuring out transitive verbs. Stealing a glance at Luc's paper, Magnus decided that grammar beat espionage, hands down. After all, he'd managed to follow Katherine into that Turkish restaurant last night without being detected, but he had no idea what the hell a transitive verb preposition combination was. And how was everyone else knocking out five of them? He was the native speaker, for crying out loud.

"Okay," said Katherine, "let's go through the questions together. My gorgeous new sunglasses, a mysterious brown package, his strange old neighbor. What do you notice about the first adjective in each example—Magnus?"

"I'm not sure I understand the question," he admitted.

"Do you want to venture a guess?"

Luc was regarding him out of the corner of his eye, as if

151

the answer was on the tip of his tongue and it was killing him not to be able to say it. Chieko and Maria both seemed to be smirking, Galina was raising her hand, and Nabil was looking off into the middle distance as if he wished he were somewhere else entirely. In short, it was like being back in high school. "Sorry."

Katherine smiled at him, looking distracted. He noticed that she had taken particular care with her appearance today, twisting her hair up and back and wearing a black knee-length skirt instead of jeans. Still, she did not look well. There were dark shadows under her eyes and she seemed to have some sort of rash on her cheeks. "Luc, how about you?"

Well, at least there was one other person in class who wouldn't have the right answer. But to Magnus's shock, the Frenchman responded promptly. "The first one is an opinion."

"Very good. The subjective judgment comes first."

Luc's smile was irritatingly smug, thought Magnus, noting that those were both subjective adjectives.

"All right, class you can put your quiz sheets away." Katherine leaned against her desk and Magnus wondered what she'd been doing, alone in the restaurant last night. Had she been stood up by a man? That might explain her wan appearance this morning. Or could she have made some plan to meet with her father? If so, Magnus wondered why Ken Miner hadn't shown up.

Shit, could he have been spotted? Maybe he was equally bad at grammar *and* surveillance. Fred had been extremely pleased to hear that Magnus was going to be moving into Katherine's apartment, but had told him that they now had an extremely tight deadline. It was just announced that new elections would be held in Kyrgyzstan in less than a week. If he hadn't made any progress with Ken Miner before Oybek's position became official, he might as well start looking in the want ads.

"So," said Katherine, drawing his attention back to the here and now, "I want to continue with yesterday's discussion. Galina, how did it go with you? Whom did you speak with in the museum, and what did you find out?"

"Well, it was strange, really. I saw a woman with a very nice pair of shoes, and you said to find out some information." Galina sounded faintly accusatory. "So I went up to her, and I said, Hello, I like your shoes, where did you get them and how much did they cost? And do you know what the woman did? She just sniffed at me and walked away!"

"Okay, this is an excellent chance for us to talk about what sorts of questions Americans consider rude." Katherine began to pace the room, looking so animated that everyone in the class sat up a little straighter. "Remember what Luc was saying about Americans telling you all kinds of intimate information right off the bat? On the one hand, Americans are extremely informal and very willing to tell strangers all kinds of things, but there are also topics that Americans consider off-limits. And they might not be considered taboo subjects in your country. In general, I'd advise you to never ask anyone how much they earn, how much they weigh, how old they are, or how much they paid for something."

Galina raised her hand. "But what if you really need to know the answer to one of these questions?"

Katherine considered this for a moment. "Well, in that case, what you can do is ask an indirect question, such as, 'How much do legal secretaries earn?' or 'What does a blouse like that cost these days?'"

Galina's hand shot up again.

"Yes, Galina?"

"So what do I do if I see a woman with problem skin? Will she be insulted if I ask her if she needs a facial? Because I am completing my cosmetology degree. I also cut hair," she added.

You should get your money back, thought Magnus. Who would want a beauty treatment from a dumpy, dough-faced woman in a wig?

To his shock, the answer seemed to be Katherine. "You're a cosmetologist?"

"Almost. Three more weeks."

"Can I speak to you after class? I used a new cream last night and I've had this terrible reaction."

"I noticed. Come to my house after class. I will give you a special rate."

"Wonderful. All right, class, I have homework for you. If you can, I'd like you to watch an American soap opera, paying particular attention to the kinds of questions people ask and the reactions they receive. The shows are on in the afternoon, but if you have cable, there's a station that replays them all night long. All right, everyone, see you tomorrow."

Magnus realized that if Katherine went to have a facial now, he would have the next couple of hours free to poke around inside her apartment and find any correspondence between herself and her father. Trying to hide his excitement, Magnus averted his face as he packed up his books.

"So," said Luc, "have you moved in on her yet?"

Magnus ignored the younger man's insinuating tone. "I'm bringing my things over later today."

"Let me know if you need any help. That was very clever, by the way, what you told her. Now you make yourself a challenge, like a priest. Women love priests, especially if they are good-looking."

"I'm not a priest," said Magnus flatly.

"But of course not! That's why I think you are so clever. I must try this technique myself."

Magnus glanced over at Katherine, worried that she might have overheard them. Luckily, she appeared to be deep in conversation with Galina. "It's not a technique," he said, nearly growling with irritation.

"Ah, no? *Quel dommage*," said Luc, looking completely unconvinced. And then it hit Magnus that if there was one thing the French knew, it was seduction. Maybe, thought Magnus, I just did something right after all.

chapter *nineteen*

•

Kat knew that some women enjoyed being groomed and happily devoted entire days to the minutiae of taking care of themselves. Personally, however, she just felt irritated by the whole intrusive, time-consuming process. She'd already spent an hour with various food-based masques on her face, she smelled of sour cream and avocado, and she was dying to get out of Galina's airless Brooklyn apartment. Unfortunately, she had stupidly agreed to have her eyelashes dyed black, which meant an additional twenty minutes of sensory deprivation.

Used to having too little free time to sit and relax, Kat had forgotten what it felt like to be so bored you wanted to scream.

"I tell you, Galina," she said, "when you think how much time and energy we put into staying beautiful, it makes you wonder. Maybe this is the reason women don't rule the world yet."

"On the contrary," said Galina. "Women know how important appearance is. In Ukraine, when the president wanted to get rid of his political opponent, did he try to kill him with poison? No, they give him instead dioxin, make him look ugly, with pustules and big nose."

"What difference would that make?"

"Look at your television set! Everywhere now is makeovers, with plastic surgery and hair dyeing and teeth bleaching, and all because people look just to appearances. You want to rule the world? Use your appearance to fool people, but don't be fooled by appearances."

Spoken like a woman who'd been burned. Kat wondered what Galina's story was—she dressed like an observant married Jewish lady, but she had the uncompromising air of a person who'd been living alone for some time.

Out loud, Kat inquired, "How much longer now?"

"Not long. Rest now, is part of the treatment."

Kat tapped her fingers on the armrest of the chair, wondering how much time had elapsed. She should have left after the moisturizing treatment, which had involved a bowl of something that looked like borscht. Who cared if her eyelashes were perfectly dark first thing in the morning, anyway? It wasn't as if Magnus were going to be sneaking out of her bed at daybreak.

Kat cleared her throat. "Galina? Are you there?"

"Yes, I'm here." Galina's husky voice came from across the room. "It's only been three minutes, Katherine. Try to relax."

Kat found herself wondering whether or not her student had moved into the maid's room yet. Now that it was really happening, she was having a few second thoughts. What if she and Dashiell had an argument in front of him? Would she ever be able to wander into the kitchen in her nightgown again?

Of course you will, said a snide little mental voice. He's celibate, remember? He doesn't care if you walk around in four-inch heels and a thong.

And that was probably a blessing in disguise, because she was more than a little drawn to Magnus. She'd forgotten that desire could be as unpredictable as gardening, some initial seeds of interest never taking root at all, others shooting up right away before dying abruptly, and most inexplicably of all, a rare few lying dormant before growing steadily stronger. And that kind of attraction was never purely physical. When you acted on it, you didn't just get laid, you got involved. A very bad idea, all around.

But why was the man celibate, anyway? If it were for medical reasons, that was one thing, but if it were simply that he was sick of dealing with women, then maybe he might change his mind. Kat certainly thought he could change hers. Suddenly, Kat's eyes began to burn and she realized she was beginning to open them without thinking.

This was the problem with sex, thought Kat. It annexed huge sections of your mind, diminished your mental capacity, and for what? About fifteen disappointing minutes between the sheets.

Kat shifted restlessly, drumming her fingers against the arm of the chair. What else was there to think about while she waited here in the dark? The fact that Logan still hadn't replied to her last email? Kat's eyes were stinging again; she was furrowing her brow. *Think of something else.*

Kat tried to think of her favorite movies, but instead found herself imagining how famous on-screen couples would wind up, if you could follow them past the last frame of the movie. Zack and Paula from *An Officer and a Gentleman,* for example. How long before Debra Winger's character got sick of her naval aviator husband's abusive temper and lack of social skills? As for Richard Gere's *Pretty Woman* character, Kat figured that fairy tale would end with an iron-clad prenup that he would terminate a month shy of the deadline. *Working Girl* Tess would find that her business merger marriage began to break down as soon as she had a kid. Tom Cruise's *Jerry Maguire* would be showing the money, the effort, and the charm to some other woman.

Now Kat's left eye really hurt. "Excuse me? Galina? I think it's time to rinse my eyes off."

There was a peculiar, sticky sound as the Russian woman moved across the linoleum floors in her rubber-soled prison-matron shoes. Kat waited as Galina leaned forward to examine Kat's eyelids with white, cotton-gloved hands. "One more minute. The lashes will last longer if the dye sits for the full time." Her breath on Kat's cheek smelled hot and slightly bitter, like tea.

Kat wondered if coming to Galina's apartment had really been such a good idea. How did she really know that the woman was a qualified cosmetologist in her country, anyway? Kat should have maxed out her credit card and gone to Georgette Klinger.

"Try to relax. Talk to me," Galina said. "It will distract you. Tell me about the man."

Kat took a deep breath and tried to unclench her eyelids. "What man?"

"Please. You pluck eyebrows, you wax chin. There is a man." Something about Galina's resigned, world-weary tone made Kat feel about sixteen, a reckless innocent about to make a foolish mistake. She flashed on a memory of Magnus holding her hand, then dismissed it.

"Actually, there isn't any man in my life right now. I'm trying out for a role—I'm an actress as well as a teacher."

"So you don't have suddenly some man in your life? I thought that maybe you do this for Magnus or Luc."

"Oh, God, no! They're my students," said Kat, managing to sound completely offhand.

"But they are interested, no? I see that they are pursuing you." Galina made the last word sound almost sinister.

"Luc is the type to flirt with every woman he meets, and Magnus probably blushes when a nun walks by. Listen, my left eye is really starting to hurt, Galina."

"That is because you keep blinking. Relax the eyes, Katherine. It is just vegetable dye, not harmful." There was a gentle hand on her shoulder. "Just two more minutes."

"But you said one more minute two minutes ago!" *Oh, Jesus, did she even know what she was doing?*

"I look, I see the dye needs a little more time. Trust me, this is not my first time doing this. Try to relax. Tell me about yourself. You grew up where in the United States, in New York?"

"Well, my family lived in Barcelona and Rome for a little while when I was growing up."

"Really? What did your father do?"

Kat hesitated. "He worked for the State Department," she admitted, certain Galina was going to have a lot of opinions about this. "Listen, about my eyes . . ."

"Yes, yes, almost done. So your father was a spy, yes? Are they still married, your parents?"

Kat decided on taking the path of least resistance. Not responding to the spy comment, she said, "They divorced when I was a kid."

"Typical. Probably your father cheated."

Kat didn't bother to contradict her, and Galina took this as agreement.

"It is always the way. Because if you are used to having double life, suddenly to be having just one identity feels too confining. You must experience this as an actress, no? When you are just wife, mother, teacher, you disappear a little, you get lost. But when you play a role? Suddenly, in this false self, you are more alive, more interesting, more honest."

"I do know that feeling," said Kat, startled. She hadn't articulated it before, but that was what she missed most about acting: the ability to lose herself and find herself at the same time.

"This is why married men and women have affairs. Not for sex. For the pleasure of keeping something hidden, separate from ordinary life, just for you."

"The commonest thing is delightful if only one hides it," said Kat. "Oscar Wilde."

"You sound like a woman who might have a secret or two of her own," said Galina, with satisfaction.

Kat decided that she'd had enough. "Okay, I really need to get this dye off my eyes now."

"You are moving too much. Wait, I get the bowl." She sounded disappointed. "Here." A plastic bowl was pressed into Kat's hands, along with a damp cotton balls. "Rinse the eyes. Don't try to open."

Kat looked up with her eyes still closed. Warm water dripped down her cheeks. "Is this all right?"

"More. You said your eyes sting, so use plenty of water." Kat could feel the intensity of Galina's gaze on her. "So, about your father. You are closer to him, or to your mother?"

Kat kept patting her eyes with the wet cotton balls. Galina, she realized, would have fit in perfectly with her grand-mother's old friends, who felt that age had given them the right to ask anything of anyone, and had unshakable faith in their own opinions. Now that Kat thought about it, her grandmother's social circle had all originally come from Russia. "I really don't want to talk about my father anymore, Galina."

"Of course, I understand completely if it is too painful."

"It's not that it's painful, it's just that I really don't have much of a relationship with him." *And at this point in my life, I don't want one.* Kat thought about the note the Turkish waiter had delivered last night. *You are being followed. Meet me this time Sunday. Tell no one.*

But Kat had no intention of showing up on Sunday to meet her father. First of all, the man was clearly not right in the head. Who would be following her, a demented fan with a fixation on old soaps? Second of all, her father clearly had absolutely no idea that Sunday was her fortieth birthday, and the thought of spending even part of that day with a parent who was completely out of touch with reality was not exactly appealing.

"By the way, you shouldn't admit that your father was a spy," said Galina, her tone severe. "I don't want to hurt you, but Americans are very naïve about such things."

"Thanks for the advice," said Kat, thinking, *If you hadn't turned my facial into an interrogation, I wouldn't have said anything about my father.* "Can I open my eyes? How do they look?"

"Much better. Of course, your face is a little inflamed now, because of all the pores I cleaned, but by tomorrow you will see a huge improvement."

That didn't sound too good. Kat stood up and walked over

to the wall mirror. What she saw made her wish she still had her eyes plastered shut. "Galina! What's wrong with my face?" There were red blotches all over her cheeks and forehead, her nose was peeling, and the black dye had stained the skin around her eyes.

"Don't worry, it's nothing. As I said, a little puffiness."

"Are you kidding? It looks like I have leprosy! And this dye—does it come off?"

"Of course, of course. I tell you, I am a professional."

"Oh, God, I have to shoot an infomercial in three days." Kat kept herself from bursting into tears in front of her student, but she couldn't manage more than a polite nod despite Galina's continued reassurances that her skin would look wonderful by tomorrow. Or the day after.

Walking to the subway, Kat was half-convinced that people around her were looking at her strangely. *God, she really wanted to be home already.*

As she made her way along the crowd that lined the platform, Kat stepped over the painted yellow safety line and craned her neck to see if a train was coming. A squat, dark-haired woman with an infant jockeyed for position with a man in pale green surgical scrubs. Three young women stood in a phalanx by a pillar, obscuring the name of the stop.

Peering down the dark track, Kat saw that the signal light had turned green. An instant later, she heard the familiar rattling of the train's approach and felt somewhat reassured. She had a good half hour to make it home before Dashiell's school bus arrived in front of her building, and as long as she got on this train, she would make it in plenty of time.

Standing at the edge of the platform so as to be first on the train when it pulled in, Kat removed her compact from her purse and checked her eyes in the mirror. The lashes looked good, but the dye around her eyelids gave her a slightly dissolute look. Licking her finger and trying to get rid of some of the dye, she didn't look up as the train began to clatter down the track. If my face doesn't clear up, I'm going to lose this Rejuvenatrix job, she thought, and felt ridiculously close to crying again.

The only bright side Kat could see was that things were about as bad as they could possibly get. Surely she was overdue for some good luck, right? And then a flash went off. For a moment, Kat thought someone had thrown a small explosive, and she cringed instinctively, but then, right before the second flash, she heard someone say, "Katherine! How do you feel about your husband's new co-star?"

It was an attack, all right, but not the kind that worried the police. Kat was being stalked by paparazzi.

chapter *twenty*

•

By Saturday evening, Kat was fed up. It was bad enough being a has-been soap star, but turning into front-page tabloid fodder really was adding insult to injury. Hard to believe that just a few days earlier she'd thought her father was paranoid to think she was being followed. Now, she was the one who was paranoid, jumping out of her skin each time the phone rang, wearing a baseball cap and sunglasses when she left the building. Over the past twenty-four hours, Kat had received ten different emails and at least six phone calls from various tabloids, and she wasn't even the reporters' real object. She was simply a sidebar.

It seemed that Logan's high-profile return to *South of Heaven*, coupled with advance buzz for his new movie, had suddenly made him a prime target for the media. It felt to Kat as though it had happened overnight, but she knew that

Logan's career had reached critical mass gradually. Fame, Kat had been told by an old Hollywood movie actor turned soap villain, was like a population of cockroaches. It built steadily behind the scenes for a long time before spilling over.

Given the choice, Kat would have preferred dealing with cockroaches. She'd explained to her doorman three different times not to simply buzz people up before checking with her, but a reporter from the *Informer* had shown up at her front door just as she and Dash were sitting down to dinner. Kat had told the reporter that if she did want to give her side of the story, she would call the rival paper. At that point, Kat realized that someone must have paid Pedro off, and she had threatened him with dismissal if he let anyone into the elevator without calling her on the house phone first.

In retaliation, Pedro called Kat each and every time Magnus came into the lobby, which he had done five times yesterday as he moved into the maid's room.

The house phone rang, and Kat flinched. "Yes, Pedro, who is it?"

"Lady says she is your friend."

"Put her on."

"Kat? What the hell is going on here?"

"Sorry, Zandra. Let her up, Pedro, and if a woman named Marcy comes, she's a friend, too."

"So I let her up?" Pedro sounded suspicious.

"Yes, Pedro, you don't have to call me when she comes. And you don't have to call me each time Magnus comes in, either."

"Magnus?"

"The tall man with the blond hair."

"But you said call you each time. You said you would fire me if I not call you each time," said Pedro, each word dripping with malicious pleasure. "So each time, I will call you."

Zandra knocked on her door two minutes later. She'd brought a bottle of wine and her nine-year-old son, Nico. "What was that all about? Did you do something to piss your doorman off?"

"You could say that," said Kat, kissing her friend on her cheek. "You look amazing," she said. Zandra's curly hair had recently been hennaed a fierce shade of auburn, and she was wearing a new, ruffled Betsey Johnson dress that made her look like an MGM version of a Wild West Harlot.

"You look great, too," said Zandra automatically.

"Take a closer look." Kat leaned forward, offering her face for inspection.

"Oh, my God, what happened to your skin? You're all broken out."

"You should have seen it yesterday. This is an improvement." Kat turned to her friend's son. "And how are you, Nico?"

Nico, who had inherited his mother's bold nose and corkscrew curls but none of her vivacity, mumbled something unintelligible.

"How're you doing? Dash can't wait to see you."

Nico shrugged, not bothering to meet her eyes. Kat thought he was a charmless toadstool of a child, and that Zandra needed to teach him some manners, but the two boys had been playing together since preschool. These days, Dashiell went to a magnet program in a nearby public school, where most of the parents were artists, writers, or actors, while Nico attended an exclusive private school at the United Nations, funded by Zandra's wealthy parents. As far as Kat could tell, the two boys were learning essentially the same things— math, English, and the biographies of people so obscure Kat had never heard of them.

Kat smiled at Nico, trying to muster some enthusiasm for the gormless child. "Go on ahead to Dashiell's room, honey, he's waiting for you."

Nico looked at his mother and shrugged again, looking as if he were heading off for a dental appointment. This was pretty much the only response Kat had ever received from Nico, who greeted birthday parties, trips to the zoo, comic books, and doctor's appointments with the same stoic indifference. Yet, according to Zandra, her child was a paragon of intelligence and popularity, and in fact, whenever Dashiell asked for a playdate, Nico's schedule seemed to be full with other friends.

"Go on, honey, have some fun," said Zandra, pushing Nico in the direction of Dashiell's room. She handed Kat a bottle of merlot and a small, wrapped present.

"Thank you, Zandra. My first present, I'll have you know."

"Open it, open it, I think you'll really love it."

Kat would have preferred to sit down and have a drink first, but Zandra was beaming at her expectantly. Unwrapping the gold-foil paper, Kat revealed a book entitled *Letting Go of the Anger: The Emotional No-Fault Divorce.* "Um, thanks, Zan." Kat kissed her friend's cheek without enthusiasm. "Looks interesting."

"My friend Celia swears by it."

Kat put the book to one side, thinking that it might just be the worst gift she'd ever received, beating out the hideous papier-mâché clock she'd gotten from Aunt Amelia as a wedding present and the monstrous deluxe foot bath that Logan had given her on their last Christmas together.

"I have to say, Zan, I think it might be easier to let my anger go if Logan stopped doing things to enrage me. And now God only knows what version of things the tabloids are going to publish."

Zandra bent down, unzipping one of her black Italian boots. "Well, you know what they say: She who lives by the sword . . ."

Kat stared down at the back of her friend's head. "What's that supposed to mean?"

Zandra looked up. "You know."

"I don't know."

Zandra unzipped her second boot. "Oh, come on, didn't you tell me you threatened Logan with doing some tell-all for the tabloids?"

"Did I?" Kat didn't remember telling Zandra about that, but her mother did say that your memory begins to fail after forty. "Well, in any case, I didn't actually contact them."

"Oh." Zandra put her boots by the door, looking surprised. "Well, never mind, then. Anyway," she said, brightening, "where have you stashed the hunky Viking?"

"Who said he was hunky?"

"Marcy. She said you just happened to rent out your maid's room to the cutest guy in your class. Have you two gotten past the hand-holding stage yet?"

Of course, Marcy must have seen Magnus at the Institute. "We are not holding hands," Kat said, before suddenly remembering that this wasn't exactly true. "Come on, I'll get us both drinks."

Zandra followed Kat into the kitchen. "Mmm, it smells great in here," she said. "What're we having?"

"Chicken, corn, and cilantro. I made Mexican casserole." Kat put Zandra's wine down on the sideboard and took her corkscrew opener off its hook. When she looked up, she saw that Zandra was pointing at Magnus's closed door.

"Is he in there now?"

Kat nodded. "He went out for some kind of marathon run and just got in about an hour ago. I think he might be taking a nap."

"Won't we wake him up if we're in here?"

"It's six o'clock on a Saturday night, Zan. I have to have a life." Kat paused, looking at the cheap bottle of merlot in her hands. Like a lot of trust-fund babies, Zandra prided herself on having peasant tastes. "How about I make sangria for a change?"

"Por qué no? We make fiesta." Zandra did a little shoulder shimmy, making Kat laugh.

"Okay, Charo, would you mind cutting up an apple for me while I peel the orange?" Kat handed Zandra a knife before decanting the merlot into a pitcher.

Zandra began chopping the apple with practiced ease. "Tell me something," she said without looking up, "don't you think the man has moved pretty fast? You put up the ad Wednesday, he moves in on Friday? Either he hasn't got a life or he has a serious case of wanting to get into your pants."

Kat looked up, appalled. "Jesus, Zandra, where did you learn to whisper, at a school for the hearing impaired?" She pointed at the door not six feet from where they were standing and then put her finger to her lips, indicating the need for silence.

"Well? Do you think he has a crush on you?"

Kat took the apple Zandra had cut up and tossed it into the pitcher. "I have no idea."

"I have an idea. Maybe you could work this into your next lesson," said Zandra, ignoring her. "Now, Magnus, what does 'get into your pants' mean? A, to try on your trousers; b, to see if you can wear your friend's size-four jeans; or c, to get your hand or some other body part into the personal genital region of the pants' occupant?"

"That would certainly get his attention. Hand me an oven mitt, will you? I want to check the dinner."

Zandra, who never cooked, gave Kat a dish towel. "If all this clattering around doesn't wake him up, then I don't see how my whispering's going to do it. Besides," she added, lowering her voice, "what's wrong with him overhearing that you're a little interested?"

Kat closed the oven and beckoned Zandra away from Magnus's door.

"Because," she said, speaking very softly, "I don't think he's interested in me that way. But I have to admit, if he had been, I might have considered it." Kat held up the pitcher. "May I pour you a glass?"

"Please." Zandra took a sip. "So," she said, looking up with mock innocence over the rim of the glass, "what I want to know is, what's the protocol if you do sleep with your boarder? I mean, do you treat him like a casual boyfriend who happens to be renting, or does he automatically become a live-in lover?"

Despite herself, Kat laughed. "Oh, neither," she said, pouring herself a glass. "I believe the common practice is to raise the rent, after all, there ought to be surcharge for hump—oh, hello, Magnus," Kat said, whipping her head around as the door to his room opened. "Did you just wake up? I hope we weren't too loud." Now, she thought, there was some badass acting for you; too bad there wasn't an Oscar for Best Actress in an Unscripted Encounter.

"Not at all. I didn't want to sleep too long, anyway." Magnus leaned against the doorjamb, looking tall and sleep-rumpled and decidedly masculine in a white T-shirt and faded army pants. Kat couldn't tell from his expression what, if anything, he had overhead, which meant maybe he deserved an Oscar, too.

"Hello," said Zandra, gasping a little in surprise. And holding her breath a moment, so that her breasts swelled up over her dress's low neckline. "You must be Magnus. I'm Zandra. Would you like some sangria?"

Classic, thought Kat, shooting her friend a silent message of irritation. Zandra was one of those women who underwent a visible personality change whenever an attractive man was around. If the man were unattached as well as good-looking, Zandra could go into full girl-reporter mode, looking up with big doe-eyes and asking endless questions. Kat wasn't sure why, but she hadn't thought Magnus would provoke this reaction.

Just as Kat was about to suggest that she and Zandra move into the other room, the intercom buzzed. Kat picked up the phone. "Thanks, Pedro, let her up, thanks."

The phone buzzed again. "A woman says she's a friend of yours," said Pedro, with infuriating slowness. "Name Marcy."

"Yes, yes, I just told you to let her up."

"Maybe she lie about who she is," said Pedro, his hostility palpable even through the tinny intercom. "I put her on with you."

"Kat?" Marcy sounded puzzled. "Did I get the date wrong? Aren't we getting together tonight?"

"Of course we are. Pedro is just being an asshole." Kat waited until her doorman came back on the phone.

"I let her up now, okay, Missus Miner. If it is okay with you, of course."

"Thank you," Kat said coldly. In the background, she could hear Pedro saying something under his breath in Spanish. I really need to do something about that man, she thought. She turned back to Zandra, who was gazing at Magnus as if she would have liked to clean him with her tongue. "Not even one glass," she said, "to toast Kat's birthday?"

Magnus grinned. "I probably shouldn't. It's very dangerous, you know, offering Icelanders alcohol. We get very stupid, lose all our inhibitors."

"Inhibitions." Kat noticed that Magnus was rubbing his right knee. "Did you hurt yourself running?"

"No, my knee just acts up from time to time."

"So you must have one glass with us," Zandra insisted.

Magnus paused, something she had noticed he often did before responding to questions. Was it just unfamiliarity with the language, Kat wondered, or did he always deliberate everything like a supreme court judge?

"Well," he said.

"It's not that big a decision," Kat said, more sharply than she'd intended. A thought occurred. "Unless you have a problem . . . ?"

"No, not at all," he said. "All right. One glass. Thank you very much."

chapter *twenty-one*

•

two glasses of sangria later, Kat realized they were all a little tipsy. She hadn't brought out dinner, because she'd figured that Magnus would have one glass and then leave. But first Marcy had started talking to him about her upcoming trip to Iceland, and now Magnus had spotted Logan's guitar. He turned to Kat. "Can I take a look?"

"Be my guest." Well, what else could she say?

"Oh, please, play us something," said Zandra, plunking herself down at his feet like a groupie. "What do you know?"

"I'm not sure what I remember the words to," Magnus said, tuning the D string. Glancing up, he added, "It's a little scary, with two English teachers here."

"Don't be silly," said Marcy, who was looking surprisingly pretty in a pastel pink blouse and jeans. Suddenly Kat was reminded of how winsome Marcy had looked when she'd first met her fifteen years earlier, in a regional production of *A Midsummer Night's Dream*. Kat had played the desperate, abandoned Helena to Marcy's much-desired Hermia.

I wonder, Kat thought, if she misses it as much as I do.

"I'm off-duty now," said Marcy. "Mangle language at will."

"All the same, I think I'll let you sing." He bent his head, and his thick, fair hair fell forward as his large fingers experimented with a few different chords.

"Your hands are so big, it's amazing how well you do that," said Zandra, which was the final straw for Kat.

"Can you come into the kitchen and help me with something, Zan?" Kat grabbed her friend's hand, hauling her off the floor.

"Back in a second," Zandra said over her shoulder. When they'd reached the kitchen, Zandra put her hand over her mouth. "What is it? Something embarrassing? Do I have something on my teeth?" She rubbed her finger around her gums.

Kat sighed. "Zan, I know Magnus is nice-looking, but this is supposed to be my birthday celebration, and I don't want the evening to be all about flirting with some man."

"I don't know what you're talking about."

"You," said Kat, exasperated. "Flirting compulsively."

Zandra put her hands on her hips. "Why are you singling me out? I'm not paying any more attention to him than Marcy is."

"Please, Zan, get real. Marcy isn't gazing up at Magnus as if he were some kind of rock star."

"I don't know where else to sit, Kat! You don't have any comfortable furniture!"

"Listen," Kat said, gentling her tone, "I know it's not serious. It's just your style. I mean, you even flirted with Logan when he was around, and I never said anything. But I wanted to spend some time with just you and Marcy."

Zandra tossed her head, offended. "I do not treat men any differently than I do women. And I just didn't want to seem rude to your student, Kat. But by all means, tell him to leave if you want to."

"Thank you, I will."

The two women marched back into the living room. Magnus was still tuning the guitar; Marcy looked up. "Everything all right?"

"Fine," said Kat and Zandra simultaneously, both sounding sharp.

Magnus looked up. "I'm sorry. I'm intruding, aren't I?"

"No," Kat said, deciding to be blunt. "But in a little while, we'll need some time to talk woman talk."

Magnus flushed and stood up. "Oh, of course. It was nice meeting you both," he said to Zandra and Marcy.

"I didn't mean you had to leave this instant," Kat said, embarrassed by his embarrassment. "I was hoping you could play us a song first," she added.

"No, I'd better be getting back to my room."

"No, really, stay a little longer." Kat felt like smacking herself. Talk about sending mixed messages.

"Well, just one song." Magnus settled himself back on the couch with the guitar on his lap. Kat perched on the armrest, so as to give him room to stretch out.

Magnus strummed the guitar, then adjusted the G chord. "It's a lovely old guitar you have here, but you might need to restring it. How long since it's been played?"

"Since Logan left. I was thinking Dash might learn." Logan had called her once, just after he'd moved out, ostensibly to arrange to see Dashiell. Then, with studied casualness, he'd asked for his guitar. Sorry, she'd said, but that's Dashiell's guitar now. Logan had not been happy about it, but Kat had remained firm. Somehow she'd known, even that early on, that Dashiell wasn't going to be getting much from his father.

"Good idea for when he's a teenager. If you're shy, it gives you something to hide behind at parties." Magnus put his ear close to the strings, checking the sound. "Okay."

How had she known that Logan wasn't going to be your typical divorced dad, anxious to stay in his kid's good graces, offering racing bikes and junk food as bribes? As Magnus started to play the first few bars to "Heart of Gold," Kat thought back and realized that she'd always facilitated Dashiell's time with his dad. Unlike her own father, Logan had known how to play the part of a father, but she had always planned the outing, packed the food, issued the instructions.

Logan had never actually volunteered for these father-son excursions, either. She'd nagged him into them, wearing him down with comparisons to other fathers, appeals to his conscience, comments about what good press it was for the soap opera magazine to run photos of him doting on his son.

"Hey, Kat," said Marcy, "why aren't you singing?"

Kat blinked and smiled at her friend. "I'm enjoying listening to you. Keep going." Marcy resumed singing in her thin, sweet soprano, while Zandra turned the empty guitar case over and used it as a drum. Kat hummed along, still trying to assimilate the idea that Logan's betrayal hadn't really come from out of left field. There had been clues. She just hadn't read them correctly.

"Oh, wait," said Marcy at the beginning of the second verse as her voice broke on a high note.

"No, keep going," said Magnus, joining in for the first time.

His voice was low and surprisingly pleasant, and he gave Kat a quick glance as he sang about being a miner for a heart of gold. Now that the song was in a lower key, Kat joined in, meeting Magnus's surprised smile with one of her own. ". . . keep me searching and I'm growing old . . ."

Magnus continued singing, too, his quieter, more consistent voice mostly drowned out by theirs. And somewhere around the third chorus, Kat felt herself relax. Maybe this hadn't been such a bad idea, having a boarder, inviting Magnus to join them. She admired the shape of his shoulders under his white T-shirt, the play of muscles in his arms as he played the guitar. Surprisingly nimble, those fingers, she thought, and then flushed as Zandra caught her looking and raised one thinly plucked eyebrow.

When the song ended, Magnus started to stand up, his knee giving an audible crack. "My fingers are stiff," he said. "I'm not used to steel strings anymore."

Paradoxically, the moment he was leaving, Kat found herself wanting him to stay. The fact that his eyes seemed to linger on her longer than on her friends had absolutely nothing to do with it.

"Wait," said Zandra, who had momentarily relinquished her spot at Magnus's feet to smoke a cigarette at Kat's open window. "Do you know 'American Pie'?"

"Oh, please no, Madonna ruined that song for me," said Marcy. "How about another Neil Young song?" She clapped her hands together. "Or James Taylor?"

Kat, about to tell Zandra to put out her cigarette, decided to just let it slide. She had a sudden mental picture of her mother in the mid-seventies, bringing out a pitcher of martinis and a tray of rumaki to a roomful of guests. In those days, Lia Miner had attracted an unusual crowd: diplomats who had gone a little native, lesbian nuns, psychiatrists with unpopular theories, ex-military men who had gone to live on house-boats. All of them a little in love with Kat's mother.

Her mother had always suggested that something of this sort would happen to Kat someday—"My thirties were my prime time, and they'll be yours, too, just wait and see." But lately Lia had started saying, "Well, nowadays forty is like thirty used to be. But you have to be more selective about your friends, Kat. Weed out the dead ones and constantly plant new seeds, that's the way to do it."

At this point, Kat usually pointed out that her mother ba-sically saw the same two friends day in and day out, in large part because one worked with her and the other lived in their building.

Kat looked around at Marcy and Zandra, still caught up in the novelty of an attractive man with a guitar. Only Magnus glanced up at her, asking a silent question.

Oh, fine, Kat thought, I'm not going to fight this. "Is any-body hungry?" she asked. No point in withholding casserole now. Besides, she was getting hungry.

"I don't want to . . ." Magnus began, but Kat waved her hand dismissively.

"There's more than enough." Before heading into the kitchen, she decided to check in on Dash and Nico. Knocking on their door, she asked, "Everything all right?"

"Yeah," said Nico, turning around. He and Dashiell were sitting on the floor, surrounded by the Yu-Gi-Oh! cards that Dash collected.

"Ready for dinner? I made some casserole, or else there's frozen pizza or hot dogs."

"In a minute," said Dash. "How about this one?" He held up a card for Nico's inspection.

Kat closed the door, but just as she was about to walk off, she heard Nico say, "Not enough. All five of your best cards, or I'm not going to be your friend anymore."

Heart pounding, Kat waited to hear her son's response. "All right," Dash said, "and then we can play?"

"Sure," said Nico in his affectless voice. "But first, I get the cards."

chapter *twenty-two*

•

It took ten minutes for the evening to turn deeply, horribly ugly. Three minutes for Kat to inform Zandra that her son was being manipulative and unkind; two minutes for Zandra to explain why she didn't believe that direct parental intervention was the answer, as children need to learn to navigate their own friendships; and four more minutes for Kat to tell Zandra that taking a million courses in spiritual growth and self-actualization wasn't worth five dog turds if you didn't know when it was time to step in and tell your kid that it's not okay to take advantage of people by pretending to be their friend.

Then it took Zandra a minute to suggest that perhaps Kat needed to look to her own son's problems making friends, Nico hadn't wanted to come, she added, until he'd been bribed with staying up past his bedtime.

In her turn, Kat suggested that it was vital to pay attention to asocial tendencies, adding that lack of empathy was a common trait among sociopaths.

This statement was followed by a long, long moment of heated silence.

"Okay," said Marcy, breaking in, "I can see that everyone's feeling very strongly about this, but let's try to avoid any premature closure." Magnus, Kat noticed, had discreetly disappeared at the onset of hostilities.

"I'm sorry," said Zandra, "but there's only so much time you can give a person leeway for getting a divorce. Kat, you have just gone over the edge. Nico," she shouted, "we're leaving. Now! Marcy, I'll call you later."

Nico ran out of Dashiell's room, looking confused. "But Mom," he said, "I haven't got my shoes on!"

"We'll put them on in the hall," said Zandra. The door slammed behind her.

And there you were, thought Kat. Ten minutes to end a friendship. "Can you believe that?" she demanded, turning to Marcy. "Can you believe that she would rather let our friendship end than stop her son from taking advantage of mine?"

"Oh, Kat, please don't look at me to take sides," pleaded Marcy, nervously pushing her fine, fair hair behind her ears. "I love you both."

Kat put her hands on her hips, furious. "Give me a break. You can't even take sides when it's this obvious who's right?

"It's not that clear-cut," said Marcy. "Both of you make valid points."

"Jesus Christ, Marcy, sometimes you have to have an opinion."

"I do have opinions, Kat, they're just not always the opinions you want me to have." Marcy's voice was wavering, and she took a deep breath. "Take my subbing for you next week," she continued, sounding a little calmer. "While I'm happy to do it, you should know that the director came up to me the last time and asked why you were absent."

Shit. That wasn't good. "What did you say to her?" This came out sounding more accusatory than Kat had intended.

"I said it was something to do with your son," said Marcy, her cheeks reddening with temper. "But if you want my opinion, Kat, you can't keep skipping classes in order to go to auditions."

"Next week is an actual job, remember? The skin-care infomercial."

Marcy shrugged. "The point is, the Persky Institute wants its instructors to make teaching a priority."

"Then they should pay a living wage! Do you know how much I'm going to make from that one day of work, Marcy?"

"But it's not reliable, is it, Kat? At least teaching provides a steady income."

For the first time, Kat found herself sympathizing with Marcy's aggressive boyfriend. "So I should just arrange my life to suit the Persky Institute because that's the way *they* want it? For Christ's sake, Marcy, you can't live your life trying to avoid all confrontation. It's okay to get angry sometimes. It's okay to get people angry."

"Yes, Kat, but you're *always* angry at somebody or something. And somebody is *always* angry at you. I mean, look at tonight. First you pick a fight with Zandra, and now you're picking one with me."

Kat had to actively fight the urge to shake the self-righteous look off her friend's face. "You know what," she said, "maybe we should just call this a night."

"I'll still sub for you on Monday, Kat. I just hope you

know what you're doing. And here, I didn't give you your present yet." Marcy handed Kat an envelope. Kat opened it up: There were two tickets inside for the new production of *The Taming of the Shrew.*

Kat looked up. "Is this meant to be a hint?"

Instead of laughing, Marcy shook her head. "I can't talk to you when you're like this."

"Like what?"

"You have a huge chip on your shoulder sometimes."

Well, Kat thought once she was alone, Marcy had taken her advice; she hadn't shied away from a confrontation. For some reason, this did not make Kat feel as good as she might have hoped. Knocking on Dashiell's door, she thought of all the things she wished she'd said to Marcy. *I'm not looking for arguments, but I'm not just going to sit here and take abuse. You can't always stay neutral in order to be the good guy. Please, let's not end things on such a bad note.* Kat knocked again. "Dash? Aren't you going to let me in?"

"No," her son shouted from behind the door. "You know, I *wanted* to give Nico those cards!"

Kat pressed her hand against the door. "Can't I sit down with you and talk about it?"

"No!"

"Dash, I know you're upset." She tried to turn the knob, only to discover that her son had barricaded himself inside. "Please move the chair away from the door. It's a fire hazard."

"I hate you. You ruin everything," Dashiell yelled. "No wonder Daddy wanted to leave."

"Okay, now, that's not fair," said Kat, suddenly furious. Banging her hip against the door as she turned the knob, she forced her way into her son's room. "Listen, Dash, not everything is my fault."

"Get out!" Dashiell's face flushed bright red.

"Not until you listen to me for one moment," Kat said, knowing she was doing this all wrong, that she should just let it go and allow her son the freedom to be angry at her.

"I hate you!"

"You don't hate me, you're just mad at me right now. But it's not really me you ought to be mad at," she added, unable to stop herself. "It's that horrible, selfish, poisonous dwarf of a child, and that miserable excuse for a father."

"Shut up! I don't have to listen to you!"

Kat reached out, and Dashiell flailed at her. "Stop hitting me," she said.

"Then get out!"

"But I want to work this out."

"Get out! Or else I will." Crying, Dashiell grabbed his pillow and stuffed elephant. "I'm going to Nana's house!"

"Okay," said Kat, thinking, maybe Zandra was right, I am going over the edge. Her own eyes welled up with tears. "Let me call Nana and tell her you're coming over."

But now Dashiell was crumbling, all his rage disintegrating in the face of her pain. "Mommy, stop, I won't go. Don't cry."

Kat wrapped her son in her arms. "You can go, Dash, it's okay to be mad at me."

"I'll stay, Mommy."

Kat smoothed her son's hair back from his sweaty brow. "No, baby, I'll stay," said Kat, finally sure she was saying the right thing. "You can push me away and be upset with my decisions and yell at me, and I will still stay right here and love you just as much as ever. I won't go anywhere, baby, no matter what."

"I'm not mad anymore," said Dash, and she hugged him

more tightly. She wanted to offer him a chance to sleep in her bed, but she knew instinctively that this wasn't what her son needed right now. He needed what children with two parents had: the freedom to push Mommy away a little, so you could listen to the little voice inside you. Dash needed to sort tonight out for himself.

Kat wiped the tears away from her son's cheeks. "Would you still like to sleep at Nana's? Just to get away from all this?"

"Not if you don't want me to, Mommy."

Kat kissed her son's forehead, then called her mother and sent Dash across the hall with his pillow and stuffed toy and toothbrush, feeling as if she were about to turn eighty instead of forty.

Maybe if she just focused on doing what needed to be done—clearing up the dishes—she could get through the rest of the evening. But as Kat walked into the kitchen, trying furiously not to think about Marcy calling Zandra up to make it clear she wasn't taking sides, Kat remembered. She wasn't alone in her home. Magnus was still around, a witness to her humiliation.

Shit, Kat thought, wanting to dig a hole and hide her head in it for the next twelve months. Okay, she told herself, quit moping. You're not sick, your home hasn't been demolished by flood or fire, and at least *you* don't have to deal with being the mother of an amoral bully.

But still, Kat thought, fucking Zandra, going around pretending she was a struggling independent documentary filmmaker when she was actually a trust-fund baby.

The more Kat thought about it, the more infuriated she became, with Nico's robotic little voice, with his mother's casual dismissal of the incident ("Oh, my God, Kat, they get into this kind of thing all the time, you should have heard them at my place last time, I had to stop Dash from paying Nico five dollars"). And to top it all off, there was Marcy, primly telling her that she had anger-management issues.

Suddenly Kat looked down at the stove, where the dinner she had cooked was sitting, congealing. So much wasted time and effort. What the fuck was the point of trying to do things for people? All they ever did was let you down.

Overcome by another burst of rage, Kat seized her untouched casserole and swung it with all her might against the kitchen wall at the precise moment Magnus opened the door to his room, startling her into turning her head, and throwing her aim off by a critical six inches.

chapter *twenty-three*

•

I am so, so sorry, Magnus," said Katherine, putting her hand to her mouth. The problem was, she didn't look sorry. In fact, Magnus thought, his new landlady looked as though she were about to burst out laughing.

"Please, don't apologize." He could feel something warm and wet dripping down the left side of his face, and as Magnus wiped his fingers across his forehead, he was conscious of just how ridiculous he must appear. "Um, do you have a washcloth I could use?" Katherine bit her lip and Magnus decided that he didn't mind looking a little foolish if it cheered her up.

"Sorry, of course I do." Katherine sprang into action, wetting a kitchen towel under the tap. As she wiped his jaw, her brows came together. "Your skin's a little red. It wasn't hot, was it?"

"Not really." Magnus licked his lips, trying to make a joke out of it. "But it was tasty."

"Yeah, well, next time I'll offer it to you on a plate." As Katherine continued to clean him off, her movements brought her in contact with his chest and arm, and Magnus grew tense as his body began to respond.

"I can do that." He tried to take the towel from her hand, but Katherine ignored him.

"I think I've got all of it. Most of it seems to have hit the wall, but, ugh, wait, I see some in your hair." As she reached up again, Magnus grabbed Katherine's wrist, wanting to stop her before she realized the effect she was having on him.

"What's wrong?"

"I just—You don't have to do that."

"Don't be silly," she said, stepping closer again. Christ, he was turning into a teenager. Part of him wanted to cheer— see, Guthrun, I haven't lost my sex drive, it just went into hiding for a while.

"There," she said, "I've got it all off." Still, Katherine made no move to back away from him. She smelled of some citrus scent, with an undertone of woman. Magnus felt light-headed as all the blood in his body seemed to rush south.

"Thanks." His voice sounded hoarse and strained, but he forced himself to meet her eyes. Her long, dark hair was tangled, her skin was blotchy, and there were traces of dark makeup smeared under her eyes. She was indescribably beautiful, and visibly upset. "Are you okay, Katherine?"

Katherine made a sound that was almost, but not quite, a laugh. "Not really, no."

Magnus hesitated. Should he put his arms around her, offer comfort? If he did, she would realize pretty damn quick that not all of him agreed with the celibacy idea. He wasn't sure why Katherine affected him the way she did. Maybe the fact that she was off-limits was part of her allure. But he had to keep in mind that she *was* off-limits, because there was no way on earth he could make love to her tonight and then turn around and tell her he was really a case officer.

The silence was stretching out too long. Kat looked up at him, and Magnus saw the sheen of tears in her pale gray eyes. He found himself instinctively folding her into an embrace, his hands stroking her dark hair, which was softer than he'd expected. Kat made a muffled sound of distress, and her shoulders began to shake.

"I'm sorry," she said, trying to pull away.

"Hush," he said, "I've got you." Battling conflicted emotions of tenderness and desire, Magnus moved his hands in slow circles over Katherine's back, trying to soothe her. He could feel how rigid her neck and shoulders were, and without thinking, he began touching her more firmly, pressing his thumbs into the knots of tension, working his way deliberately down her spine.

God, she felt wonderful under his hands, firm and well muscled, but still deliciously rounded and feminine. He moved his hands under her blouse, then experimentally spanned her waist between his fingers. "Your skin is so soft," he whispered, spreading his thumbs and inadvertently grazing the undersides of her breasts. In response, Katherine pressed her mouth against his chest, lightly nipping his nipple through the thin cotton of his shirt.

Magnus groaned, knowing that this was wrong—she was distraught, and he was here with her under false pretenses. But it was too damn hard to think clearly when her small bites were sending shocks of pleasure straight through him. Magnus kept his hands on Katherine's upper arms, afraid that if he touched her anywhere else he might lose control and take this past the point of no return. But then Katherine reached up on tiptoe, licking the hollow under his throat. "You know, you still haven't kissed me," she said, meeting his eyes. And he forgot why he'd been holding himself back.

Hauling Katherine up against him, Magnus kissed her open-mouthed, the first in a series of hard, hungry kisses that didn't cease as he turned, pressing her up against the wall.

"Wait." Katherine was looking at a splatter of casserole on the paint next to her head, but he was through with waiting. Leaning back, Magnus pulled off his shirt, wanting to feel her bare flesh against his.

"Good God." Katherine ran her fingers lightly over the muscles of his chest. "How does a scientist get muscles like these?"

"Rock climbing." Magnus closed his eyes as her hand trailed lower. "Some martial arts."

"I'll say. You could start a second career in pro wrestling."

Magnus was glad she liked his chest, but did they have to keep talking about it? Talking about her chest, on the other hand . . . Magnus opened his eyes. "Your turn."

"My turn?"

"Shirt. Off."

With a smile that could only be described as coy, Kat shook her head. "Oh, I don't know. I kind of like the idea of having you all naked and helpless, while I keep my clothes and my wits about me."

"I believe in equality." He tugged the hem of her blouse. "Off."

"I can't." Her eyes were filled with mischief.

He trailed his hands over her bare stomach. "Why not?"

"I'm under an enchantment. I can't surrender. I have to be bested in fair battle."

Magnus raised his eyebrows. "Excuse me?"

Kat lowered her chin and gave him a sultry smile. "You heard me. I'm under a curse to let no man touch me unless he defeats me in a contest of strength."

Magnus leaned over to kiss her sternum. "Not much of a contest."

"Of course it is, Viking. I'm a fierce warrior maiden. Didn't you ever read comics as a kid?"

No, Luc was the comic book guy. Was she thinking of Luc? "I'm not sure I understand."

"That's because you're thinking. Stop thinking and just react." Reaching up, Katherine tried to get Magnus into a clumsy judo hold, which Magnus prevented by the simple expedient of grabbing both of her wrists in one of his hands.

"God, you're strong." She twisted her hands, trying to free herself as Magnus kissed her neck and shoulder, his lower body pinning hers.

Magnus gazed down at her, noticing for the first time that Katherine had dimples when she grinned. "Woman, you are bested."

"Are you kidding? I'm just lulling you into a false sense of confidence," Kat said, renewing her struggles.

For a few moments, they grappled together, Katherine laughing, Magnus smiling as he removed her shirt. Then, pausing to catch their breath, they found the mood shifting, intensifying. Fumbling with the clasp on her brassiere, Magnus freed her breasts. At the sight of her, he sucked in a sharp breath.

He bent his mouth to her nipple and lost himself in the feel and taste of her. Her fingers tangled in his hair, her breathing grew ragged, and Magnus found himself getting close to the brink as he pressed her breasts together, moving from one nipple to the other, nipping her gently as she had done to him. When she cried out, arching under his hands, he looked up, confused. "Did I just hurt you?"

Katherine exhaled, dragging her hand through her hair. "Believe me, that wasn't pain."

"Do you want me to be gentler?"

Katherine replied by grabbing the back of his neck and kissing him until his head began to spin. Her hand began to work at the fly of his jeans, and Magnus reached around to help her when it hit him.

If his jeans came off, he was going to wind up inside her. Pulling back, Magnus grabbed Katherine's wrist. "Wait a moment."

She twisted her wrists, trying to close her fingers around the bulge in his jeans. "No more waiting, Viking."

"Katherine. Please. We have to stop."

"No way. It's your turn to be defeated." Her hands still held captive, Katherine rubbed herself against the front of his body, and Magnus relaxed his grip on her wrists for a moment.

"That's better," she said, reaching her hand down his waistband. Her fingers barely touched the head of his penis, but the sensation was so incredible that Magnus thought, To hell with it, I've already crossed the line.

And then the phone rang. They both paused, staring at each other as the answering machine clicked on. It was Dashiell. Untangling herself from their embrace, Kat ran to the other room to speak to her son. When she came back, Magnus had himself under control.

"Is he okay?"

Katherine nodded. "He just wanted to say good night." She had washed her face and brushed her hair, and seemed uncertain about how to proceed. "Listen," she began.

"I think we'd better say good night, too," he said gently, preempting whatever she might have been about to say.

Her smile was a little crooked. "That would be the rational thing, yes." She waited, but he didn't contradict her. "I mean, you're my boarder, you're my student, I don't even know you very well, and you're celibate, for Christ's sake!" Katherine frowned. "You aren't really celibate for Christ's sake, are you? I mean, you're not thinking of becoming a priest?"

"No, I'm not." Magnus took her hand in his, entwining their fingers. "My reasons for not wanting to have sex right now aren't religious ones."

"I see," Katherine said, and he could tell she was wondering what the hell his problem really was.

Magnus fought the urge to explain himself. She'd had enough emotional revelation for one evening.

"Well . . . good night then, Magnus." For a long moment, they held each other's gaze. Magnus caressed the back of her wrist with his calloused thumb, trying to express something he couldn't put into words.

"What are we doing here, Magnus?"

He paused. "Saying good night."

Leaning over to kiss him on the cheek, Katherine said, "Then good night."

His hand felt strangely empty when she moved away. "If it's all right with you, Katherine, I think I'll use the hall shower now."

"Of course."

As he ran the water in the hall bathroom, he could hear Kat taking her own shower. Acutely aware of the naked woman on the other side of the wall, Magnus leaned his head back, soaped himself and changed the ending of the scene.

I'm really a case officer, Katherine, sent here to find out about your father. I don't blame you for hating me. Or hitting me. No, don't cry, you didn't really hurt me. You don't need to kiss . . .

Gasping, Magnus thought he heard a moan from the other side of the wall, but the water was running and he couldn't be sure.

chapter *twenty-four*

•

Kat woke up on the morning of her fortieth birthday and instantly started fretting over what had taken place the night before. It hadn't been sex, exactly, but it had come damn close. And it had been fantastic, some of the hottest not-quite-sex of her entire life, ranking up there with the ecstatic fumblings of adolescence. So why hadn't Magnus thrown her down and done the deed on the floor?

Well, maybe it hadn't been all that great for *him*. Throwing back her covers, Kat made herself face the unsavory possibility that she might have come on too strong. Or else he might have found that whole Viking fantasy a little off-putting. Had she really told him he had to best her in fair battle? The memory was cringe-inducing. Kat realized that she had forgotten how physical desire colored your perceptions of things, lulling you into a false sense of emotional intimacy.

The next thing you knew, you'd lost all sense of dignity and were rolling around, offering your tender underbelly and begging for an affectionate touch.

On the other hand, Kat thought, as she tied her hair back with a scrunchy, it wasn't as if she'd done something out-landishly peculiar. So she'd gotten a little silly. When you came right down to it, sex was inherently silly, and the more seriously you tried to take it, the more absurd it became. If a little fooling around made the man that damn uncomfortable, well then, he needed to spend some time with Dr. Freud.

Splashing cold water on her face, Kat decided to shake off any residual hope that Magnus was a candidate for perma-nent residence. Because he was shy and quiet and a little un-sure of himself, it was dangerously tempting to see him as some new breed of male. But even if Magnus wasn't the type to intentionally inflict pain, it was probably safe to assume that he had a few unresolved issues. An obsession with Inter-net porn, perhaps, or a predilection for surgically enhanced lap dancers.

Ugh, not nice thoughts to be having before breakfast. Kat brushed her teeth and tried not to dwell anymore on Mag-nus's possible fetishes.

On the bright side, the rash on her face had finally cleared up, and whatever Galina had done, her skin now looked amaz-ing. So at least she would be able to shoot the infomercial to-morrow. And the chance to make some money in front of a camera again was really the best present of all. As she tied the sash on her ratty old terrycloth bathrobe, Kat resolved to do some sit-ups before the day was done.

Kat walked slowly past Dashiell's room, not wanting to wake him up, before remembering that her son hadn't slept in his bed last night. Which brought back the other memories of last night—the argument with Zandra and Marcy, the lousy way she'd handled her son's breakdown.

Maybe the best thing to do would be to go back to bed. After coffee, of course. Kat went into the kitchen to brew a pot, only to discover that someone had beaten her to it. She poured herself a cup, pleasantly surprised to find that Magnus had made it strong enough to suit her.

As Kat walked back toward her bedroom, she heard the sound of hammering coming from the living room. Curious, she ducked her head inside. Magnus gave the nail a last tap with the hammer.

"Good morning," she said, bemused. "Mind if I ask what you're doing?"

"Rehanging this." He indicated her large abstract oil, which was propped against the wall. "Can you tell me when I'm in the right place?" He lifted the painting and Kat came around to see when the wire on the back was lined up with the nail.

"You're good."

Magnus stepped back, then adjusted one side of the painting. "What do you think? I lowered it. Whoever hung it before put it too high up."

"That would have been Logan. He hung paintings at the right height for his eye level, but didn't take shorter people into account."

Kat noticed that Magnus had found her father's old metal tool chest, which was on the floor next to the couch. She recalled belatedly that she'd kept it up on the top shelf of the closet in his room.

"Do you want some coffee?"

"That would be great, but come see what else I've done."

"What else? How long have you been awake, Magnus?"

"Ages." Magnus wiped his face with his forearm. "I held off with the hammering till I was sure you were awake." His jaw was stubbled and his white T-shirt was slightly damp from sweat. Boy, did that man look good in a sweaty T-shirt. "Look around. Tell me what's different."

Trying to keep her mind off Magnus and sweat, Kat inspected her living room. The broken chairs she had shoved against the far wall were now resting on all four legs. And there was something else. Kat took a sip of her coffee, mulling it over. "The bookcase seems different."

"I fixed the glass bit that pulls out."

Kat ran her fingers over the glass, sliding it back and forth. "Wow. My dad's old bookcase. This actually belonged to his grandfather. I didn't want to throw it out because it's an antique, but those hinges haven't worked since the early eighties."

Magnus seemed pleased with her reaction. "Go on. See what else I did."

Kat walked slowly around the room, trying to hide how moved she was. "The chairs, I can see you adjusted them."

"I'd like to work on the molding next. And this room needs to be plastered and painted," said Magnus. "Not all in one day, of course."

"Wow." Kat knelt, inspecting one of her chairs. "You are absolutely amazing, I don't know how to thank you . . ." She stopped short, suddenly realizing that what she ought to do was reduce his rent. Except that would mean putting herself deeper into a financial hole. Still, it didn't seem fair of her to take his help without offering anything in return. "I'll tell you what," she said, making it sound casual, "how about you skip this first week's rent." She'd be all right, once she got her infomercial money.

"Katherine."

"Or skip the first two weeks, if you're going to paint the room, too."

"Hey."

Kat looked at him.

"It's a birthday present. Want to thank me?" Magnus wiped his hands on a rag and draped it over the toolbox. "You could make me some breakfast."

Katherine smiled at him. "Salty or sweet?"

"You decide."

After Magnus showered, they ate pancakes and sausage as the sun poured through the kitchen windows, and Magnus talked about all the projects he had in mind. The cabinets needed to be stripped of old paint, so they could close properly. He wanted to replace some doorknobs. Some of the bathroom tile required grouting. Kat was surprised to find that discussing home improvements with Magnus felt both exciting and domestic, a balance she had never managed to achieve with Logan. By the time Kat brewed the second pot of coffee, she knew that she'd already broken all her resolutions to keep from hoping for more from this relationship.

Magnus shook his head, refusing a third cup of coffee. "So that bookcase belonged to your father?"

"Along with a lot of the books. The John Carter of Mars novels, the Steinbecks, the books on abnormal psych."

"Interesting combination. When did your parents divorce?"

"My mother left him when I was ten." Kat took Magnus's empty plate and stacked it in the sink. "But to be honest, I never really saw my dad all that much." In response to Magnus's questioning look, she said, "he traveled a lot on business."

"Wait, you cooked. Let me do the dishes."

"You can dry." Kat handed him a towel, then tried not to feel self-conscious as he stood right next to her, not two feet away from where they'd been making out last night. What happened to the man who hadn't wanted to get within ten feet of her in the classroom? That was the problem with sex. It made men more comfortable and women more insecure.

"Did your father make an effort to see you after you and your mother moved out?"

Kat shook her head. "Out of sight, out of mind. I believe he had what's called a narcissistic personality disorder. Which was probably an asset in his line of work."

"And what was that? Actor?"

Kat raised her eyebrows. "Very funny. No, as a matter of fact, my father was a spy."

Magnus did not seem as shocked by this news as she would have expected. "Who did he work for?"

Kat resisted the urge to correct his grammar. "The CIA. And that's really about all I know. I don't know where he went or what his official title was. I don't know whether he was any good at what he did or how much he earned."

"Aren't you at all curious about him?"

Kat handed Magnus the last plate to dry. "Not really. When I was growing up, I missed the idea of a father, but I can't say I really missed him as a person. I don't even have very clear memories of him."

"Because he wasn't around much?"

"I suppose." Kat dried her hands, then squirted some moisturizer on her palms. "I don't think he was a terribly involved parent even when he was around. Anyway, I really didn't think about my father much. Until last week, when he sent me a letter saying he wanted to meet me. I waited for him at a restaurant on Wednesday, but he never showed. Whoa, watch it." Kat rescued the plate, which had looked as if it were about to slip out of Magnus's hands. "I think we've had enough wildness in this kitchen already, don't you?" Too late, Kat realized she'd just ventured into a no-fly zone. "That didn't come out quite the way I'd intended."

And then, because Kat had never been the type to tiptoe around a problem, she said, "Look, I think we need to talk. I'm more than a little confused here. Are we pretending that last night never happened? It's a little difficult when there's still casserole splatter on the wall." Kat went over the spot with a wet rag.

Magnus looked abjectly miserable. "Of course, we can't pretend that nothing happened." He paused, for a long time. A very long time. Kat maintained a stony silence. No way was she going to rescue him.

Finally, Magnus managed to get out, "I just wanted to say that I'm sorry."

"Oh, I see." Kat began to put the dried dishes away in the cupboard. "Sorry for what, precisely?" The plates clattered as she stacked them with too much force.

"Sorry things went so far and then just stopped."

Kat stood still for a moment, keeping her back to Magnus. "I see. Which part made you sorry?"

"Excuse me?"

She closed the cupboard door, which instantly sprang open. That paint really needed to be stripped down. "What part made you sorry, the going so far, or the stopping?"

Magnus coughed. "Well, I'd have to say . . . the stopping."

Kat spun around. "May I ask you a personal question, Magnus?"

He nodded.

"Why are you celibate?" Kat reached out, touching his arm. "Is it . . . do you have a medical condition, something communicable?"

"No. No, I don't have herpes or HIV, nothing like that."

"Then what is it?"

"I didn't want to get too close to anyone right after the divorce."

Touched by Magnus's honesty, Kat resisted the urge to physically reach out to him. "Your wife must have really hurt you."

"I think I probably hurt her, too. I just didn't realize I was doing it."

"How did you hurt her?"

Magnus ran one hand through his hair. "I think . . . I think she wanted me to lose control with her, and that's not something I do very easily. And there was something, I don't know, a little childish about Guthrun. So maybe I didn't pay enough attention to what she wanted." He paused. "Kat?" He took a step closer to her. "I don't want to pretend that nothing happened last night."

"You don't?"

Magnus took another step, closing the distance between them. "And I don't think you do, either."

Kat tried to swallow. The air between them felt electrically charged. "Not really, no."

"But I don't want you to get hurt." Magnus gave her a wry smile. "I don't want me to get hurt. So let's just take this very slowly and get to know each other."

Kat stared up at him. "Talking about emotions, wanting to take things slow . . . what are you, a saint?"

There was a pained look in Magnus's blue eyes. "Far from it."

This is my reward for putting up with Logan, Kat thought. The universe has sent me a good man who probably beats himself up over nothing, to make up for my time with a creep who found excuses for all his self-serving behavior.

"Hey," she said, wanting to chase the shadows from Magnus's face, "I think that's enough heavy talk for one morning, don't you? Why don't you tell me what your plans are for today?" Shit, that sounded like she was angling for him to spend the day with her, when she couldn't. Besides, she didn't want to sound needy. "I'm supposed to go out with my mother and Dashiell." Kat turned to wipe down the surface of the stove.

"What are you doing tonight?"

"Actually, I don't have anything definite." That sounded offhand, didn't it? "My dad did leave a note rescheduling for tonight, but I wasn't intending to go."

"I think you should go."

Startled by the intensity of his voice, Kat glanced up. "To be honest, I'm far more concerned with what's going on with Dashiell's father that I am with my own. Poor Dash. I've managed to provide him with an exact replica of my own fucked-up childhood."

In the harsh morning light, Kat could see the lines of concern in Magnus's face. "If you feel that way, you really should go meet him."

Kat paused. "I don't know." She did not add, I'd rather have dinner with you.

"I could watch Dash for you."

"Thanks, but I'm really not feeling like spending my fortieth birthday with the man."

"It might give you a better understanding of things. What time are you supposed to be there?"

"Six."

"So go for five minutes. Just show up and leave if you want to. You don't have to be polite to him. Go see him and yell at him if you want to. Throw food in his face. Blame him for screwing you up and making you choose a loser like Logan for a husband." Magnus touched her arm. "But don't avoid him."

Kat laughed, shaking her head. "Tell me, is this what you generally do? Go around to women's houses, trying to fix what's broken?"

"Is that what you think I'm doing?" To Kat's surprise, Magnus took her hand in both of his. "Listen, Katherine, there's something I need to tell you."

Before he could say more, the back door swung open. "Surprise," said Lia and Dashiell in unison, before launching into a chorus of "Happy Birthday."

I really need to talk to my mother about remembering to knock, thought Kat, giving Magnus an apologetic glance before throwing open her arms to her mother and son.

chapter *twenty-five*

•

by six-thirty, Kat decided that she would never set foot inside a Turkish restaurant again. Which was a shame, because her little corner of the Upper West Side didn't really have much in the way of good ethnic places. But after being stood up for the second time in a row, Kat didn't think she ever wanted to see a plate of shepherd's salad again for as long as she lived.

This time, she hadn't ordered anything, which meant that the waitstaff weren't exactly dying to see her again, either. *Oh, well.* Stepping out of the Arabian Night atmosphere of Fez, Kat took a deep breath, which was visible on the exhale. The temperature had dropped sharply in the short time she'd been waiting for her father to show, which meant that the balmy, colorful, early days of autumn were giving way to the bleak, brown finish of the season. Shivering, she pulled her thin sweater around her, wishing she hadn't worn a dress.

"Hello."

Kat turned, instantly tense, then relaxed when she saw that it was just a homeless man, shabby but mild-looking. Glancing at her watch, Kat started to walk home.

"Pardon me, but may I ask you something?"

The homeless man had peeled himself away from the wall beside the supermarket, and Katherine increased her pace.

"Please, just one quick question?" The man was dressed in a scruffy suit jacket, an ancient poacher's cap, and jeans that hung off his skinny frame. In the artificial light of streetlamps and store signs, he looked like a gaunt-faced visitor from the great Depression.

Kat stopped. "All right, go ahead and ask. But I have to tell you, I can give you directions to a synagogue where they'll give you something to eat and a place to sleep, but I am not buying you a meal or handing you money."

The homeless man smiled, clearly amused. "Oh, I'm not asking for help," he said.

Oh, terrific, another Jesus freak. "You're not going to save me, either," she said.

The man smiled more broadly, revealing gaps in his teeth. "I wasn't sure at first," he said, "but when you frown like that, you look just like your mother."

"You seem to have a lot of people interested in you these days," said Ken Miner, dipping a hunk of pita bread into his soup.

"You mean the press? They're really interested in my ex-husband." Kat watched her father eat with horrified fascination. He appeared to be sucking his soup through the holes in his bridgework.

"Are you so sure they're all press? The last time we were

supposed to meet, I saw a tall man with white-blond hair following you." Kat tried not to stare at her father's unshaven face. She wasn't sure whether his appearance was a disguise, or whether he had actually fallen so far down on his luck that he couldn't afford to get new dentures.

"That's Magnus. He's renting a room in my place, so you'll probably see him around a fair amount."

Ken took a sip of his beer. "What do you know about this man?"

"That he's not a spy," said Kat, growing impatient. She wasn't here to pander to her father's paranoid fantasies. "Look, there wasn't anyone following me tonight, was there?"

"No."

"Then why weren't you here on time?" It was a perfectly legitimate question, yet Kat felt rude to be asking it. Something in Ken Miner's mild, diffident manner did not invite angry confrontation.

"Sorry about that. You thought I wasn't coming, didn't you?"

"What else could I think?" Again, she sounded like a bitch to her own ears. Which was justified, true, but still strangely uncomfortable.

"This may be hard for you to believe, but there've been times when being five minutes late has saved my life. I find it's never a good idea to let people know exactly where you're going to be at a given time."

"Don't you think that's a little extreme?"

"Excuse me." Ken Miner lifted his napkin to conceal his mouth as he worked to dislodge something that had gotten stuck between his teeth. "You think I'm a crazy old coot, and you're probably right. But tell me, how many people did you tell about me? Besides your mother, I mean. Two? Three?"

Kat flushed, remembering her father's written admonition to talk to no one about him. "Two, I guess." Three if she included Dashiell.

"That's better than I expected. When I say don't tell anyone about something, I figure the person automatically tells four other people."

A safe assumption, Kat thought, remembering all the times friends had confided in her, revealing other friends' secrets. "Maybe it's better not to tell people not to say anything."

"Absolutely. But the need to share information is a powerful one. Terrific soup, by the way."

"Glad you like it."

"Well, to tell you the truth, it's pretty mediocre. But I like seeing you." Ken Miner leaned back, removing his tweed cap and smoothing down his sparse white hair. "It's not often I have such lovely company over dinner." His brown eyes twinkled in his ravaged face. Dear God, thought Kat, my father looks like the Crypt Keeper. "You really have grown into a beautiful woman, Katherine."

"You should have used that line on my twenty-first birthday, not my fortieth."

Ken raised his eyebrows. "Of course, October fifteenth. It's your birthday today, isn't it?

"Today is October sixteenth, actually."

Ken shook his head. "I'm a dead loss as a father, no question. But you are beautiful, probably more so than when you were younger. You have more character in your face now. You looked a bit bland back then."

"How would you know?"

Ken smiled, unperturbed by her rancor. "I've followed your career. You're very talented."

Kat felt an absurd rush of pleasure at hearing her father say this. "Thank you. It's nice to hear that."

"Doesn't anyone else tell you that you have talent?"

"Not lately. I haven't been doing much."

"You've been raising a child. That's a lot."

The mention of parenting brought Kat back to reality. "Yes. Your grandson, Dashiell. Who's going to turn ten next month."

"Good Lord, is he really? Tell me what he's like."

Kat stared at her father. "I don't understand you. You act like you've just come out of prison or something, and you're trying your best to make up for lost time. But no one kept you from getting in touch years ago, when Dash was born. No one stopped you from contacting me when I turned ten. So what's changed? Why are you suddenly so interested in getting to know me?" Ken opened his mouth to respond, but Kat kept going. "Are you dying? Is that it? Were you hoping I'd give you absolution?" She narrowed her eyes. "Or did you want money?"

Ken Miner shook his head. "No, I'm not dying. And I don't want any money from you. It's just that I have reason to believe that I have become a problem for the Agency. For years, I lived as quietly as I could, trying to keep off their radar, and then, one day, they came looking for me." Ken patted his inside shirt pocket and took out a pack of cigarettes.

"You can't smoke in here, Dad." The word "dad" just slipped out, startling her.

"You can't? Ah, of course not." Ken's hands trembled on the table, like nervous animals. "Anyway, I wasn't walking away from much—just a little one-room apartment, my usual routine playing chess in the park—but all of a sudden, I had nothing but time on my hands. Time to reflect back on my life."

Kat found herself resisting the urge to put her hand over her father's, to calm its tremors. "And what did you realize?"

Ken put his shaking hands around his beer mug and took a sip. "That my one huge regret was not being a better father to you. I don't have any easy explanations for why I acted the way I did. I did write you, at first. But I was never much good at relating to children, and the more time we spent apart, the less I knew about you." He paused, making a movement with his mouth that made him appear even older than he was. "It felt false. Being your father felt like just another fake identity."

"It wasn't about you," Kat said, suddenly remembering why she was so angry at this man. "It wasn't about your feelings. When you have children, sometimes you fake it if you have to. But you make sure you're there for them."

"You're right. You have more wisdom at forty than I have at seventy-five. But when I was your age, I felt like I was being honest with myself. I'd watch other men get sentimental about their children, their wives, their pets, and I'd feel contemptuous, because they were following a script that someone had handed them. You're supposed to love your wife, and so they did, up until the moment they fell for someone else."

Ken paused, and for a moment, Kat saw him as he must have been in his youth: lean, clever, deceptively soft-spoken. "And then, of course, they got eaten up with guilt, which made them easier to manipulate."

"And how about you? Did you ever feel guilty?"

"Not really. Regretful, perhaps. Except that I couldn't have done things any differently than I did. I would like to do something different now."

Kat found that this stark honesty appealed to her as nothing else could have. "I'll think about it." Pausing, she added, "Do you want anything else to eat?"

He shook his head. "No, no, thank you."

Kat asked for the check. When it came, her father took out his wallet, which looked as though it had been gnawed on by wolves.

"No, it's all right, let me."

"It's not right, Katsala, I should be taking care of you."

The sound of her mother's nickname for her coming from her father's lips caught Kat by surprise. "You look as though you don't have much right now," she said, then wondered if she'd insulted him.

"Oh, I just hate shopping for clothes," Ken said, winking.

And washing them, thought Kat. She paid for their dinners. "Listen," she said, "if you really want to meet Dashiell, come by after school on Tuesday."

Her father's face lit up with surprise and pleasure. "I would like that," he said softly. "Thank you."

"Well, it would be nice for him to finally meet his grandfather."

They stepped out onto Broadway, and Ken instantly lit up a Camel. The smoke smelled vaguely familiar, like something remembered from early childhood. "How is your mother these days?"

"She's doing well." Unlike you, Kat thought. She wondered why he didn't take advantage of the fact that he'd been a government employee and go see a dentist. Then she remembered that he was in hiding. "Dad?" There was that word again, unfamiliar and yet irresistible. "Do you need anything?"

"You've already given me more than I expected." Ken put his thin arms around her in an awkward embrace. "So," he said. "Tuesday it is."

"See you then." She watched him lope away, then said, "Dad?"

He turned to face her, and Kat realized why she'd initially thought he was homeless. In his threadbare jacket and old-fashioned cap, her father had that air that many homeless people have, of expecting nothing and accepting everything, of having dignity but no pride. "Yes?"

"If you want me to—if you need a job—I can ask at the Persky Institute, where I teach."

Ken Miner smiled around his ill-fitting teeth. "That's very kind, but I have to maintain a relatively low profile. Why don't we talk about all that on Tuesday?"

"All right," Kat said. "Bye." Then she wondered: Why did I do that? All the way home she asked herself why she felt as if she should have done more. Given him a hundred dollars. Invited him to sleep on her couch. Offered to cover his dentistry bills. Objectively, she knew that he owed her an unpayable debt, but when she'd been in his presence, she'd felt as if the opposite were true.

When she opened the door to her apartment, she found Dashiell and Magnus in the middle of a Scrabble game. Kat picked up the phone and called her mother.

"Well," she said, "I saw him. He looks pathetic. And no matter how mad I was, I kept having these bursts of feeling sorry for him."

"Oh, honey," her mother said, "that's how he operates. Don't let him suck you in."

"I won't."

"Don't start trying to help him."

Kat could still smell the residue of tobacco on her clothes. "Why would I?"

"Because, Kat, at the end of the day, a spy is a salesman.

He has to convince you that betraying your country is a good idea. He has to convince you that the whole thing was *your* idea."

Okay, so that explained a lot. Profoundly irritated with herself, Kat walked back into the living room. "Well," Magnus said, "how did it go?"

"It was all right." Kat ruffled her son's bangs. "Your grandfather asked about you, baby."

"Cool," said Dashiell, clearly unimpressed. "Okay, I have my word." He slipped his Scrabble tiles into place. "Equivocal. Count up the points."

Magnus gave a low whistle. "Do you know what it means?"

"Of course. Open to more than one interpretation. Ambiguous or misleading." Dashiell smiled proudly. "I study the Scrabble dictionary," he admitted.

"Okay, Einstein, thank Magnus and pack it in. You have school tomorrow."

For once, Dash didn't argue with her. Wow, it really was her birthday.

"Katherine." Magnus put his hand over hers, stopping her from folding up the Scrabble board. "Was it all right? Were you glad you went?"

Kat thought about it for a moment. "I guess so. It was a bit like climbing that rock wall with you. I didn't enjoy myself, but I feel like I faced something."

To her surprise, Magnus leaned over and kissed her briefly on the lips. "You did."

"He wants to come back Tuesday, to meet Dash. I just don't know if I did the right thing telling him he could. I just spoke to my mother, and she reminded me that he probably has a hidden agenda." Kat brushed her hand against Magnus's hair. "What do you think I should do?"

"Take some time to think things over yourself. Your mother is right. But remember, she isn't objective, either."

Kat tucked a strand of Magnus's hair behind his ears. He has nice ears, she thought. "You're good for me, do you know that?"

"I hope I am. But what your mother said . . . you could say that everyone has a hidden agenda."

"Oh, yeah? What's yours?"

Magnus swallowed. "Well, to begin with, there's the real reason why I took your class."

"Mom!" Dashiell, as usual, was hollering for her from the far end of the apartment instead of coming to get her.

"One minute," Kat yelled back. "Go on," she told Magnus.

"The real reason I took your class, you see, is . . ."

"MOM!"

Kat sighed. "Dash, can't you wait a minute?" She had a feeling that Magnus was going to tell her he had a crush on her from some old movie. Which wasn't so bad, so long as he'd gotten over feeling star struck. She remembered all too well the way some men would get disenchanted when the mystery of dating an actress they'd seen onscreen wore off.

"MOM, MY NOSE IS BLEEDING!"

"Oh, hell." Kat made an apologetic face. "Can we talk later tonight?"

"Sure."

"Oh, wait, I have my infomercial tomorrow. I should get to sleep early. Let's talk when I get back."

"MOM! HOW MUCH TISSUE DO I PUT IN MY NOS-TRIL?"

Kat glanced at the door, then turned back to Magnus. "Just tell me one thing. You're not some sort of crazed fan, are you? You don't have a shrine to me back in Iceland?"

Magnus looked a little taken aback. "No, absolutely not."

"Fine, then, we can talk tomorrow. But don't let me hear that you went cutting any more classes, or you'll get me in trouble. Marcy's a good teacher."

Magnus held up his right hand. "I promise."

But the day held one more surprise. When Kat had finished getting Dashiell cleaned up and ready for bed, she went into her own bedroom and found a carved ivory pendant on her pillow. Turning the object around in her hands, Kat thought the designs were Norse. There was also a note: A Little Viking Good Luck Charm.

For the first time since Logan had left, she fell asleep the minute her head hit the pillow.

chapter *twenty-six*

•

either Viking good luck did not work on Jewish Italian women, or Vikings had a pretty strange idea of what good luck meant. And now that Kat thought about it, hadn't the Norse believed that death in battle was the best kind of ending?

Maybe Magnus's charm was working a little too well.

Kat had arrived at the downtown studio only to find that she was supposed to shoot her segment in a cramped, poorly lit apartment with only one cameraman, a grip, and a director who appeared to be all of twenty years old.

Kat's next discovery was that the actress from *Sex and the City* was not one of the show's four stars. Instead, the pretty blonde was a bit player who had appeared in one memorable episode. Making matters worse, she was full of herself, demanding bottles of Evian and a tray of sushi, which the director kept telling her he would bring in just a moment, when the lighting was set up.

That looked like it was going to take awhile: The newbie director, who had the unfortunate name of Schnook, kept waving his hands in the air, exhorting the overweight lighting guy, who was rolling his eyes. The grip, who resembled Bruce Dern with dyed yellow hair, kept muttering something dire about the outlets.

Kat went over to the BBC actress, who was looking haggard and slightly disoriented. "Good God," she said, "what have we gotten ourselves into? I've seen porn films with better production values."

"I don't really give a flying fuck *what* you think," said the actress, her upper-class English accent slightly slurred. "I'm being paid to act, and I don't condescend to my roles."

Okay. Kat moved away from *Arsenic and Old Lace,* noticing that the former Oscar winner kept sipping something from a small thermos.

"It's *tea,*" she said sharply when she caught Kat watching.

Kat closed her eyes and wished she were back teaching her class.

The director tapped her on the shoulder. Despite his extreme youth and the acne covering his cheeks, he was going prematurely bald. Kat felt sorry for the man, but wished that he hadn't chosen to wear a flannel shirt. He reeked of sweat and fear. "You're going to be up first."

"All right. Are you also doing makeup and wardrobe on this highly professional set?"

A nerve beside the director's left eye began twitching. "You're, ah, supposed to do your own."

"You're kidding me. What is this, an episode of *Punked?*"

"No, really, it'll be fine. You look great." His eyes swept

over her black, long-sleeved T-shirt and faded jeans. "Very casual. Casual is good."

"Okay, so who's going to interview me?"

"Excuse me?" The director paled, looking as though he might throw up.

"You know, the lady in the white lab coat who's pretending to be a dermatologist. Come on, all these things are the same. There's the lady in the lab coat, there's the main celebrity spokeswoman, which of us is your main spokeswoman, by the way?"

"The main . . . well . . . that would be you. That would be you." The director swallowed, his large Adam's apple bobbing in his scrawny neck. "But we're, ah, experimenting with a different format here."

Kat was torn between compassion and disgust. "You have absolutely no idea what you're doing, do you?" She stood up. "All right. You. Grip guy. Go out and purchase a white lab coat. You can get it from any hospital uniform shop. Look it up in the yellow pages. Meanwhile, someone, take away Madame's tea and fetch her some black coffee."

"Hang on," said the pretty blonde *Sex and the City* extra. "Who made you boss?"

Kat sighed. "Look, I'd like to walk out that door, but I can't afford to get sued for abrogation of contract. So why don't we all pitch in before this becomes a complete disaster?"

"Ooh, watch out, Junior," said the BBC actress, propping herself up on one elbow. "I think she's after your job."

"Okay, listen up, guys." The director drew himself up to his full five feet, five inches. "We are going ahead with *my* plan, thank you very much."

Oh, great, he thinks I've stepped on his balls. "Fine. What do you want me to do?"

"Just face the camera and tell us why you love Rejuvena-trix products."

It had come down to this. Her acting ability, the attribute that she had once thought defined her, had become the instrument of her complete humiliation. "Fine," she said, stepping in front of the camera. "Ready? Here goes." The cameraman hastily began filming. "I can't believe how much younger and firmer my skin feels since I began using your products." Kat felt a stab of guilt for the poor, gullible woman who might actually fall for this patent falsehood. Still, an acting job was an acting job, and she summoned all the sincerity at her disposal, looked intimately into the camera and said, "You can really tell the quality of the ingredients that have gone into these creams and lotions. I'll bet you're wondering, Just how does the Rejuvenatrix line work to diminish wrinkles and pores and enhance the evenness of my skin tone?"

"And . . . cut." The director cleared his throat. "Yes. Well, um, well, that was pretty good . . . for a rehearsal."

"I wasn't rehearsing. That was it." Kat picked up her pocketbook. "I'm leaving now."

"But I never said 'action.' You can't start before I say 'action.' "

Kat just looked at him, her arms folded in front of her. "You have to be kidding. That's your big objection? So say 'action' now and they'll splice it in during editing. Then you can pretend that you were directing."

The director cast a quick glance at his other two actresses. Clearly, he was realizing that if he didn't establish his authority with her, he'd lose what little control he had left over this train wreck of an infomercial. "Ha ha. Very funny. But besides that little glitch, there was another . . ." The director cleared his throat. "That is to say, I just . . . I sensed a certain lack of conviction in your tone. I mean, to be honest, that sounded a little wooden."

"Oh, really?"

"Yes." Emboldened, the director looked her in the eye. "Now, can you say that again, but this time, can you try to give a little laugh, like you're surprised by how good this stuff makes you feel?"

"A little laugh?" Kat's voice was low with menace.

"Yes."

"What kind of a little laugh?"

"You know." The director gave a forced little laugh. It sounded like a cat choking on a hairball. "Well, I'm sure you can do much better. You're the actress."

"And you're the director." Kat smiled at him with loathing.

"That's right." He made a motion to the cameraman. "Okay, and four, three, two, one—Action!"

"Hi, my name is Katherine Miner, but you probably know me better as Helen Jessup from *South of Heaven*. Now, ever since my soap decided to replace me with a younger actress, looking youthful has been really important to me. More important than my health. More important than being a good mother. In fact, looking younger is so important to me that I'm happy to risk my life to get rid of a few wrinkles. So if someone told me that injecting massive amounts of snake venom into my face would improve my appearance, I'd do it. Which is why I was so eager to try the Rejuvenatrix line of products."

"Cut." The director cleared his throat. "Um, listen, that wasn't exactly what I had in mind."

Ignoring him, Kat continued talking into the camera. "Unfortunately, the creams caused my skin to erupt in hideous lesions. I'm not sure why, since the scientists who created this skin-care line tortured a bunch of rhesus monkeys to make sure it was safe. Well, it was probably stray cats. Rhesus monkeys cost more, and Rejuvenatrix wants to keep their prices low for you."

"Now, that's really enough, Katherine."

The cameraman, chewing gum, ignored him and kept filming.

"Just remember, if it doesn't say 'no animal testing' that's your assurance that we care enough to kill for your complexion." Kat smiled at the camera. "But that's enough from me. Let's hear from an ambitious twenty-two-year-old and a world-renowned alcoholic and find out why they love Rejuvenatrix!"

The director looked at her coldly. "I don't think this is going to work out, do you?"

"No," said Kat, "I don't think it is."

chapter *twenty-seven*

•

Searching through Katherine's underwear drawer, Magnus realized that the problem with *almost* having amazing sex was that it created more of an appetite for *actually* having amazing sex. At forty-six, he wasn't used to walking around feeling as horny as a teenager. In some ways, it was quite enjoyable. In other ways, it was just as inconvenient as he recalled from adolescence.

Take right now, for example. Fred had just made it very clear that they no longer had the luxury of time. With the situation in Kyrgyzstan as volatile as it was, every hour leading up to Wednesday's elections counted. So while Fred was thrilled to hear that Ken would be showing up tomorrow afternoon, he needed to speak with the man *today*. Magnus had to find the letter Ken had sent his daughter and use the information inside to make contact.

We don't need another situation like Afghanistan in the eighties, Fred had explained, reminding him yet again of the dangers of putting the Agency's resources behind the wrong team. What he didn't say was that he was being pressured by his own bosses to come up with immediate results. But he didn't need to. Magnus knew what it meant when you had one plan—gain Katherine Miner's confidence and enlist her help to make contact with her dad—and you exchanged it at the last minute for another—jump right in and grab Ken Miner before he could run, physically restraining him if necessary.

Maybe part of the reason I can't keep my mind on the objective is that it has "doomed for failure" written all over it. Ken Miner was paranoid to begin with; being nabbed off the street wasn't going to put him in the best frame of mind to cooperate. And when the operation did not produce the desired result, guess who was going to get the blame?

And Fred's bosses weren't the only ones who were going to jump all over Magnus when everything went bad. How did he expect Katherine to react when she learned that he'd been lying to her about his motives for getting to know her? Would she give him a chance to explain, or would he never get another chance to kiss her up against the kitchen wall?

Magnus shook his head, trying to clear it. As much as Katherine mattered to him personally, her feelings were irrelevant right now. Like it or not, he had a job to do.

Magnus returned his attention to the lingerie drawer, systematically feeling around the sides. It would have helped if Fred could have told him precisely what he was looking for—paper, computer CDs, floppy disks, a microdot, panties containing messages in invisible ink.

Magnus wasn't exactly sure how he'd even recognize this last item, but since the Egyptians had accused an Israeli businessman of smuggling information in this manner, he had to assume it was possible.

Magnus held up a pair of white silk panties to the light. They looked nearly transparent, and he had a sudden vision of how Katherine would look wearing them.

You're thinking with your dick. Ken Miner may have been a negligent parent, but surely even indifferent fathers didn't send their daughters thong letters.

On the other hand, Guthrun had always hidden her diary in her underwear drawer, and Magnus had already searched through Katherine's neatly organized box of computer disks, her two immaculate file cabinets, one overstuffed rolltop desk, and a surprisingly messy bedside table drawer.

He'd also discovered the reading material she kept hidden from view. *So that's where all that Viking stuff came from.*

Hunkered down on the wood floor, Magnus brought his attention back to the task at hand. A row of plain, neatly folded pink-and-blue cotton underwear, a row of lacy pink-and-blue bikini panties, and two red-and-black thongs, each no bigger than his palm. *Nice.* In the back of the drawer, Magnus also unearthed three pairs of flesh-colored panty hose, one pair of black thigh-high stockings, and one pair of beige fat-lady undies. When the hell had Katherine worn these?

A mystery, but not the one he'd been hired to solve.

Shutting the underwear drawer, Magnus glanced at the clock. He figured he had, at most, another hour before Katherine was due back from the infomercial. Standing up to stretch his right knee, Magnus wondered why his brain was being so uncooperative. He felt thick and slow, unable to make connections. Was it because he'd skipped his daily run to get back to the apartment sooner? Or was he just getting dulled with age?

Think. Where would Katherine put something personal? Under the bed? Nothing but what appeared to be gerbil droppings. Inside a book? He flipped through the pages of a book called *Suspects* on Katherine's bedside table, but nothing fell out but an old credit card bill. In the bathroom? Nothing but makeup, medicines, and a tube of contraceptive gel that had passed its expiration date.

Taking one last look around Katherine's bedroom, Magnus was about to turn off the light when he thought to check the closet.

After a few moments, Magnus discovered three wigs (one short and black, one shoulder length and red, and one long and blond), two dental appliances, a box of broken jewelry, a breast pump, and finally, tucked all the way in the back of a shelf, a drawstring bag.

Pulling the bag down, Magnus removed one curious object after another. There was something that resembled a silver and purple baton, something else that resembled brass knuckles, and an electrical appliance that appeared to be a strange, modernist toothbrush, except for the fact that it had three attachments, two of which were sausage-shaped. Magnus didn't have to be told that those weren't intended for periodontal care.

They probably weren't concealment devices either, but Magnus tried to unscrew the baton, just in case. There was nothing inside but batteries, two of which had corroded. Not her favorite toy, then. Experimentally, he plugged in the electric toothbrush and observed with some alarm the speed with which the bristles moved.

Jesus, if this was what it took to satisfy her, what chance in hell did he have? He could just picture what would have happened if he'd followed through on Saturday night: Oh, yes, faster, harder, harder, faster, a little to the left, no, not your left, my left—oh, dear. Don't worry, sweetheart, but would you mind going over to the closet and bringing down that bag for me?

Even Guthrun hadn't possessed an entire arsenal of sex toys. Magnus switched off the vibrator. Putting aside all questions of ethics and morality, the whole point of having sex with a potential source would be to leave her happy and pliable, not crabby and disappointed. And Guthrun had made it abundantly clear that Magnus did not have good instincts as far as sex was concerned. He was always touching her the wrong way, being too gentle or too rough, too fast or too slow, and never in the right place at the right time. Worst of all, he actually liked the missionary position, a clear indication that he didn't really like sex all that much.

The last accusation was the only one that Magnus had challenged. He didn't think he had a low sex drive. If memory served, he had liked sex plenty before he had learned to associate it with criticism.

In any case, better to leave Katherine with an illusion of wanting him, because there was, after all, a bit of power in that.

Just as Magnus was replacing the bag of vibrators, the phone rang. He froze, waiting for the answering machine to pick up, which it did on the fourth ring.

"Mommy? Mommy, are you there? I got hurt and the school needs you to come right away." There was a sniffle, and then the sound of an adult, female voice in the background, asking a question. "I don't think she's there," Dashiell replied. He sounded younger than nine. He sounded frightened.

Without considering it further, Magnus reached over and picked up the phone. "I'm here," he said. "What's wrong?"

"Daddy, I broke my nose," said Katherine's son, and then promptly burst into tears.

chapter *twenty-eight*

•

W hat are you doing?" Dashiell gingerly removed the ice pack from his nose.

"Taking another look at your hands." In addition to a bruised nose, the boy had splinters in his palms. "Okay, I'm going to need to get this one out with a needle."

"Are you sure?"

"Afraid so. Hang on a moment while I sterilize the tip." Magnus turned on the stove and held the needle to the flame of the gas burner. "By the way, I think your nose has stopped bleeding. You can take the tissue out of your nostril."

"Are you kidding? It's still gushing."

Magnus didn't argue the point. He thought that some of the child's stubbornness might have been a form of protest. The boy had barely blinked when he'd seen that it was Magnus and not his father there to greet him as he got off the school bus, but Magnus was well aware that he'd been a major disappointment. "I'm sorry that your father and mother aren't here," he'd said, taking the boy's blue backpack. "But it's okay. We can wait for your mother at home."

No visible reaction. "Where did my dad go?" Said with perfect matter-of-factness.

"I'm afraid that was me on the phone earlier." The school nurse had explained to him that she was calling because Dashiell wanted his mother to pick him up. She'd tried Katherine's cell phone first, but had only succeded in leaving a message. Not sure how to get in touch with Katherine, Magnus had told the nurse that the boy should go home on the school bus as usual, and that he would take care of him.

"Where's my mom?"

"She's on her way home now."

"Oh." The tissue had gone back in the nose, a barrier against further communication. Magnus hadn't inquired about the schoolyard fight, so all he knew was what the nurse had told him: two other boys, a minor altercation over a game of tag, no one sure who'd started it.

The needle's tip glowed red for a moment as Magnus turned to Dashiell, who was sitting on a kitchen stool, wearing a dirt- and bloodstained polo shirt and a look of trepidation. "Okay, ready to get those splinters out of your hand?"

"Why do you need all that?" Even sitting directly in a pool of late afternoon sunlight, the boy looked pale.

"The tweezers are to grab the splinter and the alcohol is to sterilize the site."

"Oh." The boy fidgeted on the stool, almost falling off. "Will it hurt?"

Magnus grasped the child's right hand, which had two slivers of wood embedded deep in the palm. "A little. But it has to come out." As he tried to gently lift the first two layers of skin from the larger splinter, the boy nervously shifted his weight and came sliding off the stool. Magnus quickly moved the needle away. "Careful," he said. "You have to keep still."

"It wasn't on purpose!"

Magnus regarded the child, trying to see something of Katherine's strong features in this boy's delicate face. He was a good-looking child, almost pretty, with startlingly green eyes and thick, wheat-colored hair, but he seemed a different breed from his mother. "Ready to try again?"

"Sure."

Watching the boy wriggle back onto the stool, Magnus was reminded of Lefty, who'd been his bunkmate in basic training. Lefty had been one of those skinny, uncoordinated kids who was always fumbling with the covers right before morning inspection, dropping his tray while on line at the cafeteria, stumbling and tripping during marches. Magnus still wasn't sure what Lefty's problem had been; all he knew was, no matter how hard anyone yelled at him, he still couldn't seem to keep his mind on where his body was going. And Lefty had gotten yelled at by everyone—the drill sergeant, the guys in the mess tent, his fellow bunkmates.

Magnus had a feeling that Katherine's son was the Lefty of his class. Feeling the tip of the splinter, Magnus pressed down hard with the needle.

"Ow!" The kid yanked his hand away. "That hurt!"

Magnus looked at the boy with a combination of surprise and disapproval. "Dashiell, we have to get that splinter out or it will get infected. There's no choice involved. And it's going to hurt a bit. No choice about that, either. So your only choice is, how are you going to handle it? Because if you remain calm, I can get this done faster."

Dashiell thought about it. "I can tough it out."

"Good thinking." Magnus managed to get the tip of the splinter loose, then used the tweezers to extract the rest. As he prepared to start on the next splinter, Dashiell asked, "Do you think my nose is broken?" He was trying to sound calm, but his voice was high and thin.

Magnus, whose nose had been broken twice growing up, did not look up. "What did the school nurse say?"

"She said she couldn't be held responsible."

Hearing the boy on the verge of tears, Magnus put down the needle and put his hand under the boy's chin. "It's swollen, but it's still straight."

"You're sure I don't need to go to the hospital?"

"I'm pretty sure you've just bruised it. But your mother will have to decide that."

"But where is my mom? Why isn't she here?" The boy's eyes brightened and Magnus thought, Christ, if I'd have cried at that age, my father would have gone through the roof.

"I don't know." Should he add something reassuring? "I'm sure she'll be back shortly." The instant he said it, Magnus found himself wondering if something truly worrisome had happened. Why wasn't Katherine calling on her cell phone? It didn't seem in keeping with what he knew of her character for her to simply not show up.

Mainly to distract Dashiell, he asked, "Want to tell me what happened?"

"Riley, who's supposed to be my friend, just pushed me off the jungle gym for nothing."

Magnus dug a little deeper with the needle, and Dashiell winced, but didn't pull his hand away. "Sorry. Nobody ever pushes anyone for nothing."

"I didn't do anything! I was minding my own business, not even playing tag with them."

Magnus met the boy's eyes. "I'm not saying you did something on purpose. I'm not saying it's your fault. And I'm sure not saying it's fair. But there's always a reason for why things happen."

"Yeah, right. The reason is they all hate me. Riley was my friend until Jamal came, and now he and Jamal are in a club I can't join, and when I play tag with them I always have to be it. So I said, fine, I'm just not playing, and then Jamal called me a crybaby and Riley pushed me."

Magnus had finished removing the last splinter without Dashiell even noticing. As he swabbed the boy's palm with a cotton ball soaked in alcohol, he tried to remember what he'd read about Katherine's son from her file. Diagnosed with language-processing issues at age two, can miss the intended meaning in casual conversation. Has difficulty in reading social cues. On the other hand, adept at math and verbal puzzles, consistently able to beat adults at chess and Scrabble by the second half of third grade.

On paper, he sounds a lot like me, Magnus thought. No wonder I'm not getting along with him. He knew from his own experiences growing up that adults find it hard to tolerate in children the things they dislike most about themselves. He paused, considering what to say next. "You ever see a bunch of puppies together?"

"Like in a pet store? Sure. I want a dog, but my mom won't let me." Dashiell's cheeks flushed bright red. "She says it's too much work for her right now! But I would do anything, everything, she wouldn't have to even feed him or walk him." Dashiell's voice rose to a high wail. "I mean, don't my feelings count at all? Don't I get a vote? I hate my mother."

Magnus had no idea what to say to this. He figured the kid really hated his dad, but it wasn't easy to hate people who weren't around, especially when you weren't finished longing for them yet.

Dashiell put his hand to his face. "Oh, no, my nose is bleeding again."

"Hang on," said Magnus, "here's a tissue." He blotted the boy's nosebleed while Dashiell looked at him steadily out of clear green eyes, and suddenly Magnus remembered his own puppy, left at ten months to fend for itself when his father was posted Stateside again. People thought being a kid meant having no responsibility; the truth was, it meant having no control over your own life. "I could talk to your mother about getting a dog," he offered. "It probably won't do any good, though. At the end of the day, she can't take on any more than she's ready for right now. And whether or not she admits it, Dashiell, the divorce is hard on her, too."

Dashiell looked like nobody had been using the word "divorce" in front of him.

"Anyway, the reason why I asked about dogs is, you can learn a lot from watching a litter of puppies that are still with their mother. Once they get to be about seven weeks or so, they spend all their time play fighting, and some of that play fighting gets pretty rough. After awhile, the pups sort it out, and they know who's top dog, who's in the middle, and who's at the bottom of the heap. But you know what happens if you add a new puppy into that mix?"

"They start fighting again?"

"That's right. Because one new member can shift all the old relationships. If he's a strong, active, dominant dog, then he'll challenge everyone, and everyone will have to challenge everyone else until it all gets settled again."

Dashiell took a deep breath. "Is there any way a puppy can become a middle or top dog once he's on the bottom?"

Magnus remembered being nine in Egypt, a big, slow American surrounded by smaller, faster kids, all of whom played a kind of football that required agility rather than strength. That was the year he'd found the stray puppies. "Sure you can," he said. "You can become the dog that's calm and confident and doesn't get involved with all the fighting."

Dashiell furrowed his brow. "How do you do that?"

"Good question. You learn to read the signals that tell you when somebody's going to pick a fight. You figure out how to stand like someone who knows how to throw a punch. And you pretend."

Dashiell smiled broadly, revealing two front teeth that appeared slightly too large for his face. "So it's like people have a secret code you have to figure out."

"Exactly."

"I'm great with codes. I just figured one out for my mom, because her dad sent her this letter that was all in code. Well, actually it was a cipher. Do you know the difference between a code and a cipher?"

Magnus felt his heart rate speed up. *Easy, easy, don't sound too interested.* "Do you?"

"Sure." Spoken with all the assurance of a professional cryptographer.

"Do you remember what the letter said?"

"Just when they were supposed to meet." Dash put his small, slightly moist hand on Magnus's shoulder. "I hate to tell you this, but spy stuff really isn't as cool as you think."

"It's not?"

"Nah. You know how my mom said they send messages back and forth? With chewing gum." Dash rolled his eyes. "I mean, that doesn't even make sense. What kind of message can you send in a wad of pink chewing gun?"

"It's not a message," said Magnus. "It's a signal."

"Oh, yeah?"

"Yeah. So when your mom put the pink chewing gum . . ."

It only took Dash a moment to recall. "On the phone booth outside the Turkish place."

"Left or right side? High or low?"

"Um, left. I think."

"So when your mother puts the gum there, it signals your grandfather to check inside the dead drop for a message."

"Oh, I get it. But what's a dead drop?"

"A place where you exchange notes without having to be there."

Dash nodded. "Okay," he admitted, "that's kind of cool."

And then, with perfect timing, Magnus heard the sound of a key turning in the front door.

"Mom!" Dash flung himself into her arms. "I thought my nose was broken. Where were you? Magnus removed some splinters from my hand."

"Thank goodness for Magnus," Katherine said, hugging her son. "You have to tell me everything." She looked at Magnus over Dash's back, her eyes bright with unshed tears. Thank you, she said, silently forming the words. Magnus forced himself not to look away. He'd finally gotten the break he needed. And it wasn't as if he'd tricked the kid or bribed him into telling what he knew.

So why did he feel as if he'd played a mean trick on a defenseless puppy?

chapter *twenty-nine*

•

Kat bent her head so the shower could pound the back of her neck with warm water. The five hours between getting home and putting Dash to bed had felt interminable, but here she was, with the rest of the night free to wallow in guilt. Jesus, she still couldn't believe Dash had been hurt while she'd been unreachable.

What was happening to her? For years, she'd fretted over every minor detail of her son's life, carefully arranging all his classes, his therapies, his playdates. She never forgot class snack, like some of the other mothers did, and she never palmed them off with store bought crackers or pretzels. She baked fresh brownies and blondies, hoping that if the other kids liked Dashiell's mom's baking, they might treat him better.

She always showed up for school plays and sports events,

she always volunteered to chaperone class trips, and she was always home in time to greet Dash when he got off the schoolbus.

Until now. What if Magnus hadn't been here to receive Dash? What if her child had arrived home, bleeding and upset, only to find the apartment empty? The school had Lia's phone number, but Kat's mother didn't get off work till five-thirty or six. Dashiell would have had to sit in the lobby with Pedro while all her neighbors stopped and asked him what was wrong.

Oh, God, Kat thought, I really am a terrible mother.

She tilted her head up, letting the shower spray her directly in the face. It didn't help. She still felt wretched, her head still ached and she kept fighting waves of dizziness. And no matter how many times she tried to convince herself that there had been extenuating circumstances, she couldn't forgive herself for not being there for Dashiell when he needed her.

On the other hand, if there ever were an excuse for temporarily losing your mind, discovering that you were front-page tabloid news had to be it.

Kat had been on the subway coming home from her career Armageddon when she had glanced up and noticed someone reading the *Informer.* At first, Kat hadn't recognized the haggard actress on the cover. She had thought, *Whoever that is, time has not been kind.* Of course, it could also be that it was the photographer who was unkind, by choosing a shot that deliberately highlighted all the woman's flaws. Kat had noticed that when the tabloids couldn't fill their photo gallery with older actresses who'd become obese, emaciated, or face-lifted into a rictus of perpetual surprise, they hunted for the one bit of cellulite or neck droop on an otherwise lovely woman.

Kat started reading to see which poor actress was being fil-leted this week. It really was a horrible picture, made worse by the fact that the woman appeared to be cringing, her mouth gaping open in surprise.

And then Kat had realized, to her complete horror, that *she* was the cringing, gape-mouthed, middle-aged woman on the cover. Aghast, Kat had gotten off the train at the next stop, bought the tabloid from the underground newsstand, and read it three times in a row.

It did not improve with repetition. In fact, it got worse, as she discovered that she'd inadvertently memorized the damn thing as if it were the script to her next show. Which, in a sense, it was.

SEXY SECRETS
OF THE SOAP STARS

While his estranged wife looks more like a bag lady than the siren of the small screen she once was, Logan Dain appears fitter than ever as he consoles himself with up-and-coming soap star Bo Johnson. Pretty brunette Bo has taken over his wife's old role as *South of Heaven*'s spoiled heiress Helen Jessup, and Logan is making a number of guest appear-ances on his old show. Sources close to the stars say that the two have spent a lot of time "rehearsing their lines" in his private dressing room. But Bo had better not get too used to co-starring with Logan: Our INFORMER tells us that when Logan was on location filming an action movie in Prague, sexy European star-let Alessandra Mili was keeping him entertained . . . and Miss Mili is about to shoot her next film right here in the U.S. of A.

Kat had even warranted her own sidebar:

In a desperate attempt to restore her faded beauty, Katherine Miner has elected to try injections of an untested serum from Brazil. Thousands of rare Brazilian toucan eggs are harvested each year to produce this exclusive treatment, but as this photo shows, in her case, the results have been disastrous.

Kat couldn't even remember if toucans came from Brazil, which was hardly the most relevant question. In any case, she thought, turning off the shower, maybe there's a bright side to this. Maybe the Rejuvenatrix people won't sue me when they learn that they almost had a crazed toucan-killer as their spokeswoman.

Kat's foot brushed up against something hard, and she glanced down to find one of Dashiell's bath toys. Bending down, she put it outside the tub.

Now, that would be ironic, falling victim to a three-inch plastic shark. Although at this particular moment, the thought of being stuck in a hospital with all her limbs in traction was almost appealing. At least then she wouldn't have to walk around Manhattan knowing that thousands of *Informer* readers across the nation were looking at her picture and thinking "vain Brazilian-bird-killing bitch."

Kat stepped carefully out of the shower and instantly slipped on the toy shark that she'd just removed from the bathtub.

Stunned, she sat on the floor for a moment, then put a hand to the back of her head, where an unpleasant burning sensation told her she was probably bleeding. She must have hit the corner of her little bathroom table on her way down. Staring at the vivid red blood staining her palm, Kat remembered reading somewhere that head wounds bleed a lot. But do they bleed a lot and then you're all right, or do they bleed a lot and then you die?

She tried to stand up, then stopped, frightened by a sudden rush of dizziness.

"Magnus?" She had no idea if he would be able to hear her from the other side of the apartment, so she shouted his name the second time.

Right before she drew a breath to try a third time, the bathroom door opened. "Katherine? What's wrong?"

To her own surprise, she burst into tears.

chapter *thirty*

•

Magnus's first impression was that there was a lot of blood. His second impression was that Katherine was naked and possibly hysterical. "It's all right, take a deep breath, there you go." He checked her eyes to see if her pupils were dilated and tried to slow his own breathing down. *Don't panic, don't conjecture, take this step by step.* There was blood on the tile floor, on the white porcelain sink, on Katherine's neck and right breast.

"Can you tell me what happened?" He couldn't tell if her skin was clammy or if she were just chilled from being wet and naked. Magnus pulled down a towel and tucked it around her, then gently inspected the back of her head.

"I slipped."

"Stay still. That's a nasty cut. Did you black out?"

"I don't think so. No. But when I tried to stand up just now, I felt like I was about to."

"Let me take another look." Ignoring the sharp pain in his knee as he shifted his weight on the hard tile, Magnus searched carefully through her long, dark hair. "Actually, it's not as bad as I thought. The edges are a little farther apart than I'd like, but I don't think you need stitches."

"So I'm all right?" Her voice was too breathy. *Shit.* Something must have happened to upset Katherine. She didn't strike him as the kind of woman to turn weak at the sight of a little blood.

Magnus glanced at the bathroom walls. Well, more than a little blood. "You're really fine. Although . . . do you have a butterfly bandage?"

"I might. There's a first-aid kit in the medicine cabinet."

Magnus went to fetch it. When he sat back down, he saw that Katherine had drawn the towel more carefully around her, drawing his attention to the fact that it didn't conceal all of her breasts, and barely covered the tops of her thighs. Catching his look, she said, "This is pretty embarrassing."

Instantly, he felt his body respond to her self-consciousness in a way it hadn't when he'd thought there might be a real medical emergency. Feeling overdressed in a long-sleeved shirt and jeans, Magnus began to sweat in the humid bathroom. "If you lean forward, I can clear away some of this blood from your scalp."

"Sure. It's just—I'm a little light-headed."

"Putting your head down should help." As Katherine bent over, the silver pendant he'd given her swung out of the towel. *She'd kept it on.* Which meant that she was wearing it all the time, even when she bathed. And if she felt like that, then maybe she wouldn't just write him off when he confessed who he really was. Feeling a little light-headed himself, Magnus began to clean the blood off Katherine's hair with a gauze pad.

"First you had to patch up Dash, and now me."

"I don't mind."

"How do you stay so calm?"

"It never does any good to panic." Magnus dabbed some antibiotic ointment on the laceration before applying the butterfly bandage.

"I get the feeling you'd be good in an emergency. Good under fire."

Magnus stopped moving his hand for a moment. "Well . . ."

"That's why you'd make a good father." An awkward silence. "I meant theoretically."

Magnus rocked back on his heels. He had always worried that he might turn out like his own father—an aloof figure, impossible to read, good enough as an adjunct parent but woefully inadequate to the task of raising a son on his own. *Maybe that's why I didn't push the fertility issue with Guthrun.* But here Katherine was saying she thought he'd make a good father. Unsure how to respond, Magnus changed the subject. "There, you're all fixed up. Let me help you to bed."

Was Katherine right about his potential to be a decent dad? She certainly knew enough lousy fathers. Slipping his arm around her waist, Magnus thought, I do not have time to think about this right now. He'd left the chewing gum in the phone booth just after Katherine had gotten home, and his note, typed in null cipher, had suggested they meet tonight at ten. He'd picked the late hour because Fez was one of the few restaurants around that remained open on Mondays, and it was packed with people until nine-thirty or so.

Since Ken would be expecting Katherine, Magnus figured his best bet was to simply slide into the seat alongside him and make his pitch fast, before Ken could get away.

"Magnus?"

Only problem was how to begin. "I don't want to hurt you" sounded like a threat. "Don't get up" sounded worse. Magnus settled Katherine on the edge of her bed, distracted. "You all right?"

She inhaled, as if gathering courage. "That necklace you gave me for my birthday." She touched it with one hand.

"You already thanked me." Magnus checked the back of Katherine 's head. "The bleeding has stopped."

"It's not just something you picked up from the store, is it?"

Magnus paused. "Well, no. It belonged to my mother." He'd given his mother's engagement ring to Guthrun, of course, but the silver charm actually held greater sentimental value for him. His mother had given it to him when he was nine, the day she told him that the cancer had come back. For strength, she'd said.

Katherine was watching his expression. "Maybe I shouldn't keep it."

Magnus shrugged, uncomfortable. "It's not as if I ever wear it." He wanted to say something else, about feeling a connection to Katherine that made it all right for her to have it, but he couldn't.

And yet, looking into her eyes, he had the feeling that she understood.

"Magnus? I want to ask you something."

Oh, dear God, she was going to ask him about his mother. That wasn't a place he wanted to go. He didn't even like to think, let alone talk, about it. Magnus glanced at the clock, wanting to be out of this house, out of this room, out of this heavily charged moment. Given the choice between discussing his dead mother and capturing an unstable secret agent, Magnus thought he preferred the latter.

But to his surprise, all Katherine said was, "Could you put your arms around me for a moment?" When he hesitated, she added, "I've had a really bad day."

And just like that, Magnus forgot about his own anxieties. Sitting down next to her on the bed, he drew her in close. Katherine rested her head against his chest, and he inhaled the clean, citrus-soap smell of her. Her hand crept over to rest on his chest, and he wrapped his fingers around hers.

Katherine ducked her head into the crook of his neck. "I'm cold."

He tucked her into his body, gently rubbing her back and shoulders. He was aware that it was a sign of trust that Katherine was letting him see her like this, quiet, vulnerable, in need of his comfort. He pressed a kiss to her damp hair, and She turned in his embrace. Her movement caused her towel to slip. And suddenly a different kind of comfort came to mind.

Magnus tried to pretend that he hadn't noticed, running his fingers circumspectly over her arms and down her back as if he weren't getting hard inside his jeans. Katherine apparently had a different idea. "Magnus?" She stood up, gloriously, unabashedly naked except for his silver pendant around her neck, and walked across the room. Shutting her bedroom door and locking it, Katherine turned to him. "I've decided I don't want to take things slow."

Still riveted by the sight of Katherine's nude body, it took Magnus a moment to compute. When he did, his erection became almost painful. The problem was, if he acted on it, he was the dickhead. *Oh, Jesus, this was really unfair.* "Katherine, I don't know if this is such a good idea right now."

Katherine closed her eyes. "Ouch." Picking up her towel and wrapping it around herself, she gave him a wry smile. "You know, that wasn't quite the reaction I was hoping for."

Shit. He'd hurt her, made her feel self-conscious. "Katherine, I . . ." Magnus had no idea how to finish the sentence. Have to be ambushing your father in about forty-five minutes? Excuse. He needed to think of an excuse.

"You know, I keep hearing how the culture has become saturated with sex and how explicit everything is and how everyone and their grandmother are having affairs with people they met in internet chat rooms. But you know what? Not in my reality." Tears were running down Katherine's face now. "I want to feel sexy again. I want to feel passionate and hopeful and . . . I don't know." Katherine swallowed. "Young."

His mind racing, Magnus silenced her with a kiss. Maybe, if he could just communicate how badly he wanted her, that would be enough. He kissed her with all the pent-up frustration inside him, and as she clutched his shoulders, Magnus lifted her onto his lap, so that she was straddling him. Pulling the towel away from her body, he wanted to tell her how beautiful she was, but all the words felt canned and fake, like imitating something he'd seen in a movie. So he tried to tell her with touch instead, admiring her breasts with his fingertips, complimenting her taut waist, her full hips, showing her how much he approved of the firm roundness of her rear.

Actually, he might have gotten a little carried away approving of her rear. Which was probably a mistake. How do I even know whether she likes this, he thought. Guthrun hated it when I touched her there. During the first year of his mar-

riage, he'd learned to think of a woman's body as a mine-
field—two inches to the left was safe to explore, two inches to
the right and you'd blown it. But then Katherine arched her
back, and just like that, Magnus knew.

It was like the moment when he'd stopped mentally trans-
lating English into Icelandic, when everything had clicked and
become natural, fluid, instinctive. He might never have mas-
tered his ex-wife's signals, but he appeared to be fluent in
Katherine.

He drew her nipple back into his mouth, letting her feel
the edge of his teeth this time.

"Oh, God, Magnus."

Katherine strained against him as he moved from one nipple to the other, wondering if he could make her come like
this. Jesus, it was possible he could make *himself* come like
this. Winding her hands around his neck, Katherine pressed
herself against him, his jeans the only barrier between them.

He'd really begun to hate those Levi's. And he wasn't too
fond of his shirt, either.

As if reading his mind, Katherine started dragging his
shirt over his head. "I want to feel you."

Magnus gave a low groan when she pressed her breasts to
his bare chest, helplessly holding her hips and grinding himself against her. "Shh, you have to be quiet. Dashiell's asleep."

Nobody in his entire life had ever implied that Magnus
was too loud. "But he's on the other end of the hallway."

"Don't argue with me." Katherine bit the pad of muscle
where his throat met his shoulder.

Magnus inhaled sharply as that small pain sent a shock
wave of sensation straight down to his dick. *Jesus.* He pushed
his hand down between them, wanting nothing more than to
unbutton his jeans and enter her body. But as he came into

contact with her slick inner flesh, he hesitated. How could he take her like this, under false pretenses? On the other hand, how could he leave her like this, trembling on the brink?

Katherine broke his train of thought by rolling her hips. "Magnus." Unaccustomed to having his partner take such an active role, Magnus was too surprised to react when Kat began to unbutton his jeans. It was only when he found himself staring down at his own erection, peeking over the top of his snug black boxers, that Magnus stopped her, covering her hand with his own. "I think I'd better keep these on for now."

"But I want to touch you." She reached for him and Magnus grabbed her wrist. Raising an eyebrow, she reached for him with her other hand, and Magnus pinned that wrist, too. "Katherine, we can't."

She lowered her chin and smiled, her look as provocative as it was insolent. "Don't tell me I need to best *you* in fair battle?" She kissed him, hard, twisting her wrists, trying to get free. And maybe he was perverted, but this whole Viking versus warrior maiden scenario was pushing him over the edge.

I have got to get back in control of this, and quick. Cradling the back of her head with one arm, Magnus flipped Katherine over onto the bed, so she was lying on her back beneath him. She continued to struggle, but now . . . oh, man, now he could feel her better.

"Stop fighting me," he told her, his voice sound unusually gruff. It was hard enough fighting his own need to thrust. But he couldn't allow this to go any further until he'd broken cover and told her the truth about himself. What they'd done up till now was intimate enough, but according to his ex-wife, all women had one category for the men they'd fooled around with, and another for the ones they'd actually allowed inside their bodies.

Of course, at the moment, the distinction was getting a little blurry. Katherine was twisting her body, and her movements slid him along the channel between her thighs. Magnus gritted his teeth at the almost painful pleasure that the friction was causing. "Katherine, please, you have to stop." All it would have taken was a slight shift in the angle of his hips and the tip of his erection would be pressing against her entrance. As much to stop himself as to satisfy her, Magnus reached around and slid his free hand over Katherine's flat belly, slipping a finger inside of her.

Katherine looked up at him. "If you're trying to be gentlemanly, forget it."

"Forget what?"

"Ladies first."

"Forget ladies first?" He wondered if she wanted him to forget all the other women he'd been with. If so, he already had.

Katherine let out a sigh of exasperation. "Look, it takes me a long time to relax enough with a man to have an orgasm. And I'm not talking about hours, I'm talking weeks or months. So don't think you have to satisfy me before we make love."

Magnus considered what she was telling him. "That sounds like a challenge."

"It's not, I swear, please don't take it that way . . . hey, what are you doing?" She tugged at him, trying to haul him back up as he slid down her body.

"Accepting the challenge." Magnus pinned Katherine's wrists at her sides. "A Viking never backs down."

"Magnus, I'm not joking, I feel self-conscious about . . . oh, my God." For a moment, he thought he had her, but then Katherine lifted her head. "Did you hear something?"

Magnus listened. "Not a thing."

"No, really, I'm sure I heard something. Let me up."

Magnus stopped moving and concentrated on detecting any sound outside the bedroom. "Nice try," he said, nipping Katherine on the inside of her thigh, "but I had the best hearing on my sub, and I detect absolutely nothing."

"You know what, I'm thinking this is a bad idea, what if Dashiell does wake up . . ."

"I'd hear him before he opened the door to his room."

"You might be distracted."

"Katherine, I've been trained in hand to hand combat. Nobody is going to sneak up on me." Too late, Magnus realized what he was revealing.

"When were you trained in . . . oh. Um, Magnus, listen, can't we just . . ."

Magnus tried to think of a way to distract her. "Wench, be silent."

"Excuse me?"

"Now you must do as I command." Still holding her wrists captive, he bent his head and breathed in the earthy, intimate scent of her. Katherine started to struggle in earnest, and he looked up at her.

"Listen, Magnus, I know all women are supposed to love this, but to tell you the truth, I'm not such a huge fan."

And Magnus, who had suffered through three attempts on his ex-wife's part to take him into her mouth, instantly understood. Even if everyone didn't like giving oral sex, everybody was supposed to love receiving it. But there was nothing less sexy than watching a woman gag and choke as she tried to please you.

"This isn't about your pleasure," he said. "It's about mine."

Then, before Katherine could protest, Magnus pressed a

kiss to her inner thigh, then moved higher. He made the first touch of his tongue a question, deliberately not on her most sensitive spot. She remained motionless, but as Magnus continued to trace a circuitous path, he could feel the subtle beginnings of her response—a loosening of the thighs, a tilt of the hips—and Magnus paused, overcome by a tenderness so fierce that all the forbidden words bubbled up inside him. *I love you. I'm a spy.*

But Katherine misread his hesitation. "Oh, listen, that was great, you don't need to go on." She tried to sit up, drawing her legs together. "I know a lot of men really don't like the taste."

Magnus tried to think of some way to reassure her. "Why would I start this if I didn't want to finish it?"

Katherine flushed. "Do we have to talk this to death?"

Magnus watched her pull the covers over herself. "Logan didn't like performing oral sex." He made it a statement.

Katherine closed her eyes for a moment, then shook her head. "With me. He didn't like it with me, especially after I had Dashiell. He said . . . I had a stronger taste than other women."

Magnus shook his head. "I like the way you taste."

"Let's just forget about it, all right?"

"I don't want to forget about it. I like the feeling of putting my mouth on you. I like the way you smell."

"Why don't we just move on?"

Magnus shook his head. "You don't understand. This is the first time I *have* liked it. It was something I did for my wife, because she liked it, because that's what men are expected to do these days. I didn't mind it. But I didn't feel anything like this."

"Like what?"

"Like I wanted to roll myself around in the taste and scent of you."

"Oh. But I . . ."

"Shut up." Pulling the covers away from her body, Magnus leaned over and plunged his tongue between her folds, thrusting inside her, feeling her small, involuntary muscular contractions. For the first time in his sexual life, he felt an animal wildness building inside him.

"Oh, Jesus, Magnus, wait, wait, it's too much, I can't, I can't . . ."

She was pushing him away, trying to grasp his arms to haul him up, over her, but Magnus was immovable. Sliding his hands under her rear, he held her captive, something strangely primitive driving him now, seeking her satisfaction, her submission, her surrender. Holding her hips, he licked inside her with long, slow, determined strokes and Katherine gave a strangled gasp, and then he could feel her orgasm quaking all through his jaw, down his throat.

For a long moment, Katherine just lay there, her breathing uneven, and then he felt her body stiffen.

"Oh. My. God. Was I too loud? I wasn't loud, was I?" Magnus kissed his way up Katherine's body until he reached her face.

"You weren't loud." He brushed the hair away from her face, cupped her cheek and kissed her mouth, reveling in the fact that he had pleasured her so completely. And it wasn't taking advantage, not really, since he'd been the one doing all the giving.

"Oh, God." His hand felt something wet. Katherine was crying.

"Hush, Katherine, hush." She rolled in his arms, spreading her legs beneath him, and Magnus realized that his unbuttoned jeans had slid down his hips, taking his underwear with them. There was nothing between them now; the head of his penis was one push away from entering her. In the back of his mind, Magnus knew there was a meeting, a timetable, a rapidly approaching deadline. He knew this was wrong.

And he was going to do it anyway.

Katherine gasped as he entered her in one long stroke. Stunned at the intensity of the sensation, he watched her expression as he withdrew. Then it hit him.

"Shit. Katherine, I'm not . . . we forgot birth control."

"It's okay." She locked her legs around his waist. "I have an I.U.D."

He pushed into her a second time, and it felt like the top of his head was going to come off. "Wait."

She smiled. "I told you, I don't want to wait."

He thrust into her again, harder than before, and Katherine dug her heels into the small of his back, driving him on. She said something. His name. I love you. Magnus stopped holding himself in check. His rhythm picked up speed and force, became instinctive, animal, raw. His vision blurred and he had an incoherent thought about wanting her to have his baby.

He might have said something out loud.

She made a startled sound and arched up against him, and that was it, the beginning of the end, a wave of pleasure so intense that it bordered on pain. Katherine kissed his chin, the side of his neck, his chest, and for the first time in his life Magnus didn't have to ask whether that meant what he hoped it did.

Magnus rolled over, chest heaving, stroking Katherine's head where it lay across his heart. God, his hand was shaking. He felt as if he'd been shattered into a million pieces and put back together so that some of Katherine's atoms were mixed in with his. How else to explain this acute awareness that made him feel as if he was still fused with her?

And then Magnus glanced at the clock and felt his body go ice cold.

Katherine propped herself up on one elbow. "Are you okay?" She touched his face. "What is it?"

He had done exactly what he'd promised himself he wouldn't do. And in doing so, he'd lost all track of time. It was ten o'clock. Sitting up, Magnus buried his head in his hands. He couldn't not go to the rendezvous. Ken thought the message was from Katherine. If the man thought he'd been stood up, would he even bother to come back the next day?

"Magnus, are you in pain? Tell me, what's wrong?"

"I have to leave."

"You have to leave?"

Magnus forced himself to meet her gaze. "For Chinese food. I'm starving. Aren't you starving?" Yanking his jeans up, Magnus tried to smile.

"You know, we can always order in."

"Takes too long." Magnus kissed her abruptly on the forehead and pulled his shirt over his head. "Be back soon."

As he ran out the front door with his shoes in one hand, Magnus realized there was one thing worse than having to tell Katherine he'd been lying to her all along.

And that was having her think whatever she was thinking about him right now.

chapter *thirty-one*

•

At five past ten, Kat got herself up off the bed and started to clean the blood off her bathroom tile. She wasn't sure that she wanted to think about what had just happened. It wasn't that she had had some *When Harry Met Sally* fantasy of being held all night long. But having the guy pop out of bed before the wet spot on the sheet had dried did seem a little abrupt.

So Magnus was frightened of intimacy. Kat scrubbed a last bloodstain off the tile floor and sighed. What else was new? She wasn't some naïve little virgin, expecting that a few moments of incredible closeness in bed would translate into closeness outside of it.

Kat rinsed herself off under the bath taps, too exhausted to take a full shower. She found her favorite Mr. Bubble nightshirt in a drawer and put it on, then pulled back the covers and got into her bed. Okay, so he'd freaked out. She was a big girl. She knew how to be alone. And the sex had been great. In fact, there was something quite nice about having some privacy to savor a triumphant return to the land of carnal pleasures. Maybe this was an unexpected benefit to being forty. She could be attracted to a man, enjoy fooling around with him, and not feel possessed with the desire to insert the DNA of her life into his. Also, she didn't have to worry about whether or not he snored. Or worse, whether or not she did.

Feeling too distracted to read, Kat turned off her light. It wasn't as if she would have invited him to spend the night in her bed. After all, how would she explain it to Dash in the morning?

It might be nice if he stopped by her room when he came back, however.

At eleven-thirty, Kat began to wonder where Magnus was. He'd been gone an hour and a half now. Sitting up, she turned on her bedside lamp. Exactly how far had he gone for Chinese food, anyway? Had he been mugged? Kat contemplated other possibilities—an illicit drug habit, a gambling debt, a standing appointment with another woman.

Okay, so they all sounded pretty unlikely. But where was he? Even if she assumed that he'd eaten at the restaurant, this was taking way too long.

Maybe, Kat thought, I'll just stay up to see if he brings back a bag of leftovers.

At midnight, Kat happened to be standing next to the front door when she heard the rattle of the elevator. Ducking quickly back into her bedroom, Kat then heard the front door close very gently. She considered a casual foray into the kitchen.

At twelve-fifteen, Kat acknowledged to herself that there was no way to pull off a casual foray into the kitchen.

At twelve-seventeen, she went anyway, opening and closing the refrigerator door, opening a new bottle of seltzer so there was a loud fizzing sound, clinking the glasses around in the cupboard.

Nothing. Could he be asleep already? She glanced at the clock, something which, she realized, was becoming a compulsion. Should she just give up and stop obsessing? It wasn't as if he'd seduced her. She was the one who wouldn't wait. She was the one who had to feel passion, and to hell with the risk of getting hurt.

Screw it. She deserved an explanation.

Katherine knocked on Magnus's door.

"Katherine? I thought you were asleep." He leaned against the door frame, bare-chested, wearing only a pair of low-slung, faded army pants.

"Look, I know we're not starry-eyed young lovers, but you have to admit, what we just did was an extremely intimate act." She tried to keep her eyes from focusing on his broad, muscular, almost hairless chest.

An expression of acute discomfort crossed Magnus's face. "I know it must seem a bit strange, the way I ran out the door."

Kat folded her arms across her chest. "You think?"

Magnus took a deep breath. "The thing is, I haven't been completely honest with you."

Kat felt cold. "You're not . . . it's not medical?"

"What? Oh, God, no, nothing like that." Magnus held out his hand, and after a moment, Kat took it. "Can we sit down?"

Kat shook her head. "No. It's bad enough I'm standing here in a pink T-shirt. If there's bad news, I want it standing up."

"Katherine, the first thing I want you to know is . . ."

"I never meant to hurt you," Kat said automatically. Then, seeing the expression on his face, she understood. "Oh, my God, you really were going to say that, weren't you?"

Magnus flushed. "I'm not much good at this kind of thing, even in the best of times."

"This kind of thing? What kind of thing is this? Is this a breakup kind of thing?"

"No." Magnus closed his eyes. "Okay. Listen. What happened between us tonight . . . what's been happening between us—that's real. That necklace I gave you?"

Kat reflexively touched her bare neck. "I took it off when you bolted."

"Of course." It took Magnus a moment to regroup. "That was my mother's. It's important to me." He hesitated. "You're important to me."

Awash with relief, Kat put her arms around Magnus's neck. "So why the hell did you just run off like that? I have got to tell you, that was not a good move. I mean, I've gotten to the point where I figure, well, men vanish, that's what they do." Her voice wobbled a little, and she felt Magnus's arms come around her waist. "But I wasn't quite prepared for you to do it, too."

"Oh, God, Katherine." Magnus pressed her cheek against his warm chest, his hand stroking her hair.

Kat felt her eyes fill with tears, and she thought, I haven't cried this much since I was pregnant with Dash. "You had me scared there for a minute."

Magnus stopped caressing her hair, and for a moment, it was very quiet, the charged quiet that precedes the first clap of thunder." Katherine, I'm not a scientist. I work for the CIA. I was sent to get your help in contacting your father."

Kat pulled back. "You're kidding, right?" He was delivering it like bad dialogue, without conviction. "Is this Icelandic humor? If so, I could live without it."

His face, like his voice, remained oddly devoid of emotion. "I'm sorry, but I'm telling you the truth. There's a situation right now in Kyrgyzstan and we need your father's expertise."

In the end, it was his stilted delivery that convinced her. Actors and con men knew how to act natural under unnatural situations. Everyone else tended to behave as though they were acting. "Oh, my God. You're serious."

"The reason I had to leave tonight was because elections have been called and our timetable was moved up. I had to meet with your father immediately."

"Wait a minute, if you needed me . . . how did you even know how to find my father?" She stared at Magnus, suddenly remembering the hours he'd spent with Dashiell. "You interrogated my son." Her eyes widened in horror. "What did you do? Threaten him? Bribe him?" She slammed her fists down on Magnus's chest. "What did you do?" Magnus made no move to defend himself and she hit him again.

"I swear, Katherine, I didn't do anything to him. He just—He trusted me, and he just told me."

"Oh, that makes it all right, does it?" Kat sounded as bitter as she felt. "He trusted you. I trusted you. Was sleeping with me part of the job? God! And I thought you were shy!"

"It's not like that." A muscle was jumping in Magnus's jaw, as if he were clenching it. "Other than lying to you about why I was here, I've been completely honest."

Kat snorted. "Please. So, tell me. How did it go with my father? Did you convince him? Or do you still need my help?"

"He listened to me. I let him go, which will probably get me in trouble, but I wanted to prove to him that we aren't going to hurt him."

"Very noble. Of course, I can't really believe anything you say, can I?"

"Of course you can."

And that was it. The final straw. Shoving Magnus hard in the chest, she said, "Pack."

"What?"

"You heard me. Pack. It's what you're going to do in the morning anyway, right? So I'm saving you some time. I mean, you have to go get debriefed or bug someone's house or torture their dog or whatever it is you do when you're not impersonating someone, right? So get a move on."

"Katherine, please . . ." Magnus looked at her imploringly.

"Please what? Please be okay about this? Please excuse my deceiving you and using you? What for? Are you suggesting that you might actually want a real relationship with me?"

Magnus looked her right in the eye. "Actually, yes. I would."

Kat laughed, an ugly, humorless laugh. "And how the hell would I know I wasn't some tool for you? Maybe you figure I'd be some kind of long-term asset. A teacher of English as a second language, that has to be pretty useful. Maybe I can point out potential terrorists."

"No. I mean, yes, by all means, if you think someone in your class is a terrorist, you should point them out, but that's not why I want to be with you."

Kat stormed past Magnus into his room. "Get out." Opening his suitcase, she threw things inside. His jeans. A book. His underwear.

"Kat, wait . . ."

"I decided I don't feel like waiting." Deliberately repeating the same words she'd used earlier. Shutting his suitcase, she shoved it into his arms. "Now move it, before I call the cops on you." She pushed him toward the back door.

261

Magnus looked over his shoulder. "Katherine, I'll come back when you've had a chance to calm down."

"Fuck off!" She shoved him and he stumbled into the hallway.

"I don't blame you for—"

"Asshole!" Kat slammed the door in his face.

A moment later, the phone rang, and Kat snatched it up. "What the hell is it?"

"Kat?" It was her mother, sounding groggy from sleep. "I thought I heard shouting. Is everything all right?"

Sinking down onto the wood floor, Kat began to cry. "No, Mom," she said, her voice coming out thin and small and very young. "Magnus was using me. He works for the CIA. All he wanted was to get to my dad."

"Oh, honey. Do you want me to come over?"

Kat looked around the living room, at the chairs he had fixed, the painting he had rehung. "And the worse part is, I think it hurts more than when Logan walked out, because I always sort of knew that Logan was selfish and egocentric." Her vision blurred with tears. "I thought I'd learned and I'd made a better choice this time."

"Kat? Do you want me to come over?"

"I don't know. I don't know what I want."

"Then let me make the decision. Open the door, I'm coming over."

Too worn out to argue, Kat sat back and let her mother take charge.

PART THREE

expressing anger
and
resolving conflict

•

There are many things that make people angry. Some of these are fairly predictable given the situation. Others are highly personal and idiosyncratic. In this unit, we will outline some of the things that make many Americans angry. You must be cautious when expressing or reacting to anger in a language not your own. If you say the wrong thing, the situation could get worse.
It is best to try to resolve the issue.

—SPEAKING NATURALLY:
COMMUNICATION SKILLS IN AMERICAN ENGLISH

chapter *thirty-two*

·

For the first time in his life, Magnus hit the six-mile mark without experiencing any discernible lift in his mood. Slowing to a jog, he stretched his arms behind his head and looked up at the sky, which had finally lost its bruised blue color.

His cell phone rang. "Yeah?" He stopped in the middle of the empty sidewalk, the sweat on his arms and legs rapidly cooling in the brisk, early-morning air.

"Magnus, where the fuck are you? I thought you were asleep on the couch."

Magnus stretched his right calf, which had just seized up with a cramp. "I needed some air."

Fred made an exasperated noise. "Well, get your ass back over here. Your gamble just paid off. Ken Miner showed up on my doorstep five minutes ago, ready to do business."

Magnus wiped his face with the hem of his shirt. "That's great, Fred." The sky didn't seem to be getting any lighter; Magnus thought that it might rain.

"I still say it was a hell of a chance to take, letting him walk off." This was a lot milder than what his handler had said last night.

"I'm glad it worked out."

"But I still have a little problem. Namely, the fact that the agent in charge of selling this deal to him is missing."

"Fred, you told me that my judgment was too poor for me to continue on this or any other case." After Katherine had kicked him out, Magnus had gone straight to Fred's apartment and spent hours filling his handler in on the meeting with Ken Miner. Magnus had informed Fred that Ken struck him as bored and depressed, adding that Miner was deeply gratified to learn that the Agency wanted his expertise, not his head. Certain that Miner was going to agree, Magnus had let the old spy go to think things over.

Fred had been less than impressed with this line of reasoning, calling Magnus a genius of an idiot before slamming the door to his bedroom.

Figuring it might be better not to be around when Fred woke up, Magnus had gone for a run. He still wasn't sure how far he'd meant to go, or when he'd meant to come back.

"Are you even listening to me, Magnus?" Magnus realized his boss was telling him something.

"Yes," he lied.

"Listen, all I'm saying is, you have to learn to take a little healthy criticism. Now, where the hell are you?"

Magnus looked around him, taking in the uneven cobbled streets, the empty warehouses, the metal garbage cans overflowing with rancid meat. "Downtown somewhere."

"So how long will it take you to get back to my apartment?" Fred lived in a one-bedroom on Fifty-fifth and Eighth Avenue, right above a Chinese takeout place. Everything inside was tainted with the smell of garlic sauce, from Fred's leather sofa to his custom-made Hong Kong suits. Magnus would have paid less for the furnishings and tried for a different location, but Fred had different priorities.

"Magnus? Is your cell phone fading out? I asked how far are you?"

"I'm not sure." Maybe it was the thought of all that garlic, but Magnus found his stomach turning at the thought of returning to Fred's place.

"Well, get back here as fast as you can. Miner's sitting in the kitchen, going over the Oybek file and trying to get up to speed, but he's going to have some questions."

"You can tell him whatever he needs to know." Magnus watched a brown rat peek its head out of a trash can. "I need to talk to Katherine. She feels that I betrayed her trust."

"Unfortunate, but not uncommon."

The rat lifted up on its hind legs, sniffing the air. "Fred, I slept with her."

"Okay, look, I'm not speaking officially here. But sometimes, when we're befriending an agent of the opposite sex, certain lines get crossed. As long as you keep your mind on the objective, it's tacitly accepted."

"To be perfectly frank, my mind wasn't on the goddamn objective, and I don't really give a shit what the Agency thinks. I just don't want Katherine to think I was using her to get to her father."

"You're not making any sense, Magnus. That's exactly what you were doing."

Magnus ran his hand over his face. "I mean, I didn't have

sex with her to get to her father." The rat wrinkled its nose at him as if it, too, was appalled at his behavior.

"Okay, I get it. You got emotionally involved. Not ideal, but in this case, nobody's going to raise a big stink over it. But don't forget, the father has always been our ultimate goal. And it's him you have to get close to now, Magnus. So come on back here and fill him in on what we know and what we need to know from Oybek before our plane takes off."

"Wait a second, are you telling me you're taking Miner to Kyrgyzstan today?" The worst part about working for an intelligence agency was never knowing whether you hadn't been cleared to receive important information or whether executive decisions were just being made up as you went along.

"Miner says Oybek will respect us if we show up in person, and that having us there for the elections will remind him that there are good reasons to turn to Washington instead of Moscow or Damascus. The plane's departing at fifteen hundred hours."

Which meant they were making decisions as they went along. Magnus's mind was racing. "Has Miner called Katherine yet? Because she was expecting him to come over and meet her son this evening."

"Oh, for fuck's sake. No, he hasn't called his daughter yet. Unlike you, Ken Miner seems to have a clear sense of priorities. Meeting with Oybek and cementing relations between our countries? Important. Hanging out with the nine-year-old can wait a week or two." The phone went dead and the rat scampered away, off to find a better class of trash.

For one long, lovely moment, Magnus was filled with righteous anger—that unfeeling bastard, how could he just use people like that. And then Magnus remembered that it hadn't been Fred in bed with Katherine. Fred hadn't been the guy encouraging her to meet with her father, or acting paternal to her fatherless son.

It wasn't Fred currently topping Katherine's list of men who'd betrayed her.

"You looking for some love, honey?" Magnus turned in surprise. He'd been too preoccupied to hear the sound of someone approaching. "Easy now, big fella." The speaker was a suspiciously tall redhead with thinly plucked eyebrows and shoulders the size of a lumberjack's. "You looking for fun?"

"Sorry," Magnus said. "I'm just taking a break from running."

"And don't you look good doing it. But you should be careful, standing around with your head in the clouds. It's not exactly Disneyfied here yet."

"Thanks for the warning." He gave the giant redhead a brief wave of acknowledgment as she stumbled along the uneven cobblestones in her platform heels and miniskirt.

Magnus started to run, glad to be moving again. Clearly, not all the rawness had been drained out of the Meatpacking District. By the time he reached Rector Street, he'd acknowledged to himself that he had no intention of going back to Fred until he'd spoken with Katherine again.

If he needed to be on a plane later today, then fine. Since he'd signed on for this, he'd follow through. But that didn't mean he had to leave Katherine thinking that everything he'd said and done had all been a big act.

Magnus glanced at his watch. Just over forty minutes to go before class started, too much time to just stand around doing nothing.

Four blocks from the Persky Institute, Magnus found a small Cuban cafe. As the radio wailed something in Spanish about *amor loco*, he ordered a coffee and an egg and ham sandwich and tried to rinse himself off in the tiny bathroom. In the oxidized mirror, he discovered that he looked as bad as he felt—half-lidded eyes, stubbled chin, hair that was standing up in all directions.

For some reason, the sharp-faced waitress kept smiling flirtatiously as she served him his coffee. Trying to smooth his hair down with his hand, Magnus wondered if he was ever going to understand women, although he wasn't exactly sure the tall redhead counted as a woman. After a moment's reflection, he decided she did. There was a fine line between pretending to be something and becoming it, and Magnus didn't think he was in any position to judge where a person fell on the spectrum.

Perched on the counter, he took a bite of his egg sandwich. The roll was saturated with butter and the ham was fatty, a heart attack on a plate. But he felt marginally better after eating. *I'm getting too damn old to function without sleep,* he thought. His cell phone rang, and after a moment's consideration, Magnus answered it. "Fred, I'm going to class."

"The hell you are."

"Look, you are perfectly equipped to tell Miner whatever he needs to know. I can join you after I've had a chance to speak to Katherine."

"Magnus, you know damn well that it's not that simple. Miner feels you've earned his trust." Fred paused, and Magnus sensed that he was editing himself, choosing what to reveal and what to keep hidden. "He says he's willing to work with you, but not with me."

Ah. "So I'll meet you both at the plane. Just explain to him that I needed to straighten things out with his daughter. He should be able to accept that."

"Magnus, the man is not thinking about his daughter

right now. He's thinking about walking into a highly volatile situation in a country he hasn't set foot in for over thirty years. And he's worried that we're going to treat him as disposable." Fred sighed. "Come on, Magnus, get it together. There's time to sort things out with Katherine Miner when you get back."

"Give me twenty minutes. I'll try to speak to Katherine before class." Magnus ended the call without waiting for a reply. His head felt like it weighed a ton, and he spent a moment propping it up with his hands.

"More coffee?"

Magnus looked up and found the waitress smiling at him again, coffeepot in hand. Despite the fact that she was probably no older than he was, she had a disconcertingly cronelike appearance. "Excuse me?"

"Coffee?" It was her face, Magnus decided. Underneath the short, hennaed hair, she had the kind of face that belonged in a different century, wearing a black kerchief and a scowl.

"Sure, thanks." He held out his cup. In the background, a man on the radio said something about *muy rápido* in an excited tone of voice. Without understanding any other words, Magnus knew he was selling something. Funny what you could tell without actually speaking a language.

The waitress pointed at his empty plate. "You want something else? Sandwich? Pastry?"

"That would be nice." Now the voice on the radio was female, saying something in a tone of voice that suggested a desire to lick the listener's body from the toes on up. Magnus figured she was selling something, too. He wondered if she'd had to convince herself that what she was selling was any good, or if she just felt comfortable lying.

Looking out the window at the overcast sky, Magnus felt

an inexplicable wave of nostalgia for Iceland. He imagined what it might be like to take Katherine there.

Now, that was one thing they hadn't mentioned in spy school—the fact that sexual intimacy could be a double-edged sword.

Although maybe he was overreacting. There was always the possibility that Katherine might forgive him for lying and manipulating her and her son in order to get to her father. Okay, so it wasn't the best basis for beginning a relationship, but neither was blind romantic illusion.

The waitress returned with a plate of something glazed and sticky. Magnus thanked her and realized that he had completely lost his appetite. Twenty more minutes before class. What the hell was he going to say to her?

His cell phone rang again.

"Fred?"

"Magnus, how long have you and I been friends? Four years? Five?" Fred sounded tired.

"That sounds about right."

"What is it, you're in love with this woman? Is that what's going on?"

"That's not the point, Fred."

"Well, what is the point? Explain the point to me, so I can understand and figure out what to tell Ken who keeps asking me when you're going to arrive!" Fred lowered his voice. "Magnus, if you don't show up soon, I think he's going to walk."

Magnus rubbed his forehead. "Did you tell him that I just want to speak to his daughter? How hard can that be to understand?"

"Hey, I'm your friend, and I don't understand it. This isn't a Hollywood movie where you have to tell the girl you love her before the plane takes off or else you lose her forever. It's real life. You call her in a week or so, you guys will work it out. But Ken Miner here has got a case of galloping conspiracy theory, and the only person he trusts is you. He says you're different, you don't operate like a typical asshole government agent. That was a direct quote, by the way. If you don't walk through that door in the next few minutes, Ken Miner says he's going to walk out of it."

There was a burning sensation in Magnus's stomach. "Fine. Tell him I'll be there by nine-thirty." Magnus figured that gave him just enough time catch Katherine before class began and at least tell her that he was going away. As long as he caught a subway or a cab back to Fred's apartment, he should make it before Miner's nerves got the better of him.

"That's way too late—" Fred began, but Magnus was already switching off his cell phone.

If I hadn't agreed to work with the man, Magnus thought, I might still be under the impression that we were friends. But friends weren't prepared to drop you the minute you messed up. That was what case officers did. They smiled at you like friends, and they went fishing with you like friends, and they drank beer with you like friends. They even offered advice and gave you a nifty job. But when the relationship no longer served their interests, case officers cut you loose and closed your file.

No wonder Dashiell wants a dog. Magnus thought he might want a dog, too.

"You don't like the pastry?" The waitress was leaning over the counter, displaying either her gold cross or her cleavage, or possibly both.

"No, it's great." Magnus hoped he'd have time to pick up some antacid before heading off to Kyrgyzstan.

"You want anything else?" The waitress looked hopeful.

"Not right now." I'll leave her a generous tip, thought Magnus. He reached behind him and discovered that he'd forgotten to take his wallet, which was kind of funny, since part of his homework assignment had been to rate apologies from the more formal to highly informal. "I owe you an apology," he said, picking a phrase from the middle of the stack. "I seem to have left my money at home, but I'll be back here tomorrow."

The scowl he had sensed behind all the waitresses' smiles finally made its appearance.

"Fine," she said, giving him a look that said, Men have been disappointing me from the time I was a young girl.

Without money for transportation, he was out of options. As it was, he'd have to run the whole way back to Midtown on a full stomach. *Shit.* Magnus took a deep breath of air that tasted like cold rain. As he picked up his pace, a garbage truck rattled past, splashing him with foul-smelling mud.

Magnus wiped his face on the front of his T-shirt without breaking stride. Was he doing the right thing? He had no idea, but it didn't seem right to put his personal happiness ahead of matters of state. Jesus, his stomach hurt. Not that he was complaining. All things considered, Magnus thought he deserved a case of heartburn.

chapter *thirty-three*

•

five minutes late, Kat thought, I am only five minutes late. Not so awful by American standards, certainly not even close to insult time. She would have been even later had she listened to her mother, who'd kept insisting that everyone at the institute would understand that she'd just been through a terrible emotional upset.

Sure, Kat had responded. I'll just say that the student I was sleeping with turned out to be a spy. The administration is sure to be filled with compassion over that one. Besides, she'd realized that she actually wanted to go to work. For three hours, at least, she wouldn't be thinking about the perfidy of men. And she was actually quite curious to see whether anyone had completed her soap opera assignment. Maybe she could write little scripts for her students, and let them act out various scenarios. Going for job interviews. Settling arguments. Handling awkward social situations.

Kat walked into her classroom and found Marcy standing in front of her class, wearing a hideous purple sweater dress and an expression of extreme consternation.

"Oh, hi, Marcy. Thanks for filling in for me. Sorry I'm a little late, everyone." She noticed that Magnus wasn't there— no big surprise. What could he possibly want from her now, and why would he take the chance that she'd publicly blow his cover and destroy his career? Not that she would ever do that. She wasn't vindictive. Bitter, yes, but not vindictive.

Kat turned back to Marcy. "I can take over now."

Marcy bit her lower lip. "Nobody called you?"

"Called me about what?"

"Um, I don't think you were supposed to come in today."

Kat felt a sinking sensation in her stomach, and willed herself to ignore it. "Somebody must have gotten mixed up. The infomercial was yesterday, and I only took one day off."

Marcy looked profoundly uncomfortable. "Maybe you should speak to the head office."

"Now? But I'm here already, so I might as well teach. I can straighten this out after class ends."

Marcy opened her mouth, but before she could respond the door opened and Arabella Simms stuck her head in. "Hello, Kat. I was hoping to catch you before you got in, but I got a call from London."

Kat took one look at the Persky Institute's regional supervisor, neatly pretty in an aqua maternity dress, and knew she was in deep trouble. "What's wrong?"

"Why don't we step into my office for a sec," said Arabella, as if they were two good pals about to look over some wallpaper patterns.

Kat took one last look at her classroom. There was Nabil, looking as if he expected her to be hauled off and interrogated, and Maria, who was either extremely upset or having a contraction. Chieko appeared embarrassed, while Galina seemed ready to do battle. "Do good work, guys." She wondered what he was doing now; writing up a report, probably. She wondered if she'd get in trouble with the U.S. government for throwing his spare shoes out in the trash.

Luc, as usual, hadn't arrived yet.

Kat walked into Arabella's office, acutely aware that she was wearing her faded work jeans and an old Billy Idol sweatshirt. The institute didn't have a precise dress code, but looking like an over-the-hill teenager probably wasn't helping her cause.

"Look, Kat," said Arabella as she settled herself behind her desk, "it's not easy for me to say this. I think you know how highly I think of you, but you've been absent an awful lot lately."

"There've been some unusual circumstances." Sitting across from her flushed, pretty, fertile boss, Kat felt inadequate in almost every way.

Arabella nodded. "Yes, I know. You took a personal day yesterday to act in some commercial, another last week for an audition, and yet another personal day a fortnight ago when your son was sick. Now, while I'm well aware that raising a child on your own can't be easy, we do expect a certain degree of consistency from our teachers. And I am aware that you also continue to pursue acting opportunities." She let that sink in before adding, "and from the amount of coverage you seem to be receiving in certain papers, acting would seem to be your priority right now."

Oh, dear God, Arabella had seen the tabloid story. Kat noticed the diamond eternity band sparkling on the English-woman's left hand, which was demurely clasping her right. Kat tried to recall how long her boss had been married—two years? Three? A very brief eternity. But there'd be another diamond for her after she gave birth, along with all the Baby Gap gifts from work, the Tiffany's silver rattles from her New York friends, and good wishes and a deluxe pram from her pals back in England.

She'd probably get her figure back right away, too.

"Now, Kat," Arabella went on. "You know that we pride ourselves on the high caliber of our teaching staff. It takes more than just good language skills to be a Persky instructor. It requires a high degree of people skills to respond to a wide range of cultural and personal differences, as well as a lot of charisma to hold the disparate group together."

Kat felt a rush of relief. *She's not going to punish me, otherwise why give me the training manual speech? This must be my official reprimand.* Kat figured she just had to look contrite for two more minutes and it would all be over.

"And you know, like many of our admin staff, I started out as a teacher myself before becoming an instruction supervisor, then a program rep, and finally a district director."

"I think I know what you're getting at," said Kat, "and I want to tell you that I'm giving up acting. I've decided to focus all of my creative energies on teaching." Kat figured this sounded better than "No one wants to hire me as an actor so I'm going to cling to this pathetic little job like a life raft." But strangely enough, Kat found that she didn't feel like she was just handing Arabella a line.

Kat sat up straighter in her chair. "I've actually gotten to the point where I'm more interested in utilizing my acting experience as a teaching tool. I know a lot of great techniques for overcoming self-consciousness, observing details, picking up on cultural nuances." As soon as the words left her mouth, Kat felt a burst of real enthusiasm. She could give the students something that other teachers could not. Kat was suddenly reminded that in life as well as on stage, pretense can be the key to unlocking real emotions.

Arabella looked unhappy. "That's admirable, Kat, but it sounds to me as if your interests may be taking you in a different direction. We have our way of doing things here, and they've worked really well for us." Grasping the sides of her chair, Arabella got awkwardly to her feet. "And while we are very sorry to see you go, I am certain you will find a way to put your talents to good use."

Kat's heart gave a little stutter. "Pardon me?"

Arabella placed a protective hand on the high mound of her belly, clearly fearing unpleasantness. "If you wish to remain on as a tutor for individual students, I'd be happy to add your name to the list of available teachers for private instruction."

"I'm sorry," said Kat, still sitting. "I don't understand. Are you trying to tell me that this isn't a warning? You're firing me now, as in today?"

"I am sorry, but you left us with no other choice. You have not shown the commitment to our students that we require, and have not adhered to the curriculum."

Kat stood up, suddenly furious. "I can understand punishing me for missing too many classes, but are you actually telling me I'm being fired because I took my students on a class trip?"

"You never even tried to clear it with me first. And then I hear that you're assigning television programs as homework. Quite frankly, Kat, that is not the kind of teaching we're looking for."

"But don't you want to leave any room for your instructors to innovate?"

"My dear, the Persky method is an innovation. Do you know how many countries all over the world have a Persky Institute? We don't need a bunch of loose cannons, Kat, we need team players."

Kat, who had always prided herself on taking rejection in stride, suddenly wondered if she had entered a new phase of her life where no one wanted anything she had to offer.

chapter *thirty-four*

•

the moment Kat stepped outside, a cool wind whipped her hair across her face and the sky gave an ominous crack of thunder. Lovely, it was going to rain on her now.

"Katherine? What is the matter?"

Kat looked up to find Luc looking at her with concern, his unruly dark hair falling over one eye, an unlit cigarette dangling from the corner of his mouth. With his five o'clock shadow and battered black rancher's coat, he lacked only a black Stetson and a six shooter to complete the picture of sexy desperado.

"I've been fired."

"But why? You are a wonderful teacher. The soap opera assignment you gave? I really enjoyed watching, and look, I made a list of expressions I did not understand." He held up a small pad, on which he'd written: I'll have to make do, You're not cut out for it, I have to get this off my chest. "That other teacher, the mousy blonde? She bores me."

Kat squeezed her eyes shut. There was another rumble of thunder. "Thanks for being so nice, Luc, but Marcy is really good. Give her a chance."

Luc traced the shadows under Kat's eyes with a gentle finger. "You are not well. You need sleep, and I think maybe also some food?"

Kat looked at Luc, thinking, he is so impossibly young, this is probably the first time he's ever tried to take care of someone. "I'll be fine," she told him. "Go on and get inside."

Luc shook his head. "I'm not going to leave you like this."

"I'm fine," she insisted.

"Yes," Luc said, looking intently into her eyes, "you are. And that is why I am not letting you leave on your own." Kat suddenly realized that he wasn't just flirting; Luc had a crush on her. It was such a balm to her wounded ego that she was tempted to say yes. Almost.

"You're very sweet, Luc, but I just need to be on my own."

And then it started to rain, a few fat drops rapidly turning into a downpour. It was such a clichéd capper to a horrible morning that Kat started to laugh. At least she thought it was a laugh. It did come out a little ragged, but her face was so wet even she wasn't sure if she was crying.

"Come." Luc took her by the arm and led her to the subway.

Kat wasn't sure what she'd been expecting from Luc—not a four-star restaurant, certainly, but possibly a quaint little bistro, someplace with tiny tables and a wood-fired oven, where the coffee was served in oversized French cups and the menu was written on a chalkboard.

Or possibly something ethnic—a Thai noodle shop, California Mexican, a falafel joint.

Instead, Kat found herself following Luc around the supermarket as he pushed a cart around, disparaged the meat and complained about the state of the vegetables.

Luc, whose long black coat had repelled the worst of the rain, held up a tiny, vacuum-packed filet mignon. "What do they do, embalm the meat for future generations? It will have no flavor. I know, I will make you a steak with Roquefort." Luc suddenly looked perturbed. "You do have Roquefort in America, yes?"

Kat pushed her wet hair back off her face. Her jacket and jeans were soaked through from the walk to the subway, and she wished she could just go home alone and jump into a bath. "It's probably in the gourmet foods section. But listen, Luc, I'm afraid that dish sounds a bit rich for me. And where are you planning on cooking this meal anyway?"

"At your place, of course." He gave her a comically wolfish look. "Unless you are too anxious that I may try to seduce you?"

Kat folded her arms under her chest. "Here's an expression for you! That dog won't hunt. Do I need to explain it?"

"Why is it that Americans always want to explain everything? When you explain, explain, explain, you take something away, *n'cest-ce pas?* Sometimes it is enough to feel the hint of a possibility." Luc paused in front of a display of imported cheeses. "Ah, Roquefort does exist here, and not just the nasty blue stuff."

Feeling a bit humbled by his previous observation, Kat gave him a smile. "See? We're not complete barbarians."

"No, of course not. So how is life with your new boarder?" Luc picked up a bottle of balsamic vinegar. "He has moved in already?"

Kat shivered, her damp clothes chilling her. "He's moved out."

Luc raised one eyebrow. "Very interesting. Am I allowed to ask the reason?"

As Kat started to reply, she saw a familiar, masculine shape in an oatmeal-colored sweater, standing between a pyramid of canned goods and a display of artisanal cheeses.

Logan. Standing next to some strawberry blonde who had her back to Kat. As Luc burbled on about trust and the French and food, Kat stared. Luc finally noticed Kat's expression. "What is it, Katherine? Is something wrong?" Kat turned to Luc. "Put your arm around me."

Luc raised one eyebrow, but slid his arm around her waist, making the gesture look easy and natural. "We are performing for someone?"

"My ex-husband is here." She couldn't bring herself to call him anything else. In her heart, he was ex, even if the courts hadn't made it official yet.

"Ah. And has he seen you yet?"

"I don't think so."

"Well, let's make him notice us." Luc's hand slid down to cup Kat's ass, and she gave a startled laugh.

"Now, hold on one moment . . ."

Luc's smile was full of mischief. "But I am holding on. You do comprehend that I intend to take advantage of this situation?" His arm tightened, and Kat felt her body respond. Whether or not she was attracted to Luc as a person, there was a certain chemistry here. Not the total mind-body connection that made you feel like taking up permanent residence in the other person's life, but something more insidious—the promise of breezy, self-contained, guilt-free pleasure, the infamous Jongian zipless fuck.

Except that Kat was aware that in the real world, true zip-less fucking was as rare as true love. In the end, clothes and phobias and sometimes even ovaries got in the way, leaving you with unexpected repercussions, such as being thirty-one and pregnant. And then it was all too easy to think, Maybe there's something more here than meets the eye, maybe this relationship does have legs.

Ten years was a long time to spend learning otherwise.

As Luc continued to inspect fruit with his right hand, Kat noticed Logan turn in their direction and become aware of her presence. At first, she thought he was going to say something, but then, to her shock, she saw him begin walking away, pushing his wagon down the fruit and vegetable aisle.

"That shit!" Kat felt her breath hiss out of her clenched teeth. "I can't believe it! He's going to pretend he didn't see us." Although why she shouldn't believe it, Kat wasn't sure. Perhaps it was just that she'd thought that, faced with the physical reality of an estranged wife, he wouldn't be able to just continue acting as though she and Dashiell had no connection to him.

"Calm yourself. You wish a confrontation, yes? But how do you wish to appear—bitter, furious, miserable? Or do you prefer him to see that you are happy in your life, and that to you, he is dirt, he is underneath your contempt?"

"Beneath my contempt sounds great, but he's the father of my son, who wants to see him." Kat dragged her hand through her hair. "Christ, I don't know what to do."

"Then allow me."

So Kat followed along as Luc took charge of their shopping cart, moving them purposefully down the fruit and vegetable aisle. He spotted Logan before she did, and before she could ask him what he planned to do next, Luc called out, "Hey!

Oh, my God! It's that guy from the soap opera! Look, *chérie*, it's him!"

Instantly, every head in the store swiveled to stare, first at Luc, and then at Logan. Kat felt her face heat, completely at a loss. In Manhattan, a place where Oscar winners, notorious criminals, and even Woody Allen could walk around the streets unmolested and unremarked on, there was a strong, unwritten taboo against outing the famous in public.

Logan was regarding her with such cold fury that Kat had to stop herself from apologizing for Luc's behavior.

"Hello, Kat," he said. "I see you haven't lost your taste for making scenes in public."

Okay, that took care of any lingering feelings of embarrassment. "And I see that *you* still prefer running and hiding to confronting any kind of unpleasant emotion."

"Oh, I don't know," Logan said, his voice heavy with sarcasm, "I managed to hang in there for ten years of unpleasant emotions."

"Oh, please, you checked out of our marriage way before you walked out the door. Just admit that you're a coward when it comes to facing the consequences of your actions."

A strange expression crossed Logan's face. "Actually," he said, his voice dripping with venom, "I was thinking of your feelings. But by all means, let's have it all out in public. It's not as if you ever had a thought or a feeling you didn't share with everyone." For the first time, Kat noticed Logan's companion.

"Hello, Kat," said Zandra, stepping out from her partial concealment behind a display of canned olives. Kat felt as though she'd been sucker punched in the gut.

"You didn't need to hide," she said slowly, taking in the changes in Zandra's appearance. "I barely would have recognized you." At some point in the past few days, Zandra had straightened her hair and lightened it to strawberry blond. It didn't suit her. "What is this, all of a sudden you two are best buddies?"

Zandra shrugged, unrepentant. "I had a fight with you, Kat, not with Logan."

"That's it? That's your excuse?"

"I wasn't aware I needed one."

"But you know what he's done. You remember how you felt when your husband left you. Don't you have any loyalty to another woman?"

Zandra and Logan exchanged glances. Something about the quality of that shared look—some intimacy, or complicity—suddenly made Kat see this whole scene in a different light. "You're sleeping with him, aren't you?" Neither Zandra nor Logan denied it. "Jesus, you are." Her first thought was absurdly shallow: But you're not pretty enough. And then Kat realized that pretty had nothing to do with it. Zandra was always outspoken about how uninhibited she was sexually. And God knew she pulled out all the stops when it came to pleasing a man—serving up the guy's favorite meals, giving him little gifts, wearing sexy little outfits to bed.

Like she had for her mystery lover, the semi-famous, semi-married guy.

I am such an idiot. Kat shook her head in disbelief. "How long has this been going on?" When had Zandra started looking so much better? Last winter? Last fall? *About the time she started drawing closer to Marcy and away from me.* Once you knew, it was strange to think you hadn't seen the obvious clues all along. "How could you pretend to be my friend while you were sleeping with my husband?"

Zandra rolled her eyes. "Oh, stop it, Kat, it's not a scene

from your soap. You knew he had other women, just as he knew you had other men."

"You're wrong about me. But even if I had cheated, how could you lie to my face and not feel any guilt?"

Not a flicker of remorse crossed Zandra's carefully made up face. "The part of me that was your friend was completely separate from the part of me that became his lover."

Kat shivered, both from cold and distaste. "All those self-help courses and spirituality weekends, you really did need them, because there's something missing in you. You don't have a conscience."

"Come on, Kat." Logan sounded irritated and impatient, a familiar combination. "I mean, here you are, shopping with your boy toy, so stop making out like you're Mother Teresa."

Kat had forgotten Luc was even there, but the comparison brought her back to life. "It's hardly the same thing."

"Of course it is," said Luc, and underneath his sly, provocative tone, Kat heard something she hadn't before. A hint of steel. "He is cheating on you, you are cheating on him—it's just the way of the world. Am I right, my friend?"

Logan did not look thrilled at being called Luc's friend.

"Although I have to say about your choice, *quelle horreur*. But, let's face it, most of the time, we wind up fucking some-one we know—a co-worker, a wife's friend, a friend's wife. It's not nice, but it's real life, eh?" Luc dropped his bantering tone completely. "But when you leave the child along with the mother, you do harm."

Logan narrowed his eyes. "Yeah, well, if I'm such a shit, maybe the kid's better off without me."

Kat put her hand on Luc's shoulder, silently thanking him. "You know what, Logan? Maybe he is. But it's hard for me to watch him when he's in pain, and he is in such pain over losing you. Even if you're mad at me, how can you take it out on your son?"

"Now, look, Kat." Logan was using his reasonable, even-tempered, North Madigan voice, the one he'd used when she'd start to cry, sleep-deprived and overwhelmed, that it was always her turn to go to the baby. "You're the one who has turned this into a fight. You know what you need to do to make things right between us."

"Are you talking about putting the apartment up for sale?"

"Look, it's not the money. It's the principle of the thing. You're sitting on our single biggest asset and pretending that the apartment hasn't gone up in value, and that it shouldn't even be considered as part of the settlement."

Kat wondered if she looked as disgusted as she felt. Had Logan changed, or had he always been like this? "How can you talk about principles? Your son asks for you, and I don't know what to say to him. 'Sorry, Dash, your dad's too busy screwing my best friend to see you for an hour.' "

"Maybe I would find time if you weren't such a suffocating mother. I guess you couldn't help it, since your mother never gave you room to breathe. Quite frankly, I'm doing you a favor by making you move away from that apartment."

The pain and anger were so overwhelming that Kat was blindsided. She couldn't find a single thing to say. This, she thought, was the kind of rage that led women to reverse their SUV's over their husbands, put their cars into drive, and then shift back to reverse in order to do it all over again.

And Logan wasn't finished yet. "After we've sorted out this divorce, then I'll be free to form my own relationship with Dashiell."

"You mean after I cave in to your demands. How much is

it going to cost me to have you spend an afternoon with your son? What's the going rate for your personal appearances?"

Logan sighed. "This is why I kept trying to communicate through my lawyer. There's no way to speak rationally with you."

For a moment, there was a ringing in Kat's ears, and then she became aware of her surroundings—the hum of the store's air conditioner, the canned soft rock coming from hidden loudspeakers, the shoppers pretending they weren't listening to every word.

"You know what, Logan? You may sound calm and logical and like you simply have an alternate point of view, but let's boil it all down to actions. You've abandoned your son both emotionally and financially. You want to fight this out with lawyers? Fine. I can't really afford it and it'll hurt Dashiell, but you know what? It's going to hurt you, too. Because you play nice guys on TV and in the movies, but in real life, Logan, you are a piece of shit."

Kat turned to Zandra. "And as for you, I hope you know he has other women. He's not in love with you, because he's not capable. But as far as I'm concerned, you both deserve each other because you're both morally bankrupt."

Whatever Zandra or Logan might have wanted to say in response was cut off out by the sound of Luc, slowly clapping his hands.

After a moment, a heavyset woman joined in. "That's right," she said in a big voice. "You tell it, sister." One of the other shoppers gave a sharp whistle of approval. As if that were a signal, other people began applauding, and shouting out things like "deadbeat" and "he's not even that good-looking in person."

Her burst of angry adrenaline spent, Kat closed her eyes.

When she opened them again, Logan and Zandra were gone, and Luc was smiling. "Brava," he said, "well done. How do you feel now?"

Kat put her arms around her stomach. "Like I'm going to throw up."

chapter *thirty-five*

•

twenty minutes after her initial bout of post-traumatic stomach disorder, Kat turned the key in her lock. Dear God, she thought, finally home and finally alone. Getting rid of Luc had been the high point of her day. He had kept smiling at her as if she'd performed a scene from some romantic farce for his benefit. Were all young men that oblivious? And if so, how could any woman over thirty-five endure it?

Kat let the front door slam behind her, taking stock of herself as if she'd just walked away from a terrible accident. Strangely enough, she didn't seem to be feeling anything in particular. Not hurt. Not angry. Not even terribly upset. In fact, Kat felt a little as if she'd been given a shot of Novocain, only it wasn't her mouth that felt thick and numb, it was her whole being.

Dropping her pocketbook on a chair, Kat discovered that

she wasn't queasy anymore. In fact, she thought she might have regained some appetite. Which was good. Appetite was good. Kat consumed a cinnamon bun, a peach, and four slices of turkey bacon before it occurred to her that maybe the hollow feeling in her stomach wasn't hunger.

Perhaps this sudden burst of compulsive eating was really a displacement activity, in which case the healthy thing to do would be to slow down and find some other way to take care of herself.

Kat found a box of individually wrapped low-calorie cookies and tore open a packet.

The phone rang, startling her. She listened as the answering machine picked up. "Kat? Is that you? It's Marcy. Just wanted to see how you're doing."

Kat waited for her friend to hang up. All she wanted to do was disappear inside herself. She took off her jeans, which were cutting into her waist, and lay down in bed. The sheets were cold, and the windowpanes were rattling. Across the street, Kat saw that the slender trees on the penthouse opposite were swaying in the wind. With each gust, a few more leaves blew away.

Kat burrowed under her covers, shivering. It had been bad enough to know that her friendship with Zandra was broken and couldn't go on, but this loss was worse. This was the loss of everything that had gone before, because now the past had to be reinterpreted to make sense of Zandra's betrayal.

Kat remembered the two of them pushing baby carriages down Broadway, struggling to eat lunch in a diner while the boys threw food on the floor, learning how to fold strollers before the bus drove away. Those fraught, early days of motherhood had been like boot camp, creating an instant, wartime intimacy.

God, she'd adored Zandra back then. All the other new mothers she'd met had taken it all so seriously: buying the right diaper, making homemade baby food, speaking to their child in clumsy college French so the kid would grow up bilingual. Zandra had been different—fun, irreverent, relaxed, playing old Beatles tunes instead of nursery rhymes, shouting out the chorus to "Maxwell's Silver Hammer" with vindictive delight.

In retrospect, Kat conceded, vindictive delight didn't seem like such a terrific quality.

But at the time, Kat had taken a great deal of comfort from Zandra's tart sense of humor. She'd been so frank and funny about being on her own, and since Kat had basically felt like a single mother herself, they had joked about how irrelevant men were, how they really needed to be married to each other. She'd told Zandra about hating her postpregnancy breasts; Zandra had talked about her own adolescent insecurities about her looks. She knew that Zandra had been put in a mental hospital for two weeks when she'd been sixteen.

So how could Zandra have slept with Logan? For some reason, it didn't surprise her that Logan had cheated on her with her best friend. If a man could justify dropping out of his son's life, then he could justify anything. But Zandra had come to her house, eaten her food, offered advice. Being capable of that level of duplicity was a talent. Maybe Zandra should get a job with Magnus.

Kat rolled over in bed, clutching her bloated stomach. She didn't want to think about Magnus. It stung too much, remembering how she'd dismissed him at first as some big, earnest clod, a nice guy, but not smart or edgy enough to really push her buttons.

The wind blew hard against the windows again and Kat pulled the covers over her head.

You had to hand it to the CIA; they might not be able to distinguish a weapon of mass destruction from a goat farm, but they sure had seducing women down to a fine art. First, find a guy who could slide right under her defenses. Then, let him slowly reveal his intelligence and sensitivity and strength, giving her the impression that she was the one peeling back the layers. Boy, had that been effective. Maybe the U.S. government should try that as an interrogation technique. Amnesty International couldn't really object to a lot of lovelorn prisoners complaining that their feelings had been badly hurt, and that their pride had suffered irreparable damage.

As far as Kat could recall, dumping your lover was not proscribed under the Geneva Convention, no matter how humiliated and ill-used the dumpee felt afterward.

The phone rang. "Kat? Are you home? It's Daphne. Listen, I meant to call you to find out how the infomercial turned out, but I also have to tell you that we've just had a rather unusual offer. I don't know how you're going to feel about this, but the *Hollywood Report* TV show wants to interview you for their segment on messy divorces. I hope you're not offended, but I did feel I ought to relay the message, since they're offering a nice sum of money. Well, call me back."

Oh, crap, somebody must have already found out about the supermarket incident. Kat wondered if there were going to be photographs in the tabloids tomorrow.

The phone rang again. "Katsala? Honey, are you there?" *Great. Her mother.* Kat put a pillow over her head and muttered, "Leave me alone."

Silence. Kat sat up. And then, just as she was swinging her legs out of bed, she heard the front door slam. Kat walked out into the hall and found her mother carrying a meatloaf pan.

"Mom? What are you doing here?"

Lia smiled broadly. "Oh! Honey! You're here! I called, but no one answered. I was reading manuscripts from home today, and I thought we could eat dinner together."

"So you just decided to waltz into my apartment and stick food in my fridge?" Kat knew she was being bitchy, but she couldn't stop herself. Today, she felt fifteen again, filled with a roiling mixture of irritation and anguish and, underneath it all, the sneaking suspicion that there must be something very wrong with her, because why else would so many people be treating her so badly?

"No need to take that tone with me, Katherine. You have more room in your fridge, and it's not like you ever cook. Besides, I wasn't expecting you. Aren't you supposed to be teaching today?"

"I was fired."

"Oh, honey." All trace of irritation was gone from Lia's voice.

"And I ran into Logan. With Zandra. Turns out they've been having an affair." The words came out stiffly, like badly rehearsed lines. I'm going to have to learn how to tell this better, thought Kat.

"No wonder you're so upset. Your father had a fling with our landlady in Rome, and I remember how mad I was."

Kat buried her face in her hands. She didn't want to hear this. She was already on emotional overload. The last thing she needed was more information to process. "Mom, please, why are you telling me this now?"

"It seemed pertinent. Tell me something. Are you beginning to have any signs of perimenopause? Because sometimes mood swings can be brought on by hormone surges."

On the verge of tears, Kat found herself laughing. "I think I still have that to look forward to, Mom. Listen, I am sorry if this sounds harsh, but at this particularly horrible moment in time, I would like to be able to lie in bed and stare at the ceiling without having to deal with anybody."

"I understand completely," said Lia, heading into the kitchen. "I won't be a sec." Kat counted to three before following. She found her mother regarding her refrigerator shelves with clear disapproval.

"You have no space in here. Don't you ever organize things?" Lia pulled out a Tupperware container. "What's in here, for example? I bet this can be thrown out."

Kat started to tremble. Suddenly, the sight of her mother poking around in her fridge seemed a symbol of all the ways in which her life was not under her control. "Mom."

Lia, her head still inside the fridge, waved the container behind her. "Just smell it. If I know you, it's probably old tunafish."

"Mom, I'm going to have to ask you to leave now. And I also want to suggest that instead of just knocking and entering, which is considered polite in France, you knock and then wait to be invited in, which is considered polite in this country."

This brought Lia out of the refrigerator. "Well, excuse me for worrying about you."

Translation: I don't think you're competent to handle your life right now. "I don't need you to worry about me, Mom."

"Oh, yeah? When is the last time you and Dash had red meat?"

"Mom, I do not want to eat your meatloaf tonight!"

"Fine," said Lia, her accent becoming distinctly chilly and vaguely British. "Maybe Dash would like some. I'll just come by around six to take a little for my dinner. We don't even have to eat together."

Kat felt like a very small boat bobbing along in the wake of an ocean liner. And then she remembered what Logan had called her: a suffocating mother. *I guess you couldn't help it, since your mother never gave you room to breathe. Quite frankly, I'm doing you a favor by making you move away from that apartment.*

Ouch, Kat thought, finally able to identify the strange, hollow feeling in her middle. It was the sensation of a criticism that had hit its target. Logan might be a selfish, self-serving bastard, but in this instance he was not entirely wrong. Of course, loving your child so much that you tended to get a bit too involved wasn't a mortal parenting sin. In fact, it wasn't a sin at all. But it wasn't completely benign either. Because when you tried to do too much for a grown child, you wound up sending some unintentional messages.

Or maybe you didn't send the messages. Maybe "excuse me for worrying about you" didn't really mean "I don't think you're feeding your son properly." Kat's advanced English students often got confused at the distinction between *implied* and *inferred,* and with good reason. When you get too close to someone, you can forget that all forms of communication are fraught with mixed signals, errors, misunderstandings. What you think is a hint of anger in someone's voice might be nothing more than fatigue. What seems like indifference might be caution. What feels like criticism could be concern. *What if I've been assuming all the wrong things about my mom?*

Kat realized that her mother was talking to her. "But if you do decide to eat the meatloaf, all it needs is half an hour at three hundred degrees."

"Mom, this isn't going to work."

"What? The meatloaf? It's delicious, I put in a packet of dried onion soup and Worcestershire sauce."

Kat reached out and took her mother's hand. "Living next door. I can't do this."

"Oh, for God's sake. Talk about your wild overreactions! Katherine, think for a minute. You're in the middle of a divorce. How many changes do you think you can take on at once?"

Kat took a deep breath and looked her mother in the eye. "As many as I have to."

To Kat's surprise, Lia didn't argue. Instead, she cocked her head to one side, as if trying to make sure she was hearing everything correctly. "I see. Do you know what your next step will be?" Her tone was carefully neutral.

For some reason, her mother's calm acceptance made everything seem perfectly clear.

"I'm going to call my lawyer and tell him that I'm willing to put the apartment up for sale, provided that Logan is willing to agree to alimony in addition to child support."

"I thought you'd decided against asking for alimony." Lia had been quite vocal in her disagreement with Kat on the subject.

"Well, I'm reconsidering. At the time, I thought I'd be able to pick up my career where I left off. Now that I know better, I figure I'm in the same position as any woman who got off the career ladder in order to raise her child. If Logan wants to be symbolic about selling this apartment, fine—so long as he provides me with enough money to buy a place in the neighborhood. I'll make sure we're still in easy walking distance, so Dash can visit you on his own when he's a little older."

"That sounds lovely, but have you considered what you'll do if Logan simply moves back overseas and reneges on his side of the bargain?"

No, she hadn't, but Kat wasn't about to admit that to her

mother. She smiled, and it felt a little crooked on her face. "Well, I've just gotten an offer to sell my story to tabloid TV. It wouldn't be my first choice, but it remains an option. And a way to threaten Logan."

Lia nodded slowly. "All right, then," she said. "It sounds like you have a plan."

Kat shook her head slowly in disbelief. "You make such a fuss about the small stuff that I always forget how great you are in a real crisis."

"That's the way it's always been with the women in our family. My mother was more upset with my bad grade in home ec than she was with my getting a divorce."

Kat kissed her mother on the cheek. "I love you, Mom."

"I love you, too."

And for once, they managed to leave things on that note.

chapter *thirty-six*

•

as expensive as it was to make lawyers repeat things, Kat decided it was worth it. "Say it again, Mr. Tatelbaum," she said. "Say it slowly, so I can savor the moment."

Her lawyer laughed, the first time Kat had ever heard him do so. "As I stated previously, if your husband is in noncompliance with the separation agreement, there are legal steps we can take, such as getting a court order to prevent his leaving the country. Why didn't you call me when you first discovered that he was in the city?"

Kat sank into a chair, shaking her head. "I just didn't think of it. My God, do you know what this means? We have leverage. We have a great, big, crowbar of leverage. The producers of Logan's film are not going to like the idea of their star being stuck on the wrong side of the Atlantic."

"Yes, well, I'm happy to be the bearer of such good news."

Kat's lawyer sounded like a man for whom "happy" was a relative term. Kat supposed that practicing divorce law would make anyone wary of too much emotion, whether it was good or not. "Now, I'd better get to work."

Kat said good-bye and checked the clock. Hard to believe it was only two o'clock. The day felt like it had already lasted for more than twenty-four hours.

What should she do now? Kat knew she should probably start figuring out exactly how she was going to earn a living, but the question was just too overwhelming. Should she be practical and take a temping job, or get some kind of computer training? She'd been in her early twenties the last time she'd worked as a temp, back before computers and the Internet became part of everyone's daily life.

Oh, God, I am old. Kat splashed some water on her face, brushed her hair back into a neater ponytail and decided that she'd done enough for one day.

Fresh air and exercise, she thought, that's what I need. Maybe I'll pick Dash up from school. Still a little full from her misery binge, Kat changed out of her jeans and into a comfortable red skirt with a dropped waist. She put on a pair of Frye cowboy boots, which gave her walk a little swagger, grabbed a denim jacket and imagined the expression on Dashiell's face when he saw her.

Kat signed in with the guard in the school's lobby, then made her way to Mrs. Rizer's fourth-grade classroom. The pervasive, slightly sour smell of cafeteria food and sweaty socks filled the corridors, reminding her of her own school days and giving her a strange feeling of nostalgia mingled with dread.

She was half an hour early, but instead of dealing with the standard chaos of dismissal, Kat had decided to take Dashiell home immediately. She figured he could use a little treat—an ice cream, some Pokémon cards, maybe even a game of Super Mario Smash Brothers. There was nothing Dashiell liked better than instructing his video-game challenged mother in how to do battle.

Kat peeked into the glass insert in the door to see what Dashiell's class was doing, not wanting to interrupt in the middle of an activity. She spotted Dashiell immediately, as he was sitting in the front, as usual. Teachers learned quickly that if Dashiell wasn't sitting in the front row, he was essentially sitting in his own universe, completely oblivious to what was going on in front of the blackboard. Usually, his friend Riley sat to his left, but today, for some reason, a gaggle of students was gathered around her son. Kat moved to one side, trying to get a better view.

Now she could see that there was a rapidly growing pile of books, papers, wadded up tissues and other detritus around Dashiell's desk. As Kat watched, Dashiell pulled out a pack of playing cards, a notebook, about ten wadded up tissues, and a rubber-band ball. Mrs. Rizer, a tall, thin woman of around fifty or so, said something that made the other students laugh. The scene was vaguely reminiscent of the circus act in which a preposterous number of clowns emerge from an absurdly small vehicle, except that in this case, the performer did not seem to be in on the joke.

Dash looked up at his teacher, his face swollen with unshed tears. He asked her something, and Mrs. Rizer shook her head, pointing back to the desk. The other children laughed, and Kat opened the door with enough force to make the glass pane rattle.

"Excuse me, but exactly what do you think you're doing to my son?"

Mrs. Rizer turned to Kat with a look of hauteur. With her dyed auburn Gibson girl pompadour and her reading glasses permanently perched on the tip of her nose, she did hauteur very well. "Excuse me, Mrs. Miner, I wasn't aware that you were going to be picking Dashiell up from the classroom today. As you can see, we have been having a chronic problem with the untidiness of your son's desk. His inability to find things in a timely fashion has been interfering with both his schoolwork and that of his classmates."

The class, glancing up at Kat uneasily, tittered at this. Dashiell's expression was harder to read—resignation, suppressed anger, a faint hope of rescue. Kat turned back to his teacher. "Mrs. Rizer, do you honestly believe that humiliating my son in front of his classmates is the correct course of action? Do you think the principal would agree?" In some part of her mind, Kat was aware that challenging the teacher's authority in front of her class was not the smartest thing to do, but another, more primitive part of her brain was in charge right now. Her young was being threatened, and Kat wanted to sink her teeth into this bitch.

"If your son is humiliated by the state of his desk, then I would suggest that he organize it." Mrs. Rizer's face was mottled with angry color.

"Did it occur to you that you might have to teach him how? Are you really trying to tell me that Dashiell is the first child you've ever taught who had some difficulty in this area?"

"Of course not," said Mrs. Rizer, looking slightly defensive. "But you're not doing him any favors by coddling him. Children need a firm hand, clear expectations, and to be held to the same standard as their peers."

Kat looked at her son and was reminded of something she'd long forgotten—how powerful teachers are in the lives of children. For a good six hours a day, five days a week, nine months of the year, this woman created the culture in which her son lived. For three quarters of a year, he was hers, ruled by her opinions, subject to her moods, profoundly influenced by her strengths and weaknesses, be they academic, psychological, and emotional. "Mrs. Rizer," Kat said quietly, "whatever you think you're doing here, you are actually encouraging the rest of the class to think that Dashiell is fair game for teasing. And I won't permit it."

As she held the older woman's gaze, Kat could see the moment that Mrs. Rizer realized that she might have overstepped her bounds. "Why don't we talk some more about your son's problem after school," she offered, and then smiled down at Dash. "I think we can come up with some good solutions for keeping your things tidy, don't you?"

Dashiell nodded, clearly grateful.

"I'm sorry," said Kat, "but that's just too little too late. I'm going to have to speak to the principal about this. Dash, grab your things and let's leave."

Dashiell's mouth dropped open. "But we haven't been dismissed. It's not time to go yet."

Kat looked directly at his teacher. "Oh, yes, it is, Dash. Any time you find yourself being mistreated, it is always time to go."

"I can't believe I got out of school early to do this."

Kat tried not to look as queasy as she felt, watching her son clambering fifteen feet over her head on the rock climbing wall. But she'd given him his choice of treats, and this was what he'd wanted. "After what happened to you today, you deserve it." What he didn't deserve, she thought, was the principal's carefully crafted, ingeniously ambiguous reassurances that Mrs. Rizer was a wonderful teacher, al-though of course these were, indeed, valid concerns. The school firmly believed in treating students with dignity and compassion, and Mr. Rivera said he would certainly look into this matter.

Kat's request that her son be transferred into another sec-tion had been denied. "Mr. Rivera, I teach, and let me tell you, what Mrs. Rizer did was vent her own irritation and set a ter-rible precedent for the rest of the class. You can't expect my son to walk into class tomorrow and act as though nothing happened. She abused her authority."

Mr. Rivera had made it clear that to him, the words "a teacher abusing authority" implied corporal punishment or racial epithets, and that publicly shaming a child, while unfor-tunate, was not expressly forbidden by the New York State Bureau of Education.

"Mom, look, I'm at the top!" Kat tilted her head back as her son waved to her from the top of the wall, some twenty-five feet up. Instead of choosing one of the ascents inside the atrium, as she had done with Magnus, Dashiell had chosen one of the more difficult, outside walls. A nanny pushing a stroller along Broadway stopped to watch.

She turned to the young climbing instructor who was be-laying him. "I know it's safe, but it's hard to watch him."

"You should go next," said the instructor, who had short, reddish brown hair and an outdoorswoman's freckles on her face and arms. "Hey, kid," she called up. "Ready to come down now?"

"Sure." Without needing to be told, Dash leaned back on the rope, pressing the soles of his sneakers against the wall. As the instructor let the rope out, Dashiell bounced lightly down, pushing the wall away with his feet.

"That was excellent," said the young woman, slapping his palm with her own. "Do you want to go again? We could try one of the harder indoor ascents." They had bought a discount card worth five climbs, and Dash had already used up two of them.

"No, I want my mom to go. You take a turn, Mom."

Kat shook her head. "Sorry, but I'm not quite dressed for it." She indicated her skirt and cowboy boots.

"You can borrow something! You guys have sweats she can use, right? And they have climbing shoes, too." Dashiell's eyes shone with excitement, and Kat thought, *Even if he weren't my son, even if I didn't adore him, I would like him as a person. Which means that somewhere, there has got to be a place where he could fit in and make friends.*

She glanced over at the wall. "Is it really important to you?"

Dash nodded. "You said you climbed here before. I want to watch you this time."

Hoo, boy. Was she really going to do this? "I think I'm too scared."

Dashiell put his small hand on her arm. "But Mom, it's not a rational fear. You can't get hurt. And once you go up, it's really fun. I want you to see how cool it is."

"How do you know how to say things like 'It's not a rational fear,' anyway?"

Dashiell grinned as if he hadn't just had a traumatic experience not half an hour earlier. "From you, silly."

Kat took a deep breath and looked at the instructor. "Okay. Do you have any sweats I can borrow?"

The young woman hesitated, then said to Dash, "Well, it's not our usual policy, but just this once, your mother can use a clean pair of mine."

Kat changed into the borrowed sweats in a tiny bathroom.

Instead of using the school's climbing shoes, which smelled of mildew, she opted to go barefoot. Why am I doing this, she thought as she stepped into the harness and got clipped to the instructor's rope.

"I want the easiest way up," she said. The instructor led her to a wall in the middle of the atrium. Kat couldn't remember if it was the same wall she'd gone up the last time or not. It seemed higher.

"I'll shine this red light to show you where to go next," said the instructor.

"Go on, Mom, you can do it!"

Kat lifted her left foot onto a large, horizontal protrusion that resembled an amoeba. "Okay," she said. "Here goes. Hope I don't panic and wet your pants."

"You'll be fine," said the instructor. "Just take it one step at a time."

Kat found the first two moves surprisingly easy, and then she made the mistake of looking up. Up was a long way to go. "How far do I need to climb?"

"Now, stop that. Don't get ahead of yourself. Just think about the next step. Don't look up, don't look down. Look straight ahead and concentrate on finding your next foothold. That's it, that's it, when you know where you're standing, then you move your hands."

"You're a good teacher," said Kat, feeling the rush of affection she always felt when someone taught her something.

"Thanks," said the young woman, shining a thin red light on Kat's next handhold.

And that was the thing about teaching, Kat thought. Just like acting, or dance, or art, some people had an aptitude for it, and others did not. And if you had a talent for teaching, as this woman did, then training and experience could hone and focus your natural abilities, but training and experience alone could not instill the gift. Which was how you got people like Mrs. Rizer, who had probably been screwing kids up for the better part of thirty years.

If that had been my class, his desk would never have gotten into that state in the first place.

"You're almost at the top, Mom!"

Instinctively, Kat started to look down, and the sight of her son, on the ground so far below her, made her feel dizzy. "I think that's far enough."

"Just two more steps and you'll be at the top," said the instructor.

Kat felt really light-headed now. *Shit.* With all that she was going through, did she really need to be challenging herself to climb goddamn walls? "I really, really need to come down now."

"Just look at what's in front of you," said the woman calmly. "That's all there is. Just the next foothold."

"Come on, Mom, you can do it!"

Her hands shaking, Kat suddenly heard what the rock climbing instructor was saying, and thought, *The reason I'm up here is because if I can make myself do this, I can do anything. All I have to do is take it one step at a time. Take Dash out of school if I have to. Teach him at home till I can find someplace better for him. Deal with the emotional fallout when he realizes that his father is choosing not to see him.*

Kat climbed another inch. "I can't see where to go next."

A red dot appeared on the handhold above Katherine's left arm. "That's it," said the instructor. Kat reached up, and there was nowhere else to go. She'd made it to the top. She could hear Dashiell cheering and shouting, but she didn't turn around.

"Okay," Kat called out. "What now?"

"Now you relax," shouted the instructor. "This is the easy part."

I need an easy part, thought Kat. It wasn't until she was down on the ground that she discovered she'd given herself a blister on her right hand. But she didn't care. She knew what she wanted to do with her life, and that was worth a little pain.

She hugged her son. "Do you have the energy for one more stop before we head home?"

"Depends. Where do you want to go?"

"I want to pick up some catalogs from Bank Street and Teacher's College. I'm thinking about going back to school."

"What for?"

"I'm not sure yet. I know I'd like to teach, but I'm not sure exactly what."

"You mean, teach kids?"

"I'm considering it. What do you think?"

Dashiell's face darkened. "I'm thinking I wish you could be *my* teacher."

Kat knelt down and took her son's hands. "Well, you know, in the long run, I think you'll be better off with someone else teaching you, because part of growing up is pushing your mother away. But I'm thinking that we need to find a better school for you, and maybe while we're looking, I can teach you for a while."

"Mom, you've just made this the best day of my life. Seriously. I don't have to go back to that school? Really? Awesome. Hey, if I don't have to go to school tomorrow, can I have dinner at Nana's? She said she was going to make meatloaf and I'm dying for some red meat. Oh, and can I sleep over at her house, too? We sure are lucky, living right next door."

Kat kept her smile in place, reminded yet again that parenting was another occupation that required good acting skills.

chapter *thirty-seven*

•

after Dash was settled down in her mother's house for the night, Kat uncorked a bottle of dry Sardinian wine. She didn't normally drink alone, but there was nothing normal about this day. Kat had just poured herself a glass and was about to start reading the Teacher's College course catalog when the phone started ringing. Kat closed her eyes and waited for the answering machine to respond.

"Kat, if you're there, please let me know if you're okay. I've been trying to reach you all day and I'm starting to get worried."

Kat picked up the phone. "Sorry, Marcy. Yeah, I'm all right. I'm just having some wine and trying to figure out what to do next."

"I am so sorry about what happened. They had no right to

fire you like that. I'd quit myself, in protest, but with Steve not working right now, we need the money."

Kat rubbed her right ankle, sore from rock climbing and cowboy boots. "Well, I appreciate the thought, but I would never want you to leave your job because of me. Besides, it's partially my fault. I guess I should have listened when you told me not to take so much time off."

"But she just fired you! Without giving notice!"

Kat glanced at the fat course catalog in front of her. She'd already discovered from the table of contents that there were all kinds of teaching specialties that she hadn't known existed, some of them clearly in great demand. Knowing she had options made her feel a bit more philosophical about losing her old job. "You know how it is. When you're a new queen, you tend to look for someone to execute. Plus, I'm sure the fact that I was breaking with company policy and going out on field trips probably didn't help me any."

"I think it was a brilliant idea. All my students have been asking if we can leave the classroom, too." In the background, Kat heard the sound of a man's voice in the background, sounding faintly irritable. "Just two more minutes, Steve, I'm almost done. Kat, I think I need to go. Steve needs to get on the internet and we still have the old system."

"Sure," said Kat, thinking, What Steve needs is a hard kick up the ass, preferably administered by Marcy. But Marcy seemed incapable of making a stand, no matter how badly Steve behaved. Which made Kat wonder: Was there anything her friend would *not* tolerate?

And suddenly Kat thought of something that made her stomach contract. "Listen, I have one question I need to ask you." Kat took a quick gulp of her wine to brace herself. "It's about Zandra and Logan. Did you know she was sleeping with him?"

"What?" Marcy's voice had risen to an indignant screech. "You're joking."

Kat felt her muscles relax. "Oh, thank God. I had this awful thought that maybe you knew and felt you couldn't tell me."

"How could you think that?"

"Because I know you don't like to take sides, and this is a take-sides kind of deal."

"I still can't believe it. Are you sure?"

"I saw them together and she admitted it. Turns out Logan was the semi-famous man."

There was an audible click, the sound of someone picking up another line.

"Steve? Is that you? I'm still on the phone." There was no response. "Steve? Honey, I'm just finishing up, but this is important."

"That's all right," said Kat, thinking, Jesus, this guy is even creepier than I thought. "I just wanted to know whether or not Zandra had told you."

"No," said Marcy, "I swear to God, Kat, I had no idea." There was another click, presumably Steve hanging up. Kat heard the sound of his voice again, this time a little louder and more impatient. She caught the words "endless, pointless gossip" and "priorities."

"This is not gossip, Steve, and I need two more minutes!"

"I'll let you go now."

"I'm sorry, Kat." Marcy sighed. "He has a bad cold and it always turns him into such a bear."

That, thought Kat, is an insult to bears everywhere, even the ones that eat camera-wielding tourists. On the other line, Kat heard an angry shout, then a clanking sound. "Steve, get your hand away from this phone. If you dare hang it up . . ."

There was the sound of the phone banging against something.

"Did something break? Marcy, is everything okay?"

But it seemed that Marcy had dropped the phone. Kat caught the words "Immature, I've had it" and "You care more about your goddamn girlfriends than you do about me."

"Marcy? Marcy? Are you all right?" She'd never heard her friend lose her temper before.

"Hi, I'm fine, but I'm going to have to call you back in the morning."

The phone went dead in Kat's hand. Throwing back her head, Kat finished her wine. *Maybe being single wasn't so bad, after all.*

After a moment, she picked up the Teacher's College course catalog, but after three tries at reading the requirements for Reading Specialists, Kat accepted the fact that she was unable to focus. Despite the wine she'd drunk, she felt as though she'd just come off a three-day caffeine binge. Too many highs and lows, thought Kat, and way, way, way too much tension. She looked at the remaining half a bottle of Vermentino and decided that the last thing she needed was to wake up with a hangover.

Kat dialed her mother's number.

"Mom? I don't suppose you have any Valium?" Like many women of her generation, Lia had her own unofficial dispensing pharmacy in her bathroom.

"Come on over to my back door."

Standing just inside her back door, Lia whispered, "This isn't Valium, but it'll relax you."

"What is it?"

"A sleeping pill."

Kat handed the pill back. "I can't, I've already had a glass of wine."

"One glass won't hurt if you eat something. It's extremely mild."

Kat looked at the pill. "Are you sure it's okay?"

"Absolutely."

"All right, thanks. I just feel so overexhausted that I don't think I can sleep."

Lia brushed a lock of hair away from Kat's face. "It's been quite a day for you. But you know, just because some people don't live up to your expectations doesn't mean that no one will. Some people surprise you by surpassing your expectations."

Kat said good night and walked back across the hallway to follow her mother's advice. She was just getting herself a late-night snack of Cap'n Crunch when the doorbell rang.

Kat opened the door. "Mom?"

Magnus cleared his throat. "Hello, Katherine." He looked tall and grave and ridiculously handsome in a Scandinavian sweater that made his eyes look very blue. "I would have come by earlier, but I had some important business to take care of."

"Pedro didn't ring you up on the house phone."

"He probably thinks I still live here."

For some reason, Kat found she couldn't stop staring at the pattern on Magnus's sweater. She reached out a hand and touched one of the little blue knots, then found her hand splayed over his heart. "Nice sweater," she said.

"Kat? Did you hear anything I just told you?"

"What?" Kat looked up into Magnus's concerned face. "Tell me again." She stumbled a little, and Magnus caught her by the elbow. "Are you all right?"

"Just tired." She let herself sag against him, and he felt wonderful, strong and supportive. The wool was a little scratchy, though. "Can you take this off?" She tugged at the sweater.

"Kat, are you drunk?"

"No, I just had one glass of wine." Kat closed her eyes and felt pleasantly dizzy. She remembered being a kid and lying back in the middle of the merry-go-round and watching the trees spin. Magnus's arms came around her.

"Are you all right? You seem kind of loopy."

"I took a pill."

He stiffened. "How many?"

Kat opened her eyes. "One, you idiot. I'm not committing suicide."

"Oh." Magnus didn't remove his arms. "But you said you also had wine?"

"Just one glass, but it was ages ago." Kat thought about it. "Of course, I haven't eaten much today." No, wait—she'd forgotten her little post-Logan binge. The whole day was beginning to blur around the edges.

Magnus held her for a moment, his mouth pressed to the top of her head. " Katherine, I want you to know, I came here to apologize. And I wanted to tell you that I'm leaving the Agency. I just . . . I didn't like the kind of choices I had to make."

"What do you mean?"

He pulled away enough to look her in the eye. "I don't want to be opportunistic about my emotions."

Kat thought about it, then made up her mind. She closed her eyes and gave him a hug. "You're a good man, Magnus."

Kat sat up in bed and blinked. She couldn't remember falling asleep. The last thing she could recall was standing in the entryway with Magnus. What time was it, anyway? The room was dark, but she could make out a shadowy form sitting in the corner, and she could feel a gentle, familiar presence. "Magnus? Are you still here?"

The mattress dipped as he sat down. "I'm here. I'm watching you."

Kat pushed her hair away from her face. "You are? What for?"

"You seemed a little out of it. You started talking about someone stealing the prize out of the cereal box, and I got worried."

"Oh." She noticed that he'd taken off his sweater and was wearing a white T-shirt. She looked at his neck, and thought about kissing it. "I feel fine now. Just a little cold."

Magnus put one hand on her arm. "Do you want a warmer nightgown?"

Kat leaned into him, inhaling his clean male scent. "Just hold me for a second."

"I don't think I should."

Kat blinked. She must have missed something. She seemed to be topless, lying in Magnus's arms. He was naked from the waist up, too. She ran her hands over the flat muscles of his chest, feeling warm and drowsy and aroused. "What?"

"I said I don't think I should take off my jeans."

Kat slid her hands around his shoulders. "Why not?"

"Because you're under the influence of a drug, and you might not really want to do what you're doing."

"Actually, I think the pill's worn off." Kat pressed her body alongside the length of his, thinking how good it felt to be in his arms like this, and how nice it was that he was so concerned about her.

"I don't think it has worn off."

Kat licked his ear. "Test me."

Magnus tried to hold her at arm's length. "All right, who am I and why are you mad at me?"

"You're a secret agent, and I'm not mad anymore."

Magnus cupped Kat's face in his hands. "Actually, I'm not an agent anymore."

Tired of the conversation, Kat pulled his mouth down onto hers. She couldn't remember the last time she'd kissed a man like this, as if there were all the time in the world. She loved kissing him. She would be perfectly content to do this all night.

Magnus was naked, his arms braced on either side of her shoulders, his face inches from hers. His expression was indescribably tender, but there was also something fierce in it. She could feel him between her legs, at the entrance to her body. Kat wasn't sure how they'd gotten here from kissing with his jeans on, but she wasn't complaining. In fact, she thought she might pass out if he didn't hurry up.

"Oh, God, Katherine, I love you."

"You do?" He pushed himself inside her, and it felt uncanny, as if they really had become one being. She couldn't ever recall sex being like this. She felt the intensity of Magnus's emotions in the touch of his hand on the small of her back, in his shuddering breath, in the way his warm, naked skin felt wherever it came into contact with hers. It was a little overwhelming. Magnus was barely moving, and the pleasure was already almost more than she could bear.

His breath was coming in ragged gasps, and then she was ambushed by a sensation that swept from the soles of her feet to the crown of her head. Wrapping her legs around him, she pressed little kisses to his neck and shoulder and face. "Tell me again."

He smiled. "I love you."

"Tell me in Icelandic."

He caressed her cheek. "You tell me first."

Kat closed her eyes. "I don't know Icelandic."

She smiled as she felt his chest rumble with laughter.

chapter *thirty-eight*

•

In the morning, Kat opened her eyes and discovered that there was a man in her bed. She gasped, and Magnus opened his eyes.

"What are you doing here?"

Magnus gave her a slow, sleepy smile. "What do you want me to do?"

"I'd like you to explain why we're both naked."

"Because it seemed a little too early in the relationship for leather?"

Kat hit him, and Magnus blinked. "You're not joking, are you?" He looked stricken. "You don't remember?"

Kat pulled away from him. God, the whole bed smelled like sex. "How did you get into my apartment?"

There was a knock on the door. "Mom? Why is your door locked?"

"One minute, honey." Kat scrambled out of bed, bringing the sheet with her. "Do not show your face to my son. I don't want him getting confused. And you'd better have a good explanation for this."

Kat gave herself a quick wash in the bathroom before throwing on an old pair of black yoga pants and a long-sleeved pink T-shirt. For some reason, she was wearing the Viking charm again. Too rushed to take it off, Kat scraped her hair back into a ponytail, unlocked her door, and slipped out before Dashiell could come inside. "Did you have a good night at Nana's, honey?" Kat smiled, trying not to look like a woman who'd just lost an evening.

"Yeah, but now she says she has to go to work. And I don't have to go to school, remember?"

Oh, crap. All her decisions seemed a little more complicated this morning than they had last night. Kat walked Dashiell back across the hall. "Mom, could you please hang on to Dash for a little while longer? It's an emergency."

Lia frowned. "I have to get into work this morning. What's going on?"

Kat glanced down at Dashiell and tried to think of a way to convey the nature of her dilemma. "It's a little hard to explain right now. But it's important."

Lia looked skeptical. "All right, I'll reschedule my day so that I can watch Dash for another hour. That will have to be enough, and I can't do this all the time."

Kat hugged her mother in gratitude and raced back to her apartment, where she picked up the house phone.

"Pedro, did you send a man up to my apartment last night without calling me?"

"You say send tall blond man up, no checking. I listen."

At that moment, Magnus wandered into the kitchen. Kat

narrowed her eyes at him, radiating hostility as she spoke into the phone. "Well, he is no longer residing here. Next time, call me before sending anyone up."

"If I remember. You change your mind so much."

Kat hung up and turned to Magnus, who was sitting on a stool and looking pale and resolute. "Well? What have you got to say for yourself?"

Magnus took a moment to respond. "I don't know how much of last night you remember."

"I don't even recall you coming over! What did you do, take advantage of me in my sleep?" She didn't really think that he would do something like that, but Kat had been more than a little disconcerted to wake up next to Magnus. Having him here was like smoking a cigarette after you thought you'd quit the habit. Suddenly, all the healthy reasons for throwing this man out seemed less important than the desire to touch him again.

"It wasn't like that. I didn't want to make love to you."

Kat folded her arms over her chest. "Oh, no? What happened then—did I force myself on you?"

Magnus frowned. "You'd taken a pill. I was trying to take care of you." His eyes looked very blue, entreating her. "Please tell me you remember something about last night."

Belatedly, Kat realized that the sleeping pill must have affected her short-term memory. *Last time I do that.* "What am I supposed to remember?"

Magnus indicated an empty stool. "Sit down." He inhaled deeply, and Kat leaned forward, waiting to hear what he had to say. Except he didn't say anything. Instead, he just frowned, as if searching for the right words.

"Well? Well? What is it? If it's bad news, just tell me."

"Right before we got on the plane yesterday, your father had what we thought was a heart attack."

"Oh, my God."

"But it wasn't his heart. It turned out to be arrhythmia brought on by an acute anxiety attack."

"So he's all right?" She felt curiously blank, as if she were doing a cold read of a scene, and hadn't gotten a handle on her character yet.

Magnus hesitated. "He's not in any imminent danger. But he is in the hospital. The doctors discovered that some of the arteries leading to his heart are partially occluded. I think he may need some surgery."

"Oh." She met Magnus's steady, compassionate gaze. "But he's not dying?"

"No." Magnus watched her face. "He asked for you, you know. He very much wants to see you."

"He does?"

"I think he's scared."

Kat thought about that. She didn't owe him anything—God knows, he'd never been there for her when she'd been scared throughout her childhood. And yet the thought of him lying alone and frightened in a hospital room was deeply disturbing. "Is there someone with him now?"

"We have an agent there keeping him company."

"That's good." Kat wasn't sure whether or not she was having a delayed reaction. She felt relief at knowing her father wasn't about to die, but that was about it. And maybe that was the saddest thing of all, that her father had given her no reason to care. "I guess I must seem kind of cold."

Magnus shook his head. "I don't think *you're* cold." Was he implying that her father was the one who was cold, or did he mean something else? She was half-afraid to ask, in case he was about to launch into one of those classic male speeches that went, If I were capable of being in a relationship with anyone, it would be you, but I'm not.

Had she said something to him last night that had implied she wanted a relationship? Oh, Christ, had she told him she was still in love with him?

Magnus swallowed hard, and Kat realized he was nervous. "I want you to know that I left my job."

Kat felt her heart speed up. This wasn't how the brush-off speech usually began. "You did? Why?"

"Because I didn't want to turn into the kind of man you couldn't trust." Magnus shook his head as if that was beside the point. "No. That's not right. I didn't want to turn into a person *I* couldn't trust."

Kat stood up. "What else did I forget?"

"Making love? You remember that, don't you? It was the most incredible . . ." Magnus searched her face. "You don't recall any of it?" He raked his hand through his hair. "Aw, shit."

He looked so utterly forlorn that Kat felt sorry for him. He was absolutely the least articulate man she'd ever been with, and she knew that if she wanted to hear everything he felt summed up in an eloquent speech, then she would be endlessly disappointed. But she also knew, standing there in her kitchen, that however badly he expressed himself, she could believe what he said.

Kat walked over to Magnus and smoothed his hair down where he'd left it standing up. And then she did remember something: a sense memory of Magnus moving inside her. A feeling of abandon and safety and joy.

"You know what?" She lifted Magnus's chin up. "You'll just have to refresh my memory."

"All right, well, to begin with—What are you doing?"

"Taking my shirt off." Kat laughed when she saw his reaction. "When I said refresh my memory, I didn't mean with words."

But as the moment dragged on and Magnus still didn't make a move toward her, Kat began to feel uncomfortably exposed. His expression was maddeningly unreadable. *Maybe he thinks I'm being inappropriate.* Maybe, despite his assurances, he really felt that she ought to be rushing off to the hospital immediately. It was what she would have done if her mother were even a little sick.

But my father didn't raise me, Kat thought, and this isn't a made-for-TV movie, where everyone winds up reconciling and the final scene is shot through a gauze filter. This is who I am, and if he's disappointed that I'm not more forgiving, it's better I find out now.

Magnus met her eyes. "First, I have to ask. Is there any possibility that you are still under the influence of a drug?"

Kat began to smile. "None whatsoever."

"In that case . . ." He was just reaching for her when the house phone rang.

Kat made a sympathetic face at Magnus as she answered it. "Pedro, is it a delivery? If so, you can leave it downstairs."

"People coming up."

Kat looked at Magnus, puzzled. "Which people?"

"Wait a minute, I get names." Pedro sounded disgusted. "Galina, Cheeto—sorry, Chieko, Nabil, Maria, and wait, here comes another one. What's your name? Luc."

Kat hung up and pulled her shirt back over her head. "It seems that the rest of your class has decided to show up on my doorstep."

Magnus's smile seemed a little forced. "That's . . . very nice."

Kat leaned over and kissed him on the mouth, giddy at the prospect of all these new possibilities. "You know something? For a spy, you don't lie very well."

"I'm not a spy anymore, remember? I quit."

Well, Kat thought, that makes us the perfect unemployed couple. Unless, of course, he did this for me and then spends the next ten years regretting it.

"Don't look so worried. I have a friend who works in the business sector, doing competitive intelligence for various companies. I can find another job. But for the time being, I thought I'd try my hand at carpentry. I figure I can start with your apartment as a demonstration of my abilities."

Kat smiled. "I can't pay you."

"That's all right. I'll take it out in trade."

"Excuse me?" Kat raised her eyebrows.

"I mean, you can rent me out the maid's room. The deal we had before?" He held out his right hand, and after a moment's hesitation, Kat took it.

But of course the deal was more complicated now, because sex had the power to tear down old connections and build up new ones. Magnus might be offering to fix things in exchange for room and board, but the way his hand felt on hers told Kat that he was really talking about creating a home.

The doorbell rang and Kat went to answer it. As she opened the door, she thought that forty felt like the beginning of a very good decade.

ACKNOWLEDGMENTS

•

This book could not have been written without the daily (sometimes more) calls to and from Joanna Novins, my critique partner, dog training consultant, and friend. Meg Ruley, my agent, gave me encouragement and feedback whenever I needed it, for which I am eternally grateful. I want to thank Greer Kessell Hendricks, my editor, for being quick to spot problem areas and then for being so patient and supportive while waiting for the finished product. Thanks also to Greer's associate editor, Suzanne O'Neill, for sweating the small stuff (and sometimes the medium-to-large stuff as well). Anna Adams provided wonderfully peculiar details about life on the NATO military base in Iceland, the kind folks at New York City's Berlitz Language Center and Fordham University's Institute of American Language and Culture allowed me to sit in on classes, and Courtney Clark Schiff supplied me with some background information on the fine line between diplomacy and espionage. Neil Gaiman encouraged me, Alexandra Grant gave me a place to write in Manhattan, and my husband, Mark, and children, Matthew and Ellie, kept me grounded in this year of change. My half-sister Anya should have had her name here a whole book ago, while our father, science fiction writer Robert Sheckley, kept reminding me that life is infinitely stranger than fiction. Last but not least, thanks to my mother, Ziva, who told me not to get an enormous Chinook puppy right after moving house, but wound up letting Magnus drag her around the park so that I could finish this book.